Totally Bound Publishing books by Kate Deveaux:

Platinum Pleasures

Totally Five Star
A Vixen in Venice

Anthologies
At Your Service: The Butler Did It

I0663076

Totally Five Star: Venice

A VIXEN IN VENICE

KATE DEVEAUX

A Vixen in Venice
ISBN # 978-1-78430-616-8
©Copyright Kate Deveaux 2015
Cover Art by Posh Gosh ©Copyright May 2015
Interior text design by Claire Siemaszkiewicz
Totally Bound Publishing

Published in 2015 by Totally Bound Publishing, Newland House, The Point, Weaver Road, Lincoln, LN6 3QN, United Kingdom.

Totally Bound Publishing is a subsidiary of Totally Entwined Group Limited.

A VIXEN IN VENICE

Dedication

Mr. Deveaux—
For one magical night
in the most romantic of cities.

Chapter One

The cobblestones proved an unsuitable terrain for both her suitcases and the four-inch heels Monique had unwisely chosen to wear for her arrival at her brand new job. She dragged her luggage behind her, jet lag combined with frustration mounting for Monique Le Bres as she traversed the maze of canals, making her way impatiently through the narrow passageways of Venice. The vaporetto driver had said that her hotel was just a short walk away when she'd departed at her stop on the Grand Canal. But now, deep in the thicket of Venice's many twists and turns, Monique would be damned if she could tell where she was.

After glancing down at the small map she clutched in one hand, Monique looked back up at the tiny storefronts crammed along the waterway, trying her best not to be overrun by the barrage of tourists filling the tight corridors that ran between buildings and the canal's murky edge. Searching for landmarks and any discernable signage, she bumped her way between tourists who were busy ogling the unusual architecture that, at that moment, proved more of an impediment than an attractant.

Tugging at her suitcases, Monique forged on.

The last thing she wanted to do was be late for her new job.

Lurching sideways to avoid a family clutching ice cream cones and pointing enthusiastically at the sights, Monique teetered on her heels to escape bearing the brunt of their gelatos as they passed. Oblivious to the obstacle they presented to Monique, they carried on, leaving her in their wake.

The wheels on her cumbersome luggage stuck on a rogue stone at the same time her heel gave way. Tumbling downward to the uneven cobbles, Monique gasped.

Just as her bottom grazed the ground, someone reached out, swooping her back onto her feet in one swift motion.

"*Mademoiselle, soyez prudent.*" A deep voice urged her to be careful in French.

Monique squinted into the late-day sun at nothing short of a vision. A majestic man, early forties, with chin-length sandy blond hair, a goatee and deep-set blue eyes that were rimmed by thin metal glasses stood before her, her hand clasped in his. The man's tailored, camel hair overcoat told her he was distinguished, as did the flash of his fancy watch, probably Swiss and very expensive from the sparkle of the crystal that caught her eye as she steadied herself.

"*Stai bene, Signorina?*" He asked if she was okay in a beautiful swoosh of Italian. The words slipped between his lips and seemed to pool like honey on the cool stones.

First he spoke French then Italian. It was official. Monique must be in heaven. She'd heard the stereotypes and the holiday stories of her friends vacationing in Europe, but nothing had prepared her for the man who still had her hand in his.

"Fine, yes, thank you, *merci* – I mean *grazie*," she offered, flustered and realizing she was quite able to stand on her own. Reluctantly, she let go of his hand to reach down and remove her broken-heeled shoe. "Just tripped on a stone. *Una scarpa verso il bass...dieci per andare.*" She hoped her Italian wasn't too rusty.

He just looked at her. *Oh damn, it must be more rusty than I thought.*

"One shoe down, ten to go," she repeated in English with a nervous laugh, motioning to her luggage. She hoped to make a joke of how many shoes were crammed in her overstuffed bags to cover her embarrassment of nearly splaying out on the canal sidewalk if not for the efforts of her handsome savior.

"Are you sure? I can fetch someone for you if you need assistance, *Signorina*," the man pressed. He then glanced anxiously over his shoulder.

Monique suspected from his unease that he must have a wife who no doubt would appear at any moment and be less than happy to find her hubby fraternizing with Monique. It wasn't the first time that had happened.

"No, I'm fine, really. *Mille grazie*," she thanked him. The depth in his eyes setting her off balance, as well as having only one shoe on and the way he called her *Signorina*. The words slipped from his lips like silk.

"Just tell me where I am. That would be very helpful." She shifted her weight to the shoeless foot and immediately dropped down a few inches, making her even shorter against his tall stature.

"*Calle Ostreghe*." He said the name of the street as she dipped her head down to remove her other shoe.

"See, much better," she said, now even-footed in her stockinged feet firmly planted on the cool stones.

But her words were met by empty space.

The man was gone as quickly as he'd appeared, the swish of his long coat disappearing through the crowds, barely visible around the corner as Monique looked on as if he had been an apparition. *A tall, handsome apparition.* And one that was seemingly desperate to get away from her before his wife showed up. *Lucky woman, having a man like that.*

Shrugging, Monique resigned herself to the fact that not only had she always had lousy luck with men, but also that her favorite pair of shoes—the ones she'd blown a good chunk of last month's paycheck on—were now of no use to her. Trudging over to a store window with her luggage, she then hunkered down and rooted through her suitcase in search of another pair of shoes to wear to her new job at the Totally Five Star Venice. That was, if she ever found the damn hotel. Gathering her belongings, she hastily stuffed her things back into her suitcase, then she hurried off in search of the hotel.

* * * *

Now in her second most favorite pair of shoes, with a smidge less of a heel, a gust of spring air pushed Monique Le Bres through the revolving glass door, abruptly depositing her in the lobby of the Totally Five Star hotel.

Stumbling, she took her first steps to her brand new job. Not exactly the initial impression she'd wanted to make as the newly hired art curator for the hotel, a sixteenth century gothic building rumored to have once been the home of Casanova. Centuries later, under the shrewd stewardship of CEO James Conroy III, the once dilapidated grand dame of the canal had been restored and renovated into a succulent feast of elegance. The latest addition to the top-notch Totally Five Star Hotels.

Surveying the lobby, Monique hoped no one noticed her less than graceful arrival. She wasn't in Kansas anymore — that was for damn sure. She could barely believe the hotel's refined opulence as she took in the bird's-eye maple paneling and the swaths of white sheers that ringed the lobby, hinting at the more intimate bar and dining areas concealed beyond. The whole effect gave the hotel a sexy, clandestine feel.

Leaving her cumbersome baggage off to one side of the lobby, she clutched her brand new attaché under her arm, the leather still stiff. Monique hoped she'd remembered to remove the price sticker as she walked smartly to the reception desk. Striding across the cream mosaic marble floor, she couldn't help but notice that despite the striking décor, there was a sparse assortment of paintings and sculptures. They definitely were in need of her help. With a budget of forty million euros and just three months to complete the task, Monique was quite sure she could establish a collection that would please the impossibly impeccable CEO James Conroy III.

The competition for the art curator position had been steep, but Monique had an 'in'. Her boss back in the States was not only an old flame, but he also knew one of Mr. Conroy's advisors and had not hesitated to put in a very good word for Monique.

Introducing herself at the reception desk, Monique was pleased when the woman behind the marble counter greeted her in Italian then efficiently switched to English for the important details. Monique's Italian was adequate for her graduate degrees in art history and later for reading art catalogues, but was sorely lacking for conversing. Something she hoped wouldn't be a determent to her employment at the Totally Five Star Venice. If she could just keep her Kansas twang under control when she spoke both English and Italian, she'd be well on her way of making a mark for herself in her field.

Smiling, the hotel clerk handed her the large gold room key.

"*Signorina* Le Bres, *benvenuti a Venezia*," she welcomed Monique warmly, "*Signor* Amatus will be here *un momento* to escort you to your suite."

Her mix of English and Italian enchanted Monique, who was so far from the small, dirt-filled town back home. The town she'd dragged herself out of so many years ago, where the only foreign language spoken was pig Latin if you grew up on the right side of the tracks. Monique hadn't even been that lucky. The rusted-out trailer she'd shared with her mother couldn't have been farther from the right side of anything.

"*Grazie*." Monique took the key, noting how large and heavy it was in the palm of her hand. No slick, electronic keys at this hotel. No, this was one hundred percent Italian luxury. The key began to heat in her grasp as she glanced around for the man who was supposed to greet her.

The elevator dinged, catching her attention.

Monique opened her mouth, but no sound came out. She quickly shut it as the good-looking, twenty-something-year-old man dressed in a suit just like the ones she'd seen on the Totally Five Star website exited the elevator. His robust laughter had caught her attention. As did his momentary flirtation with a sexy young woman dressed in the same hotel uniform. Monique smirked as the man patted the attractive young employee's ass when he passed by. He was a first-rate flirt for sure, and she made a mental note to steer clear.

Monique's smirk turned into a frown as the man kept walking straight toward her.

"There he is, *Signor* Amatus," the clerk behind the counter called to Monique.

She stood somewhat transfixed as he approached. He really was young. Could he honestly be her supervisor? Not at all what she'd been expecting. Maybe mid-twenties, if she was generous. Barely legal age back in the States, and a good ten to fifteen years younger than her, she was quite sure.

"Ah, *Signorina* Le Bres…"

"Yes, I am Monique Le Bres." She extended her hand. He wasted no time sliding it into his and placing it to his lips. His gaze stayed fixed on hers when he paused before kissing the back of her palm.

"*Incantanto*," his said, his words almost a whisper.

These Italian men were skilled at the art of flirtation—there was no denying that. But the sooner she made it clear to him that she was all work and no play, the better it would be for both of them.

"I am Donovan Amatus. Please allow me welcome to you to Totally Five Star *Venice*. I am sure you will be *molto* comfortable here."

The wicked glint in his eyes made her blush and fume at the same time. "I'm the new art curator." Monique scrambled to say something, trying not blurt out what she was really thinking—that it was actually both flattering and maddening all at the same time to have this young stud with the wandering gaze flirt with her only moments after her arrival at the hotel.

"I know, *si*. Art curator," he said, releasing her hand but not before running it lightly again over his lips. "I will be your liaison while you are here, answer any questions you have. Work with you side by side. *Fianco a fianco*," he repeated the words in Italian, his tone so intimate that she was lost for a moment as she studied his nametag.

Donovan Amatus, Del controllo qualità – *Quality Control Manager.*

A vague memory of her letter of employment and that name stuck in her head, but she was damned if she could reconcile the young man in front of her with her supervisor. Surely, there had been some mix-up. This young man couldn't possibly be supervising *her* and the forty million euro budget the CEO had entrusted her with.

"The key, *Signorina*?" he prompted.

Speechless, she just stood there.

"*La chiave*, the key, *per favore?*" he repeated, then reached to take the key from her grip. "Follow me, *Signorina* Le Bres."

"Oh, please call me Monique."

"You Americans are so friendly," he said with a smile as he led her toward the elevator, placing his hand firmly around her waist.

Summoning her most professional demeanor, she slipped from his hold and stepped into the elevator.

"I am sure you will be very happy working here at the hotel Totally Five Star Venice," he said and punched the fifth floor button.

Monique tried to focus on what she was there for—her dream job and not the leering gaze of her so-called supervisor. "Yes, I'm sure I will. Mr. Conroy's letter of employment said I could start to work tomorrow."

"*Assolutamente*," he confirmed. "Tomorrow. But first, I show you your room. *Bene*?"

* * * *

The suite wowed Monique. A penthouse really, and only five floors above the Grand Canal. Virtually a skyscraper in Venice. And it was all hers.

Admiring the wall of windows overlooking the waterway below, Monique poked her head out to catch a glimpse of the busy goings-on in the canal. She couldn't keep herself from looking for the man who had saved her from falling only a few blocks from the hotel on the *calle*, the *Calle Ostreghe*. A name she wouldn't soon forget, along with the handsome blond-haired man who had intrigued her then had slipped away as mysteriously as he'd arrived. But he was not there, just the usual tourists and shopkeepers filling the narrow passageways as she scanned them for the illusive man in the camel hair coat.

Signor Amatus stepped closer, breaking her reverie. Monique remained facing the window, hoping to hide the flash of fire that burned her cheeks from reminiscing about her mystery man from the *calle*.

"Everything okay?" her supervisor inquired.

"Oh yes, it's gorgeous, really," she said slowly and turned away from the window to meet his unwavering attention.

"Yes, it is, *Signorina* Monique."

Taking in the suite in an effort to divert his attention from her, and hers from the man in the *calle*, Monique stopped for a moment to appreciate her new home.

The room was so elegant, in keeping with the rest of the hotel with its light wood paneling and soft, white sheers that framed the windows and billowed in the breeze. The moment was surreal. It was everything she'd always dreamed of all those years ago when Italy had been somewhere far away from her white trash existence.

Signor Amatus followed her as she walked about the living area.

"And my office?" she asked, moving away from him to make some space between them.

"*Un momento.* You haven't seen the bedroom yet."

"No, I haven't Mr. Ama… I mean *Signor*…Amatus?" she queried, searching his lapel for his nametag.

"Please call me Donovan." He smiled then led the way to what must be the bedroom.

Well aware of the innuendo saturating the air as she followed him, she paused, lingering in the doorway, admiring the beautifully appointed room and the luxurious king-size bed. She caught the young man's admiring gaze. *Oh, this is a bad idea.* A very bad idea to be alone with the undeniably good-looking but persistent supervisor. She turned back to exit her room as quickly as she'd entered.

"*Signorina* Monique, you like?" he asked after her.

She stopped in the doorway and smiled politely. "It's lovely, but how about showing me to my office so I can get all set for the morning?"

He paused, lingering by the bed, then cracked a handsome, sly smile. "Very well, *officio*, if that is what you want."

"It is."

"Bedroom...maybe later." It wasn't a question. It was more a foregone conclusion.

"Yes, later to *sleep*," she asserted and caught the slight upturn in his lips. Obviously, he thought his charms were so magical that she couldn't help but surrender to him, as no doubt most women did. *Well, he's in for a surprise.* Monique Le Bres was nobody's fool and least of all young Donovan Amatus'.

Chapter Two

The view from Monique's second floor office was limited, but it did offer a peekaboo glimpse of one of the narrow canals that passed by the back of the hotel. She was glad for a bit of space from young Donovan once he'd been thankfully called away.

Alone, Monique gazed at the small, dimly lit office with its heavy ambiance. Maroon velvet swags framed the small window opening. Not at all what she'd expected and a complete juxtaposition to the sleek, modern décor of what she'd seen of the hotel so far. Her office's traditional interior struck her as more suited to a classically decorated, vintage hotel rather than the ultra-chic, contemporary luxury Totally Five Star was known for.

Taking in the beautiful but incongruous theme of her office, she remembered James Conroy III had made it clear in her letter of employment that the works of art she was to acquire were to be mostly classics. He had stressed 'not too much' modern art. He wanted art his guests could relate to, identify and appreciate. He'd worried contemporary art might slip over their heads and wouldn't wow them like the more recognizable classics. James Conroy wasn't in the hotel business to do anything but make money, and that meant not only satisfied guests, but also ones who were awed by the beauty and attention to detail at each of his hotels from Vancouver to Venice. Exquisite luxury was the key to Totally Five Star.

Looking over the compact office, Monique was glad to see an iMac and a small printer, the only visible signs of anything modern as they perched on a desk that looked like it was straight of out of Christie's antique auction. Beside the desk stood a credenza, again antique, but topped with stacks of art magazines with the most current periodicals in the art business placed on top. That reminded her that she had only three months to build a collection worthy of the Totally Five Star Hotels. No small feat, but she was quite sure she could pull that off without a hitch. She already had her iron in the fire with several art dealers who would be paying her a visit shortly. She'd even reserved a few pieces in advance before she'd ever set foot in the hotel. Monique had a good idea what pleased James Conroy III, and she planned to deliver in spades.

Her attention turned to the thick, embossed leather welcome packet that sat on her desk awaiting her. Thumbing through it, she quickly realized it was more of a manual, really. A knock at the door interrupted her and she shut the binder.

"*Scusi, Signorina* Le Bres." Donovan appeared, quickly moving from the doorway directly to her desk. "I know you are probably tired from your long trip from Kansas." The way he said Kansas sounded exotic, the second syllable floating off his tongue like something secretive. "But I was wondering if I could dine with you tonight? Share a little of Venice on your first night here."

There was no denying his well-practiced charms flattered her as he waited for her answer, but Monique knew this was like playing with fire with young Donovan. A fire that was best dealt with by a hardy dose of cold water.

"That sounds tempting," she said, parsing her words. She wondered how to turn him down gently enough as to not offend him and endanger her barely broken-in job. "I *am* exhausted from the trip."

"You still have to eat—"

Monique shook her head, knowing now was the time she must set the ground rules— boss or no boss.

"Ah." He clutched his heart as if wounded. "*Un vero peccato.* Such a pity. Well, then... I wish you goodnight, *Signorina* Le Bres. I will see you in the morning. *Buonanotte.*"

"*Bene, buonanotte,*" she replied, trying to conceal her relief as he turned and stepped out of her office.

* * * *

Waiting a good half hour, Monique was quite sure the coast was clear after her supervisor had departed. Weary from her travels, she couldn't wait to get back to her nice room and fall fast asleep in the sumptuous-looking bed.

After closing her office door behind her, Monique headed down the hall for the elevator. Each door she passed along the narrow hall had a nametag with an identifier.

Sales the Direttore Vendite.
Diretorre del Marketing.
And so on.

The subdued hush of voices from an adjoining hallway halted Monique in her tracks. She listened. Soft giggles intrigued her. Tiptoeing toward the sound, she then peered around the corner. Near the end of the hall, she glimpsed Donovan's silhouette as he leaned against a woman in a dark skirt, her suit jacket discarded onto the floor. *Definitely a hotel uniform. Interesting.*

Kissing her, Donovan pinned her arms over her head with one hand as he expeditiously rid himself of his blazer, then he pressed against her. But the woman didn't protest. She was enjoying it as Monique observed. The soft murmurs of delight filtered down the hall as his young lover wriggled against him. He trailed his fingers along her blouse, tugging at the buttons to expose her breasts. In appreciation, she hooked one leg around his waist, pulling him closer, even with her wrists still bound by Donovan's grasp above her head. His captive rolled her hips to him, rubbing herself against him, their toned bodies nearly becoming one had there not been the deterrent of their remaining clothing. Monique gasped as Donovan kissed his young lover back with such abandon, pulling her blouse from her shoulders with one hand. Greedily, he grabbed her small, pert breasts from within her lace demi bra, the dark peak of a nipple pressed between the fingers of his other hand.

Monique's key slipped from her hand and tinkled noisily onto the wood flooring. Mouth agape, her cheeks flamed as Donovan looked up and nodded in her direction. Then his partner's gaze followed his. Monique immediately recognized the young blonde from the lobby with the pixie cut and the cute little body. The same one she'd seen Donovan pat on the ass when Monique had first arrived.

She merely smiled at Monique, her legs still wrapped around her supervisor's hips, her breasts burgeoning from her bra with Donovan's hand still pinching one nipple. Her lips turned up in amusement, and she returned to kissing Donovan. He released her briefly, allowing his partner to run her fingers along his wide shoulders before he spun her around and planted his palms on her ass, drawing her to him, hard. Monique looked away then back again. Strangely aroused at their unbridled passion, Monique was aware of her nipples peaking under her silk blouse as Donovan explored the woman's curves, venturing up and under her skirt.

The blonde faced the wall, rubbing circles with her ass against Donovan's groin. Hiking her skirt up farther, Donovan bared her sculpted thighs, making Monique's body quiver when her supervisor's fingers disappeared between the woman's legs.

The ache throbbed deep in Monique's groin, while she imagined what it would feel like to have eager fingers slipping into her, knowing just what exquisite pleasure could be had at the touch of a talented lover. Her panties moist, she bit her lip, consumed with watching her boss and his lover while Monique ran her own hands slowly over her body. Lightly over her breasts then down between her own thighs.

The lover reached around and undid her skirt, allowing it to fall at their feet. Monique stared, enraptured, when her boss massaged his partner's bare ass, tracing the outline of her thong with his thumb before tugging it down over her hips. His toned lover groaned with approval at his advances and kicked the thong off with flair. Turning to face him, her bra still hiked up over one breast, her lace thong lay crumpled in the hall while they went at it—

grabbing, tasting and kissing. Monique made no move to leave them alone—she was enjoying the show too much.

The woman wriggled against her lover, the hum of soft groans as they kissed making Monique even more crazed when the woman tugged impatiently at Donovan's belt. He let her remove it, and it too soon joined the other items of clothing on the floor. Slowly, he sank to his knees. Burying his face between her thighs, the soft sound of lapping reached Monique's ears as the woman arched backward and Monique was given a full view of Donovan licking her pussy.

Monique gulped audibly as her boss took one long, slow lick. Donovan cocked an eye in Monique's direction, as did the woman. They both smiled before he nodded and went back to savoring her. They knew she was still there. Still watching them. Touching herself. Monique quickly retreated, embarrassed to have been caught spying on the lovers.

Smoothing her clothes as she slinked away, Monique was well aware of the flush over her skin and her heightened arousal. She couldn't help but wonder if they always carried on like that or if they were doing it for her benefit. Who knew what turned people on, what kinks and quirks drove them to the brink of passion? All she knew was that voyeurism was a huge turn-on and something she had never done before. It seemed that Italy was going to suit her just fine.

Chapter Three

The blade slid easily over his square jaw, removing his goatee with each carefully executed movement of the razor. Wiping the remnants of shave foam from his face, the famed art collector, Alessandro Bonnard, studied his refection in the hotel mirror.

He'd already had his blond, chin-length hair cut much shorter than he was used to. Now it was not only short but dark brown after a bottle of hair coloring. Alessandro was accustomed to tucking strands of his longer hair behind his ears, but some situations called for a change. Enough so that he hoped to slide under the art world radar undetected when he went about the task at hand. It shouldn't be too hard to ward off recognition thanks, in part, to his usually low profile and keeping out of the public eye as much as possible while he went about amassing his billion-dollar art empire. Some referred to him as a recluse. Alessandro preferred private. He used his trusted and loyal staff to be his public face, managing to keep his personal appearances infrequent while he built his art empire one painting, one sculpture at a time.

With his new hairstyle and color, minus his usual glasses and goatee, Alessandro thought he should be able to pass for Luc Umbere — the cover he'd selected to fulfill his job overseeing the burgeoning art collection of his friend James Conroy's newest hotel in Venice. Some cover. Alessandro had almost blown it earlier that day when he'd helped a beautiful woman who had snapped her heel in the *calle* and almost landed on her derrière. And what a nice ass it was.

Alessandro had known better than to be on the streets of Venice without his associates to run cover for him — especially now that he had such an important job to undertake. That sexy little minx he'd rescued in the *calle* had almost made him break his rule when she'd looked up at him, wobbling on her one good shoe and grasping his hand. Her sultry eyes had tempted him to linger in the street longer than was wise.

It was moments like those when Alessandro wished he wasn't famous and could stay and woo the woman who was, without a doubt, an American. She'd given herself away when she'd trembled and answered him in Italian. The words had been perfect, but the accent had left a lot to be desired. Another lost tourist, he presumed, seeing as many countries, castles, churches and sights as she could in ten days or less. He knew better than to come to the damsel in distress' aid, especially when he was flying under the radar, but he would have liked to have had a chance to show her a thing or two about Venice and helped her with her accent one seductive Italian phrase at a time.

When his friend J — as his closest pals referred to him — had called to request a favor of Alessandro, asking him to go to Venice and check on how his precious forty million euros were being spent, Alessandro thought his friend had had a few too many scotches.

Alessandro might be able to fool the employees and local residents, as he doubted many were aware of what he looked like, but how was he to fool the in-house art curator Conroy had apparently hired to amass his collection in Venice?

The curriculum vitae of the employee he was to oversee, which J had couriered to his Brussels home, had brought an instant smile to Alessandro's face. He'd only glanced at it. A low-ranking art curator. From Kansas no less. No wonder Conroy needed his expertise on site and thought his friend stood a good chance of eluding the new hire. The disguise had been J's idea, and Alessandro smiled in delight as he studied his reflection in the mirror. Umm. Now for the finishing touch. Popping the contacts in, he instantly had brown eyes instead of brilliant blue. That should go a long way to covering his identity.

Once he pulled on the khaki pants he'd purchased direct from the store – stiffly starched, most definitely not his usual high-end, custom-tailored – he then moved on to the shirt. The store salesman had referred to it as a 'dress shirt', but it was really too plebian to be called that in Alessandro's world. The cheap fabric and the way the collar sat imperfectly irritated him. Reminding himself it was Luc who wore the clothes, not himself, he appraised his average wardrobe in the full-length mirror.

Confident no one would suspect his real identity, and disguised in his simple garb and new eye color, Alessandro was now officially Luc. He raked his hands through his hair and made the part down the side. It was something akin to nails on a chalkboard to see himself so undistinguished. He surveyed himself from head to toe in the mirror and debated whether to wear a tie. Deciding against one, he loosened the neck of the shirt by a button and rumpled it a little. The transformation was complete. He was officially Luc Umbere, the newly appointed Architectural Director of the Totally Five Star Venice.

Undressing again, he returned to his usual clothing, sans goatee, and felt better already once free of those dreadful clothes. The dress rehearsal for tomorrow was enough for one night. Tomorrow it would be for real.

Chapter Four

A fitful sleep plagued Monique. Dreams of Donovan making out with the young woman in the hallway mingled with images of the dark, murky passageways of Venice. She didn't need to be Freud to know they were tinged with sexual innuendo. Her body hummed with electricity, unable to squelch her arousal at her newfound hobby — voyeurism. Having watched Donovan and his lover pursue each other with raw, unrelenting passion, Monique couldn't help but let her mind drift back to the mysterious man she'd met on the street that day. She imagined the stranger would push her up against the wall and dip his tongue into her most intimate places.

That tall, blond stranger, who had appeared like a vision and whisked her to her feet only inches from the rough stones, was an intoxicating fantasy. Monique caught her breath as she remembered how he'd looked at her and the smooth, seductive words that had tumbled from his mouth. Unable to remember what he'd said, she recalled only the tone of his voice and the fluent Italian. Her nipples peaked under the cotton sheets. Her fingertips were now at the growing ache between her thighs.

Biting her bottom lip, she slid one finger between her moist folds, her body wound like a tight spring, aching for release. She parted her outer lips ever so slowly, imagining it was her mystery man from the *calle*. She wished he hadn't disappeared with one swish of his camel hair coat. Visions of him sweeping her up into his strong embrace then having his wicked way with her tantalized her. She imagined him doing things to her that she only dared to dream of — like making her beg for it.

Monique instinctively raised her hips to meet her own touch when she slowly circled her slick clit. It budded under her fingertip, throbbing and needing to be kissed, suckled, tasted. Panting, she stroked and teased it, giving way to the sensations that overwhelmed her, imagining her mystery man delivering on the promise of pleasure that she was sure she had seen in his eyes when he'd saved her from falling.

Pushing her finger deep inside her tight wetness, soft moans drifted from her mouth. Taking her time, she rubbed her clit as it quivered with white-hot arousal, teasing herself with the fantasy that it was him touching her. Watching her. Like Donovan had gazed up at his lover's face as he'd licked her pussy. Moving faster amid the tangle of bed sheets, Monique rocked her hips against her palm as if it were the mystery man touching her. Exploring her. Entering her. His cock stretching her. Harder and faster, she stroked her pussy, picturing the tall vision ridding himself of his overcoat and stripping down naked to fulfill her desires. Lifting her hips to meet his imaginary cock, she pumped one then two fingers in and out of her channel, panting and murmuring. Her clit, hard and engorged against her fingers, taunted her each time she slicked her hand over the sensitive spot then deep inside her, putting extra pressure against her G-spot until she could barely take anymore. Aching for a man, for *that* man, she pictured his deep blue eyes, goatee and blond hair. She grunted and her inner thighs quaked with tension until she crested, tipping her hips up in the air, yearning for him to be buried deep inside her.

Alone in the dark, she clenched the sheets to her chest, her breasts still sensitive from self-pleasure, and drew the duvet over her. Snuggling her pillow close in her post-orgasmic bliss, she dreamed of the mysterious man.

* * * *

A few hours later, Monique reluctantly cracked her eyes open and peered out from under her pillow.

The sun shone across the bedroom, illuminating the silk-patterned wallpaper. She hadn't even noticed it yesterday when she'd been fending off Donovan's attention.

Grabbing for her watch on the nightstand, she then pulled it to her in the bed. She squinted at the time under the refuge of her pillow. Eleven a.m.

"Crap!" She threw back the covers and hopped out of bed. Her brain fuzzy, she hurried into the bathroom and skipped from the cold tile floor into the soothingly hot shower.

Toweling off, she heard a loud noise. She quickly wrapped her Totally Five Star hotel robe around herself and hurried into her bedroom. Monique realized it was someone at the front door to her suite.

Knocking coming from clear across the palatial living room continued as she walked briskly to the source.

Standing in the open doorway was a pleasant-faced maid in her sixties, judging from the gray streaks framing her face. She held a large tray with what smelled like divinely strong coffee and freshly baked bread.

"*Signorina* Le Bres, *buengorino*. I have your *colazione. Si*, breakfast?" The maid scooted past her with the large tray balanced on her shoulder.

Monique's stomach rumbled. She'd barely been able to stay awake for the sandwich she'd procured from a vendor outside the hotel last night. Grateful for the promise of nourishment and much-needed caffeine to combat her jet lag, she padded after the maid as the woman placed the tray on a table in front of the windows overlooking the canal.

The maid went over the items on the tray. "*Signorina... Pane. Caffé. Con leche. Burro...*" She pointed to the butter, which looked decadent given the low-calorie diet Monique was used to in Kansas. "*Cornetto al cioccolato,*" she added, gesturing to a gorgeous basket of fresh-baked chocolate croissants.

Monique scanned the maid's nametag — Marie. Her country was listed underneath. Monique squinted to read it. Romania, that was it. With a tiny imprint of a flag that Monique could only assume must be the Romanian flag.

"Thank you, Marie. *Grazie*. Here I thought I was going to be late for my first day at work."

"No, *non tardi*. You are not late. *Signor* Donovan and the others don't start until noon. Then lunch is later in the afternoon."

"I see, well, that suits me just fine with my jet lag." Monique sat at the table and poured herself a steaming cup of caffé from the coffee press while Marie excused herself. Her head clearing with the initial sips, Monique wondered just how she was going to face Donovan after the embarrassing incident in the hall. She bit into the decadent, chocolate-covered bun, savoring the perfect bittersweet of the cocoa and butter. Flakes of the pastry fell to her robe.

* * * *

Revived by the delicious breakfast, Monique reported to her office, ready to take on her first day at work. Opening the welcome binder that sat on the middle of her desk in her office, Monique took out the letter of introduction and sat. She scanned the letter for important details. Donovan Amatus was mentioned as her supervisor. *Direttore del controllo di qualità* – Director of Quality Control. Monique let out a snort. That young man seemed only interested in one sort of quality—quality ass and tits. Some supervisor. He probably didn't know a damned thing about art. Good thing she was a self-starter, as she had a feeling *Signor* Amatus didn't spend much time on his work.

Reading further, she noted a few pertinent names and contacts. Donovan reported to his supervisor, Gabriel Sosa the lead Quality Control Manager— internationally for all Totally Five Star Hotels—then above that directly to James Conroy III. Next, there was Teresa Stiless, the personal assistant of the Venice property, reporting directly to Conroy's official PA, Claudia Bauer. Monique remembered Ms. Bauer well. She was the one who had interviewed her in London at the Totally Five Star headquarters for the job. She'd not minced words, making it clear that Mr. Conroy expected nothing less than excellence from every employee, starting with the General Managers of the individual hotels right down to the bellman, janitors and maids who kept his hotels gleaming.

Working away at her desk, she followed the list of instructions the binder included for web logins, emails and hotel protocols. Monique busily got to the task of setting up her schedule of acquisitions for the week. There were calls to make and meetings to set up with buyers. She reached for the phone, paused then flipped open the binder again for directions on how to dial out the multi-digit local number.

A knock at the door interrupted her dialing. A tall, thin-faced woman poked her head in the doorway, and Monique immediately hung up.

"*Signorina* Monique Le Bres?" the woman inquired with a perfect British accent. "I am Teresa Stiles. I heard that you had arrived last night, and I wanted to introduce myself and see how you are getting along."

The woman's plain gray suit matched her equally gaunt face. Her pale blue eyes were almost translucent as she scanned the room before returning to Monique.

Monique jumped up from her seat to greet the woman, her mind whirling back to her letter of employment. *Teresa Stiles, the Personal Assistant to the hotel manager.*

"Yes, thank you. Nice to meet you, too, Miss Stiles — I mean *Signorina* Stiles." She corrected herself then fidgeted nervously as the woman looked around the room.

"Is your office okay? To your standards?" The woman approached Monique's desk and sat in the chair across from her.

"It's perfect. The décor is...exquisite," Monique said somewhat nervously, eager to express her appreciation of her new place of employment.

The woman nodded. "James Conroy oversaw it himself."

"He did?" Monique asked with surprise.

A stiff smile parted Teresa's terse lips. "Not in person, of course, but he did approve the plans the designer sent to him."

"Well, they did a lovely job, perfect ambiance for an art curator," she said, trying to be convivial with the sullen-faced woman.

Teresa Stiles sat there, still studying Monique, then opened her mouth briefly but nothing came out. She tried again. "I trust you met your supervisor when you arrived?" she inquired.

"Donovan?"

Teresa arched her eyebrows. "Yes. *Signor* Amatus. Donovan," she said slowly.

"He was very attentive..." It made Monique uncomfortable as she remembered just how attentive he'd been to his young lover and how much Monique had enjoyed watching them rip each other's clothes off. She recalled how he'd pressed his lover against the wall then tugged her thong down over her little ass. Monique flushed at the vision of him slipping his tongue between her legs.

Teresa Stiles' posture stiffened as if with impatience. "Yes, he *is* very attentive." Her tone was reprimanding. "Anyway, I will leave you to do your work, I just wanted to introduce myself. I'll let you get back to settling in."

"Very well, thank you. *Grazie.*"

Teresa exited, and Monique exhaled a low sigh of relief. *That woman is way too uptight for her own good.*

A moment later, the door opened again. Monique tipped her head up in surprise.

Donovan threw his hand to his chest dramatically as he stepped through the doorway. "I thought that woman would never leave."

She shifted awkwardly, dreading any interaction after last night's spying game. She'd die of embarrassment if he brought it up.

"I trust you slept well." Donovan flashed a knowing smile as he sat in the chair across from her desk.

Damn, he was already making himself comfortable, and that was making her very uncomfortable.

Flustered, Monique casually shifted a few things around on her desk, purposely not looking at him, reminding herself she was at work. She had to focus on her job, not his lustful intentions.

"I'll take that as a yes," he said when she didn't answer and only dipped her head back to the papers on her desk. "Is something wrong, *Signorina* Monique?" He reached across her desk and tipped her chin up.

"No, nothing is wrong."

He leaned closer, his lips turning upward in an encouraging smile. "Please, *Signorina*, do not frown that beautiful face of yours. *Molte bellisimo.* What is wrong, you are not bothered by what you saw in the *corridoio*?" He inclined his head toward the door.

Her cheeks flamed hot. There was no way to avoid the elephant in the room — that she'd seen him making love to that woman in the hall. That she'd stood there watching — no, *enjoying* — the show. "I'm not bothered in the slightest by what you were doing in the corridor."

He came toward her desk, surprising her by sitting on the edge of it. She wasn't sure the fragile antique could bear his weight as he leaned toward her.

"*Bene.*" He gazed at her and grinned slowly, as if he was in on some secret, his mouth cocking slightly as he nodded. "She is a girl. But you are woman. *Sei donna sexy.*"

The words just hung there as he made no move to back away. The faint scent of his aftershave — lemons and musk — invaded her personal space as he leaned even closer. "I like women...no, I love women. *Amo donna, si?*" His eyes sparked in evident amusement. "I didn't want you getting the wrong idea."

"Wrong idea. No, heavens, I certainly didn't think you were gay."

"Gay? Me, *non.*" He laughed heartily.

She felt very foolish.

"No, *me non checca.* Not gay. You confuse me. How do I say...that girl was for me...?" He struggled for a moment then broke into a wide smile. "Is like appetizer is for you. How do you say in America? A starter, *prima portata.*"

Monique should have been horribly offended that he'd just referred to the sexy young woman in the hall as a starter, like the all-you-can-eat salad at Olive Garden back in Kansas. Instead, she just stared back at him, unsure what on earth might come out of his mouth next.

"Forgive me," he said, standing. The audible creak of the desk provided confirmation that his muscular physique was indeed too heavy for the tiny frame. "I say something wrong?"

Monique couldn't help cracking a grin at his charms. Damn Italian men, how did they piss you off and charm you all at the same time?

"Forgiven. All business, *Signor* Amatus."

"Ah, no *Signor* Amatus." He shook his head. "Call me Donovan, *por favore...*" He scolded her with a seductive glint in his eyes.

He came to stand behind her chair. Then he placed his hands on her shoulders, leaned in close and buried his face in her hair. She gasped when he slithered his fingers down the front her blouse and squeezed her breasts, hard.

"What the fuck—" she exclaimed just as his lips met hers.

A loud cough made Donavan pull away. Monique followed his gaze, her outrage at his advance thwarted when she saw Teresa Stiles in the doorway, one hand braced on the doorframe and a decidedly grim expression on her face.

"I...I..."

Monique stared at the expressionless Teresa, her gaze fixed on Donovan before coming back to rest back on Monique.

"*Signor* Amatus. Come. My office, immediately," Teresa said sternly.

Monique was left to feel like a child who had been caught doing something very naughty that wasn't her fault at all.

Chapter Five

So far, no marching orders. Monique worked undisturbed, making her appointment list before deciding to go inspect the rest of the hotel. She needed to make an inventory of common areas that required art placement.

She shut her office door behind her and glanced down the darkened corridor, or *corridio* as Donovan had called it. Relieved there was no sign of the rascal, she carried on down the hall to the elevator.

There had been no sign of him since he'd been summoned for his inappropriate behavior. Hopefully not *her* inappropriate behavior, although she knew it had looked bad from where Teresa Stiles had been standing. How was the woman to know Donovan had thrown himself on her, only to let Monique be caught in a compromising position with his hands firmly planted on her breasts her first day of work? Even so, Monique did not intend to speak to Ms. Stiles and tell her side of the story. It would only make matters worse, she was sure. No, Monique could manage Donovan. He was harmless, really, just a terrible flirt and no real threat to her other than that his lecherous behavior might cost them both their jobs. And besides, as much as Monique hated to admit it, she had been both appalled and slightly intrigued by Donovan's indiscretion until Stiles had walked in. It was nice to know she was as desirable to him as that sexy little thing she'd watched him make love to in the hall. It was ridiculous and vain. She knew better. Job first. Amorous supervisors second.

Since she still had a job as far as she knew, Monique decided to explore the hotel and get a better idea of what areas required her art acquisitions first. She stood in the lobby, observing the hotel's centerpiece — its first impression on guests.

Yesterday, she'd been almost overwhelmed when she'd stumbled through those revolving doors, still flustered by her encounter with the mysterious man in the *Calle Ostreghe* and nervous with the prospect of her new job. Now, twenty-four hours later, she was settled in her lovely suite and unfortunately caught in the cross hairs of Donovan's attentions.

Ignoring her concerns over possibly having lost her dream job, she carried on with her observations. A few guests milled about as she walked around, her clipboard in hand, assessing possible locations for art installations.

The large wall behind the reception desk begged for something truly stupendous. She made a note of it and moved on to the other areas. Washes of golden paint graced the walls, giving a hint of glamorous color to the large space. Creamy limestone floors and the simple gold-hued wrought iron accents on the lighting surrounded the lobby. Taupe and ivory upholstered furniture of sumptuous velvets, chenilles and linens gave the air of sophistication. The *piece de resistance* was those sheers that had caught her attention yesterday. They framed the entire lobby, making the bar and restaurants seem illicit. Secretive. So *very* Venice.

The interior design team had aced the hotel, and she was not about to let James Conroy III down now. Her art selections would wow him *and* the art world. She'd be an overnight sensation when she nailed this. *No going back to Kansas now.* Not that she ever intended to go back. After her last botched relationship, she had nothing to stay in Kansas for. She'd seized the chance at working for Totally Five Star Hotels and had nearly cleaned out her bank account on the trip to London for the job interview. Thank God Totally Five Star had included first-class transportation to Venice when they'd offered her the job. She was so skint she wouldn't have been able to scrape two dimes together to hop a freighter across the Atlantic. But here she was, thanks to her own tenacity and hard work, as she took in the amazing views of the canal from both the lobby beyond the restaurant and through the bar.

Whoever had done the design work had lived up to the demanding Five Star reputation, providing a stunning décor without overshadowing the immensely enviable canal views. This hotel must be worth a fortune. Monique pondered back to the redo at the local Best Western in Wichita when she was a girl. That had been big news in the 80s when they had switched out the shag carpeting for wood floors and braided area rugs.

This hotel was a work of art in itself, seeming to float amidst the canals, and she wouldn't sell Five Star short on her art installations. Impressed, she wandered past the sheers that sequestered the restaurant and more intimate corners of sitting areas. All had their own unique signatures. Monique yearned to reflect on her acquisitions.

Searching for the right words to capture the feel, she mulled over the first words that came to mind as she took it all in.

Luxurious. Sensual. Tactile.

The blend of modern and the rebirth of tradition was what she was looking for. "Rococo!" she blurted out as the perfect word came to her.

"Rococo?" A rush of warm breath grazed her neck and she turned around in surprise. "Don't tell me you're on to other men so soon?"

"Donovan," she gasped, unsure if she should slap him or be glad to see him. "I was worried you'd been fired." Her gentle laugh covered up the true concern that their actions might very well have got them both canned. Stiles was probably on the phone to Claudia Bauer, tattling at that very moment.

"I'm glad you were worried..." Donovan's tone grew sultry as he leaned close and slid a hand easily around her waist, using his other hand to quickly find her ass. "It will take more than a little kiss to get me fired, my sexy. *Il mio sexy.*"

Monique immediately slipped out from his embrace, realizing his reporting to Teresa Stiles' office had done nothing to change his behavior.

He gave a disapproving frown. "You're not going *serioso, Signorina* Monique?"

"You're lucky you weren't fired — both of us for that matter," she seethed her irritation. "So yes, a little *serioso* while at work would be advised, if I were you."

"I am sorry, I apologize. Don't be mad." An impish smile filled his face. "Of course. Whatever you want, *mio* sexy *Americana.*" His appreciating gaze lingered on her cleavage.

She shifted impatiently, forcing away her desire to slap Donovan for being such a Class A ass—an ass she was stuck with if she wanted to keep her job, it seemed. Stiles wasn't the type of woman to believe Monique's side of the story. Luckily, Monique was adept at handling men like Donovan. She'd had years of practice, thanks to her mother's less than stellar taste in boyfriends who'd preferred the early-to-bloom teenage Monique to her alcoholic mother.

Summoning her professional demeanor, Monique decided the best thing to do since she still had a job and Donovan was her still her supervisor was to carry on.

"Donovan, I'd like to see more of the hotel." She hoped to steer him on the right track and admonish any hint she'd be interested in anything other than work. "I have an idea for a theme with the art acquisitions, but I need to see more to make sure I'm on the right track."

"Umm hmm," he said suggestively, making no move to assist.

"Really, Donovan, you're my supervisor for God's sake. At least give me a tour so I can report back to James Conroy's office with my plan by the end of the week."

"Oh, now you are cross with me?" He didn't wait for her reply. "I will supervise, then," he said with a glint in his eye. "But first, you tell me who this Rococo is you speak of? I don't like competition."

Monique couldn't conceal her annoyance. "Rococo isn't a man. It's a period of art. Like a style." She rolled her eyes as Donovan's expression lightened in evident relief that this 'rococo' was not a man after all. "I take it you don't know much about art, even though you are my supervisor?"

"*Corretto.*" He nodded with no apparent sign of embarrassment that he was supervising a forty million euro budget and evidently knew zilch about art. "Does that concern you?" he asked.

Monique shrugged. "Not really, I know enough about it for both of us, I guess. You just stick to your supervising, and I'll stick to the art." Monique's attention was momentarily diverted by the appearance of Donovan's young lover in the lobby. She watched over his shoulder as the blonde walked to the elevator, and Monique noted the distinct shimmy of her skirt. A flush of heat rose to Monique's cheeks as the woman paused to look back at them and flashed a sexy smile their way before the doors closed.

"And another thing..." Monique tried to ignore the feeling the young woman was still watching them, even though the doors had shut. "I have questions about some of the installations. I need you to contact someone in Conroy's office who is in charge of the architectural specifications, someone I can speak with directly about my concerns."

"You can speak directly to the man they are sending here to *verificare i progressi.*"

"What?" she asked, trying to decipher the Italian he'd mixed in with his English. "They are sending someone to check up on me, on my progress? I thought that was your job?"

"*Sí.* It is...I mean was. That is what *Signorina* Stiles wanted to tell me. That they are sending some *excecutivo* from head office, some art connoisseur, whoever he is, to oversee the collection. Nothing to worry about..."

"Oh, Donovan," she said, unable to control her annoyance at his easygoing attitude and the fact someone was definitely being sent to watch her. She was sure of it.

"Don't frown, *mio Monique*. We still have much work to do. How about I give you that tour you wanted?"

Chapter Six

Changing into his workout clothes, Alessandro was ready to burn off some of his pent-up energy. Damn, he hoped there was a gym at this dinky hotel Conroy had set him up in. A three-star hotel. Unbelievable! Shit, they probably didn't even have a treadmill. He'd have to jog the narrow sidewalks and passages of Venice, which was nearly impossible. He knew it was too risky to stay at his villa—a mere boat ride away—so why couldn't he just have stayed at the new Totally Five Star Venice, where he could observe the goings-on in more detail? But his friend J had been adamant that he'd have to stay off-site and not at his Venice villa. J wanted some place Alessandro could just be Alessandro in the privacy of his own room, without attentive staff to take notice of him after a long day of him being 'Luc'. Dammit, this was really slumming it. Good thing he was going to make a killing on this venture, as he always did, undetected by anyone, even his buddy J.

* * * *

Donovan toured Monique around the hotel as she had requested. The entire time Monique was ticked off by the news Donovan had so casually imparted. It must have been Teresa Stiles who had engineered this change in command. The scene with Donovan in her office must have confirmed Teresa's opinion that Monique was incompetent. *God knows what Ms. Stiles' assessment of Donovan is, considering he still has a job.*

After they'd left the main floor's public areas, the only other locations that would require art installations were the special VIP level and the elegant rooftop terrace.

The tour continued. They stepped onto the terrace, which housed a small pool with an intimate bar set out on the most amazing rooftop patio Monique had ever seen. Again, exquisite, like everything else she'd seen at the Totally Five Star. Monique was taken aback by the splendor of the view.

The centuries-old building was only five stories high, yet the hotel was considerably taller than many of the surrounding buildings, giving the terrace a spectacular view.

Monique could easily spot *Piazza San Marco.* She recognized it from her tour books she'd pored over back in Kansas, prepping for the job interview, then from her wild goose chase trying to find the hotel yesterday. Now here she was, the tall spires of all the basilicas cascading above the rest of the city amidst a plethora of red-tiled roofs as she looked around three hundred and sixty degrees.

"Impressive?" Donavan asked Monique.

"Very. But this will be a challenge for art up here with the light and the open air."

Monique glanced back to the covered area of the verandah bar, thinking her options were limited for placement of fine art in the indoor-outdoor setting. The art would be subject to the elements and not easily guarded either. Security was a very real concern when designing an art installation and one she had to consider. No way did she want to go through Teresa Stiles if she didn't have to. The less she had to do with that woman the better.

"I will have to discuss the issues for placing art here with James Conroy's office," Monique said, thinking aloud. "Perhaps you could put me in touch with someone in his office. Someone like you, but higher up," she teased.

"Ah, higher up. I see. Now you go over my head," he teased back, wasting no time pulling her to him and placing his hands firmly on her ass.

"Really, Donovan, this is not acceptable." She extricated herself as quickly as possible from his embrace, glancing to see if anyone had seen them. Ignoring his advances, she stayed on message. "Please, get me the name of whom I can contact about art on the rooftop. Conroy specified a mix of art throughout to the common areas but I just don't see it up here. Umm, maybe sculpture, that would work. Yes, sculpture. Heavy and immovable but beautiful."

"*Bellisima*," Donovan mumbled, not paying the least bit of attention to what Monique was saying.

"Donovan, you're making this very hard."

"You make my *cazzo* hard," he growled.

"Dammit, Donovan, I don't want to talk about your cock." She spat the words out. "I want to get on with my job, and I have to tell you, you're putting my career in serious jeopardy with your...your...advances."

He looked crushed.

Monique sighed. She felt bad, but for only a moment. Her sanity got the better of her when he moved closer, whispering amorous phrases in Italian.

"You liked watching us in the hall yesterday, *sì?*" He looked like he knew damn well how much Monique had enjoyed it. "Touching yourself while I kneeled to kiss her between her legs. I could do the same for you, *Signorina* Monique, kiss you, there..." He slid a hand downward.

Startled, she stepped backward. He moved toward her, his hand still below her waist and traveling lower.

Pressing her hands between them in protest, Monique caught a flicker out of the corner of her eye. Donovan's lover — watching. Monique paused, distracted by her appearance and the sudden flush of remembrance washing over her. *My, how the tables have turned.* Just yesterday, it had been the young woman almost naked in the hotel hallway with Donovan sliding his fingers between her legs. Monique was momentarily lost as she recalled the distinct look of pleasure on the young woman's face when she'd spotted Monique watching them.

Donovan, unaware of their onlooker, took Monique's pause to his advantage and pressed against her, his hands roaming her body, his lips finding hers. Monique could see the woman over his shoulder. Standing near the entrance to the terrace. Watching them.

Pride got the best of Monique. She decided to give the little sexpot a show of her own. She kissed Donovan back. Even though Monique was a good fifteen years older and fifteen pounds heavier than she was comfortable with, she could still wow a man like Donovan, just as well as his young lover could.

The back of an outdoor couch hit Monique's thighs. She lost her balance and fell backward with Donovan on top of her, already busily undoing her blouse.

A loud clapping of hands stopped Donovan and Monique mid-kiss. The lusty Italian quickly hopped off her. But it was not Donovan's lover who had interrupted them.

Teresa Stiles stood next the young woman. Stiles' face was even grimmer—if that was possible—than it had been in Monique's office earlier.

Oh shit, not twice in one day. Monique struggled to right herself. She pulled her skirt back down and smoothed her hair. *How the hell am I going to get out of this one?* Glancing down, she noticed her button was undone and the lace of her bra was exposed. Fussing, she did it up as quickly as possible.

Silence filled the air.

Tears pricked Monique's eyes. She tried to make sense of what had just happened. How stupid she had been to rise to the challenge, a challenge she had invented because she was insecure of her age and wanted to prove to that sexy, young woman that Monique was still desirable.

Teresa shut her mouth after no sound emerged, as if she didn't quite know what was going on either. At least Monique hoped she didn't.

The tall PA started to turn on her heels, and for a moment, Monique thought she might just walk away. Then she stopped in her tracks, gazing back with a look of complete disgust. "Monique, you're fired. Have your suite and office vacated by noon tomorrow. Same goes for you, Donovan. Room vacated by noon."

* * * *

Her anger had ebbed and now plain humiliation filled Monique when she slid the gold key into the door. It immediately reminded her that it wasn't going to be her key for very much longer. She found it almost impossible to imagine that she'd be leaving the hotel tomorrow, that her dream job was over—ended before it had really even begun. Monique berated herself for being so completely irresponsible, all the while hurling insults at Donovan under her breath. She began stripping as she went through the bedroom and headed straight for the decadent shower.

The nearly scalding hot water was oddly comforting. The sting of the water momentarily replaced the pain of her dismay and anger at Donovan. At herself. And at that damned young woman who had gotten the better of Monique's ego. Monique had *let* her get the better of her ego.

She turned off the shower and stepped out, her skin bright red as she stood staring back at her reflection in the big mirror. Barely recognizing herself, her eyes ringed with red from crying, frown lines marring her brow, she reached for one of the luxurious hotel towels. *I'm better than this.* She wasn't some floozy who'd fucked up on her first day on the job.

She toweled off roughly, practically rubbing her skin raw in her frustration. Dammit, she'd worked harder than anyone had in her graduating class to get where she was, and she'd thrown it all away on a moment of lust with a sexy Italian while his far-from-innocent sidekick had watched on.

Lordy, lordy, her mother would roll over in her grave if she could see what a screw-up Monique was. Lorrinda Don told anyone who would listen that Monique would amount to nothing. White trash, growing up in that trailer park on the outskirts of

Wichita was something her mother said she'd never shed, no matter how hard her daughter tried. Monique could still see her mother's surly scowl when she'd condemned Monique for running fast with the boys. Loose. Promiscuous. That's what she called her.

Years later, Monique wrestled with the awareness that her mother had been jealous of her pretty daughter who had matured early. But the memories of her mother drowning her rage in bourbon were still fresh, and the living hell she'd subjected Monique to for the first fourteen years of her young life still stung. Then, as if caused by some weird twist of fate, Lorrinda Don had been hit by a car and killed instantly the day of Monique's fourteenth birthday. Suddenly, Monique had been free. Free of her mother's nasty voice taunting her in the night. Of the crazy-ass drunk boyfriends Lorrinda brought back to the trailer, trying to earn a few more bucks for booze, but always passing out before she saw the men visiting seemed much more keen on Monique than they were her.

The driver had saved Monique that day when he'd plowed into her mother as she'd crossed the road to buy more booze. Monique was sure of it. She had a chance. No longer Monica Don, she reinvented herself — Monique Le Bres. A name she thought sounded so sophisticated at fourteen as she'd dreamed of a life far from that trailer park. She'd taken the few dollars from the coffee can her mother had hidden behind the stove and caught the first bus to the big city of Wichita. To a young girl, it was her New York. The big apple of Kansas. She had a chance.

Monique stood in her bathroom. Tears rolled down her face as she remembered just how far she'd come.

Dammit, she'd fought tooth and nail to make her way in the world. She'd almost made it, she thought angrily, and threw the towel to the marble floor.

* * * *

Monique spent a dreadful night's sleep of tossing and turning, worrying just what she was going to do now that she was out on her ear in Venice. No job. Nowhere to stay. No money for a plane ticket home. She was royally screwed. She fisted her hands into the down pillow then punched her frustration out as the day's light signaled the start of another day for the canal. The busy sounds of commerce heralded the awakening of the day.

In no mood to slip out from under the silky duvet and face the punishment for her foolish behavior, she lingered in bed, coaxing herself with the inner pep talk that she could do it. She was Monique Le Bres, not Monica Don from the trailer park. Feistily, she flipped back the covers. She had already lamented the imminent loss of her gorgeous suite, her cushy job and her lost ticket to the big time. Time to face the piper, pack up and clear out of Dodge. Once again.

With her robe clenched around her, Monique padded barefoot to answer the knock at her door. She hesitated before she opened it, then looked through the little peephole. Relieved, she saw it was Marie, the maid. She was in no mood to face Donovan, not that she thought he'd show up anyway. The louse was probably long gone. Monique scolded herself for her frivolous indiscretions before she opened the door tentatively.

"*Buongiorno.*" Marie strode into the suite with her arms laden with the breakfast tray.

"*Buongiorno, Marie,*" Monique replied with as much enthusiasm as she could muster.

Marie gave her a wary glance and set the tray on the table by the window. Then she began placing out the steaming *caffé*, the biscotti, *pane* and a bowl full of succulent orange slices the color of rich, red rubies. "*Arancia rossa.*" Marie proudly pointed to the blood oranges. "Supposed to bring good luck."

"Thank you, *grazie,*" Monique said with appreciation. Unwanted tears welled in her eyes that this was her last day at the hotel. In her job. With no money in her wallet to speak of.

"*Si, Signorina.*" The middle-aged maid reached out and took Monique's hand, surprising her with her comforting touch. "I know it is your last day with us."

She patted Monique's hand in a motherly way. At least that was the way Monique assumed normal mothers were — they soothed their children's worried hearts.

Monique's throat clenched with emotion, her hand still in the maid's capable grasp. "I screwed up," she confessed with a sob.

"Shush, my dear." Marie took Monique instantly in the hold of her thick arms, patting her on the back to comfort her. "It is all in the past now. *E' tutto nel passato ora.*"

"*Si*, the past. I never even got past 'go' and it's straight to jail for me." Monique teased but saw the age-old Monopoly joke was lost on the Romanian. She broke away, feeling better from the woman's embrace, and smiled at her. "Oh, never mind. It's been good to know you Marie, you've been so kind."

"Where will you go? *Dove andrai?*"

"I have no idea. Nowhere to go. Nowhere to stay." The reality of being jobless and imminently homeless in one of the world's most expensive cities made her suck in her breath to steady herself.

Marie shook her head then reached into her pocket. She pulled out a business card and a crumple of euros, and then pressed them in Monique's hand. "My brother runs a *pensione*. Moved here from Romania five years ago. It's a nice, little place, nothing fancy but you can stay there. *Molto economico.*"

Monique clasped the card and the euros in her hand thankfully, unable to speak as the words of gratitude tightened in her throat.

"You're not the first one, you know," Marie said, her tone unsure, as if waiting for Monique's reaction.

"I figured as much," Monique said, her voice filled with regret. "I should have known better. It's my fault, I got caught up in the moment...it was silly and I let my pride get the better of me."

Marie clasped her hand to her bosom with such fervor it made her jowls jiggle. "*Signor* Amatus is *farabutto.*" Marie spat the last word out.

Monique needed no translation — scoundrel.

Chapter Seven

Alessandro Bonnard walked into the lobby of the Totally Five Star and noted his reflection in the simple but elegant, wall-sized platinum gilt mirror to his left. Doing a double take, he realized he was now officially Luc Umbere. Devoid of the exclusive, tailored three-piece suit, blond hair, goatee and glasses, he barely recognized himself. His brief glance at the reflection revealed a brown-eyed, dark-haired man in average clothes. His shirt was undone at the neck and the absence of a tie almost alarmed him until he smiled knowingly at his reflection, then he continued to the reception desk to introduce himself as the new *Direttore di Acquisizioni di Arte.*

"I am Luc Umbere," Alessandro announced, the thrill of saying his cover name for the first time almost as exciting as his latest acquisition. After handing over his newly printed business card to woman behind the large reception counter, he watched to see if she revealed any hint of recognizing his real identity.

"*Si, Signor* Umbere, what can I assist you with?"

Apparently not.

"*Grazie*. Could someone please direct me to the Art Curator's office? I've been sent by J." Alessandro's Italian was impeccable, as were his native French and the five languages he often slipped in and out of with ease running his global art empire.

Confusion settled over her face.

"*Scusi,* I meant James Conroy," he quickly corrected himself, realizing it was not his Italian that had stumped the woman. It was his use of his friend James' nickname. A mistake he wouldn't make again if he wanted to remain incognito.

"Oh, definitely, *Signor* Conroy, of course." The woman looked puzzled as she glanced down at the computer then back up at him.

"Umm, *un momento*." She looked at the computer then made a call.

Her tone was hushed and he couldn't hear what she was saying, but he saw from the furrow of her brow that there was some sort of concern on the other end of the line. Once she put the phone down, she looked at him, chewing her lip, as if deciding just what to say.

"I'm sorry, *Signor* Umbere, but the Art Curator is no longer in our employ."

"No, that must be wrong, I was just sent to supervise her. Her name is..." He tried to remember the name of the woman in the dossier that J's office had couriered to him in Geneva "Monique Le Bres," he said with relief, finding the name in his Blackberry.

"*Sì, Signorina* Le Bres was the art curator, but she is no longer in our employ."

"That's ridiculous," he exclaimed a little too abruptly.

The startled woman jumping back at his outburst.

He needed to calm his authoritative manner if he was to be Luc and not Alessandro, a man accustomed

56

to getting whatever he wanted whenever he wanted it. His cover, Luc Umbere, was a mere employee of Totally Five Star, hired to make sure the art curator spent the CEO's millions wisely.

"*Scusi*," he continued more demurely. "I am just surprised no one told me of this development."

"You're welcome to go see for yourself, *Signor* Umbere. Her office is, I mean was" – the woman flushed at her *faux pas* – "on the second floor. Art Curator, *Curatore d'Arte*. I can have *Signorina* Stiles talk with you, if you would like. Her office is on the same floor."

"I'm quite sure I can find it without the aid of Ms. Stiles," he snapped a little too impatiently. Reminding himself yet again not to draw any unwarranted attention to his new persona, he politely thanked the woman for her time before going in search of the elevators. The sooner he figured out what the hell was going on here the better.

* * * *

Monique entered her office for the last time. She'd already vacated the lavish suite. Her dreams of spending three months in such luxury trying to make her mark in the world had come to a screeching halt.

Leaving her luggage inside her office door, she planned to slink out of the hotel undetected once she'd cleared up a few things in her office to avoid running into Teresa Stiles. Monique looked around the office wistfully. Then she began efficiently gathering her things from the drawers, placing them in her barely used attaché. She scoffed at her naïveté, that a girl from Kansas could make it big in the art world.

The world of Totally Five Star was indeed beyond her reach. Her mother's voice rang in her ears.

She'll never amount to anything, never be able to shake her trailer trash roots. She can only trade on her good looks as long as her luck holds out.

It was all just as her mother had prophesized all those years ago. Monique's inner demon taunted her — *Monique Le Bres was just sexier and better-educated than Monica Don from trailer thirty-one.*

Exhaling, irritated at the battle raging inside her, she scanned the computer for her files. She was careful not to leave behind her contact lists. Those were her lifeline in the art world if she ever were so lucky to get another art job anywhere after the scathing letter of termination she'd received under her door that morning.

Working quickly, she transferred her computer files onto her portable hard drive, which she tucked into her purse for safekeeping when the task was complete. Monique went back to the desk and began to make a list of the appointments she had to cancel.

She rose, giving in to what she knew would be her last irresistible glance out of the window at the canal, the art galleries, at one of the most sensuous and evocative cities in the world.

Turning back to her desk, she grabbed the last of her papers and reached for her attaché. She stuffed it to the brim. Several sheets flittered out of the briefcase and down to the floor. Monique bent over, reaching for them under the recesses of the antique desk.

* * * *

Exiting the elevator on the second floor, Alessandro scanned the nameplates on the office doors as he searched for *Curatore d'Arte* to find out just what was going on at the hotel. Surely, the woman downstairs was incorrect when she'd said the art director had vacated her position. It was only yesterday that he'd received the text from the department of quality control, a *Signor* Donovan Amatus, confirming that Luc was to meet with *Signorina* Monique Le Bres later that day.

He shook his head as he spotted the brushed metal nameplate on the door of the *Curatore d'Arte*. He knocked then waited a moment. No answer. Hmm, it must be true and she was already gone. He opened the door and smiled.

An exquisite, round, tweed-covered ass greeted him.

The owner of the perfect ass and the stockinged legs was bent over the desk, apparently reaching for something on the floor.

Yum. He had half a mind to walk over and spank that beckoning bottom, but he only cleared his throat politely to get her attention.

"Shit!" She righted herself immediately and turned to him. Her face was flushed from having been bent over the desk, her eyes flashing angrily.

He gasped.

Chapter Eight

The owner of the delightful ass was none other than that woman he'd rescued on the street yesterday. *The American.* The one whose heel had broken on the uneven cobblestones. Whose hand he had clasped in his own.

Did she recognize him? No, he didn't think so. Yesterday he was Alessandro. Blond-haired, blue-eyed mastermind of the art world. But standing there in the office he was just Luc. Short brown hair, brown eyes and a definitive lack of well-tailored clothing.

Cautiously, he studied her expression for a faint flicker of recognition. There seemed none as she stood there, a hand on one hip, impertinent as hell.

"*Scusi.* I didn't mean to startle you," he continued. "You are *Signorina* Monique Le Bres?"

"*Si.*"

"Please allow me to introduce myself, I am Luc Umbere." The unfamiliar name rolled off his tongue somewhat awkwardly, almost as uncomfortable as his growing erection as she stood there defiantly, looking like she was going to throw something at him. "I've been hired to work with you on the art collection for the hotel," he continued, strategically placing his briefcase over his groin. "To help oversee the acquisitions."

"Oh," she said with an eye roll. "Well, you're too late, it seems. I am just leaving my job."

"Leaving?" he asked.

"Yes."

"So soon?"

"Yes."

Her one-word answers were going to make it very hard for him to extract any information that he could relay back to J. He stilled had the urge to kiss that impudent little mouth of hers, just as he'd wanted to in the *Calle Ostreghe*. Her ruby lips tempted him. But he was Luc—not Alessandro. He didn't just take what he wanted whenever he wanted.

"I see," was all he said. If what she said was true— that she was leaving—then that put a major kink in his plans. He'd counted on selling off some of his art collection to the highest bidder while under the guise of assisting his friend by overseeing the art installation at the hotel. Alessandro's loss for sure. Not just the business end of things, either. This art curator was way too sexy to let her walk out of that door. He'd have very much enjoyed getting to know her.

"The office is all yours," she said, grabbing the last of her papers then stuffing them into her stiff leather attaché case. Every inch of her was sensuous, right own to her delicate neck and the tilt of her jaw when she was ticked off, which she clearly was. It made his loins throb to think how the pleasure would have been all his to supervise her and report to J. That is, if they'd gotten any work done at all.

"That's a pity," he said, moving closer. For what reason, he did not know, but she was such a beautiful and scared-looking creature that he had the urge to protect her just as he had when her heel snapped on the cobblestones and her feet had flown out from under her. She would have landed on her cute little ass for sure had he not been there to save her from a fall. She looked at him. He fought the fantasy of just what he would have liked to have done to her that day if he could have stayed instead of running off for fear of blowing his cover.

The American tapped her foot impatiently and chewed her bottom lip. He would have liked to have fucked her that day, and he felt the exact same way when she looked at him like she did right now. Oh hell, there went his erection again.

She glanced nervously in the direction of her suitcases by the door then back at him. She said nothing as he stepped so close he could smell her perfume's waft of roses and spices. She fussed with her attaché case, fumbled with it, a move which bellied her grace as one of the papers floated down to the Persian rug.

He reached for it, admiring her sexy calf and the arch of her foot as he retrieved the paper and took his time standing to hand it to her.

She reached for it and he snatched it away.

She was not amused. "Look, Mr. Umbere, you have the wrong woman." There was a definite twang in her accent as her nostrils flared. Oh yes, the dossier. He already knew she was American from his brief interaction on the street the day before. But now, speaking in English, her accent confirmed it—some southern state, wasn't it? Alabama...Arkansas... His head spun with the realization that she was his

Americana in the *calle*. Just where the hell was she from again? Mississippi? Miami?

"I no longer work for Totally Five Star," she said with a *humph* of dissatisfaction. "You'll have to supervise whoever they hire to fill my job."

He couldn't stifle his bemusement at her petulance and glanced down at the piece of paper to avoid her seeing the enjoyment he was getting out of her overt hostility. Women never dared stand up to Alessandro Bonnard. He was too powerful. But standing there as Luc Umbere, he felt so turned on that Monique Le Bres felt she could challenge his authority. It was tantalizing. Years of amassing his art fortune had become stale. What he needed was something to spark his imagination. And this woman, who appeared ready to take on anyone who got in her way, definitely fit the bill.

He handed the paper back to her, but not before noticing the list of acquisitions and the dealers she had beside them. All names very familiar to him.

She reached for the paper and he held it back from her, studying it now more thoroughly, his interest piqued.

"Rococo?" he asked. "It seems most of these works are just that." He scanned the page, impressed with her unusual proposals. Thinking aloud, he pondered the list. "Is that what you were planning for the hotel before you decided to leave?"

"Yes," she answered, her eyes widening in what he could only guess was surprise. "You know rococo? You'll be a better supervisor."

Better supervisor. Than who? He was puzzled by her response. "Why a better supervisor? Because I know rococo?"

"Exactly."

She grasped the paper from his hand as he let it slide from his grip, transfixed by the spark in her eyes and the silky, chestnut hair spilling onto her shoulders. His gaze lingered on the white skin of her ample cleavage. His cock stirred again. It was really a shame that this sexy woman was no longer the art curator. He'd better find out what the situation was. There was nothing he'd love more than supervising her in his bed.

"It's genius," he said, looking at her. "Rococo is perfect for the hotel. Too bad you are leaving."

"Goodbye, Mr. Umbere, I must be going," she said, looking rather uncomfortable as she stood there clutching the shiny attaché.

"Where will you be going?" he asked with genuine interest.

"I have no idea," she said curtly then walked to the door. She reached for her suitcase. "No fucking idea at all."

The door shut behind her as she exited, luggage in tow. Stunned, Alessandro stood in her office, wondering what to do now that his tantalizing charge was gone.

Chapter Nine

Fuming, Monique dragged her suitcases through the halls, looking for the infrequently used service elevator.

"Shit!" she swore angrily as her heel caught in the carpet runner. Her overstuffed bags ratcheted her backward, almost making her topple over as she righted herself and carried on.

She stabbed at the elevator call button and seethed about that man who had come to supervise her. Obviously, he'd had no idea she'd been fired. *What was his name? Umbere or something or other.* The nerve of him, looking at her notes as if they were for public consumption, commenting that her rococo idea was genius. So condescending. Where had James Conroy found such a lout? Probably that nasty Teresa Stiles. What did a man like that know about art? Sure, he was easy on the eyes if she ignored his bad taste in clothes. Obviously all brawn and no brains, and he knew nothing about style, that was for sure. Definitely not gay. No gay man would be caught dead wearing such an awful shirt with his hair parted to one side and slicked back like that. Very *Leave it to Beaver*. She hissed at the *double entrendre*—beaver.

The man hired to oversee her definitely was straight. The way his brown eyes had lingered on her cleavage had made her pulse race despite her irritation at his unexpected arrival while she was trying to get the hell out of the hotel. At least his admiring gaze confirmed that she hadn't lost her sex appeal along with her pride.

The elevator was taking forever. Monique jabbed at the elevator button again and glanced back to make sure she wasn't going to run into Mr. Umbere.

The floor indicator above the elevator showed that it was sitting on the fourth floor. Hopefully it wasn't Donovan vacating his room. Running into him was the last thing she needed. Deciding on plan B, Monique headed for the stairwell just around the corner and proceeded down the stairs. Her luggage bumped and crashed behind her. She was desperate to get out of that hotel.

Not knowing where she was going to go or what she was going to do, Monique knew one thing. Her wallet was empty, that was a fact. Except for the roll of bills Marie had been kind enough to press into her hand. Exiting the hotel, she found herself at some side entrance that led to a narrow passageway along one of the many canals. Monique strutted along angrily, not giving a damn if her luggage bopped and ricocheted behind her off the unforgiving cobblestone.

* * * *

The Art Curator's office was dead quiet after Monique rushed out of the door. The reality of who she was unnerved him. That wasn't part of the plan at all. Alessandro chastised himself for being so careless, so distracted by her beauty that he'd spent a fraction too long fraternizing with her in the street. Luckily, the sexy *Americana* seemed to have no clue who he was, her senses hopefully clouded by her obvious anger over departing from her job.

Needing answers, Alessandro immediately pulled his phone from his pocket and dialed J to find out just what the hell was going on with the job he was no longer to supervise. It had royally screwed-up his plans. He needed to know if there was a replacement coming soon. He could only hope she would be as alluring as *Signorina* Le Bres.

After a brief call to Conroy, who was in a meeting when he finally got through to him, it was clear his friend was clueless about the departure of the current art curator. J told him to immediately find Teresa and find out just what was going on at his newest hotel.

Luc wasted no time knocking on Ms. Stiles' open door and smiling as innocuously as he could. He introduced himself as the man sent to supervise the art curator. They'd met before at one of J's legendary parties, but he hoped the woman wouldn't recognize him as he presented himself.

"*Signorina* Stiles, I was surprised to find the woman I was sent to supervise, a *Signorina* Monique Le Bres, is no longer in the hotel's employment."

"Oh, yes," Teresa said, rising from her desk, a deep frown on her face. "Someone should have contacted you and let you know. Oh, no…" She frowned even deeper than Luc could have anticipated. "That should have been Donovan Amatus, but I am afraid he, too, is no longer in the employ of the hotel."

"What the hell?" His frustration at the ineptitude of the staff became evident before he had a chance to contain it and remind himself he was Luc Umbere. "*Perdonatemi.*" He excused his outburst. "It was a long process to get here," he fibbed. She didn't need to know he'd flown in on his private jet from Geneva, dining on caviar and champagne before visiting his Venetian villa then relocating to the hotel Conroy had set him up in. "You can imagine my confusion. I arrived ready to start work with Mademoiselle...I mean *Signorina* Le Bres. *Signor* Amatus confirmed the meeting with me only yesterday. Luckily, I found *Signorina* Le Bres in her office before she departed so I wasn't completely in the dark."

"I apologize on behalf of the Totally Five Star family and Mr. Conroy himself, as I see you come highly recommended by Mr. Conroy," she said, looking distractedly down at her notes as if trying to place him.

"I was just talking to J—I mean, Mr. Conroy. He didn't know anything of it." He noted the arch of her eyebrows and he wondered if it wasn't wise to tread so closely to his real identity, but he didn't like her attitude.

"You called Mr. Conroy?" she said with apparent alarm and motioned for him to sit in one of the chairs across from her desk. "He does not need to know about any of this, the frivolous goings-on of the staff." She seemed flustered. Her hand shook as she moved some papers aside, a dead giveaway he had her right where he wanted her.

Impatient to find out just what was going on, Alessandro sat and tapped his foot, as he was prone to do when agitated. Realizing his outward appearance might give him away, he steadied his foot.

Teresa smiled thinly. "Mr. Umbere, again, I am sorry for the confusion and the trouble it has caused you. It just didn't work out with the new hire, Monique Le Bres."

"And this Donovan Amatus?" he asked, curious why two employees were let go. He sensed there was something going on. Perhaps some sort of indiscretion between the lovely Monique and Mr. Amatus.

"I don't see that he is any of your concern, *Signor* Umbere," she said haughtily.

Shit, this incognito thing really blows. Maybe he didn't even want to do this favor for J after all. There were easier ways to keep an eye on his less than savory art transactions.

"I am sure there will be a new hire soon, just as soon as I have a chance to go over the short list of applicants with Claudia Bauer."

He didn't really care about a new hire. His mind was still stuck on that little number they'd let go. He paused, reflecting for a moment. "You know, Miss Le Bres was working on a rococo theme for the art installation. Quite ingenious, actually. It's a shame that's all gone to waste now."

Teresa looked at him, her eyebrows still arched high as if in disbelief that he would sit across from her and sing the praises of the new employee they'd just sacked. Then her face softened, and she offered a wide smile, almost like the Cheshire cat, and leaned closer to the desk. "Perhaps you'd like to suggest what qualities you would think are pertinent to this job, now that you've seen the hotel firsthand and had a brief acquaintance with *Signorina* Le Bres?"

Her tone was so condescending it took him aback for only a millisecond before he responded with equal impertinence. "How about you tell me just why *Mademoiselle* Le Bres—*Signorina* Le Bres," he corrected himself, "was let go."

The woman gasped. "The nerve," she said, "first calling Mr. Conroy yourself then questioning me on why she was let go. I don't think I need to remind you of this, *Signore* Umbere, but none of it is any of your business."

He'd had about enough of J's snarky personal assistant. "How about I call your boss and see what he thinks about you letting Monique go? Why don't I just do that?" He knew it was risky, but he pulled out his phone and pretended to dial, calling her bluff when she leaned across the desk, red-faced, and grasped for the phone.

"There's no need for that, Mr. Umbere." Her gaze darted from side to side and her neck flushed red. He was used to that. It went with the territory. He must act within character.

"Luc. Please call me Luc," he said, laying on the charm.

"Luc," she started tentatively. "There are privacy concerns."

He pretended to dial J again.

Teresa acquiesced. Whatever the reason Monique Le Bres was let go, Teresa Stiles sure didn't want him telling J about it, that was for certain.

"Discretion is the motto of Totally Five Star," she began.

"I thought it was superb service," he sparred back.

"Of course, but being discreet must be exercised in any account. Let's just say that Miss Monique Le Bres did not practice it and leave it at that, shall we?"

Oh, now his interest was really piqued as he shifted in his chair. That sexy little minx. It sounded like she'd been a naughty girl. But with whom? And had it warrant getting fired?

Luc said nothing, just stared Teresa down, waiting for more.

But the woman was hard as nails and said nothing more.

"And this Donovan, was he not discreet either?" he said, poking a stick in what he suspected was the reason for the firing.

Now it was Teresa's turn to squirm in her seat.

Luc was delighted. He pressed further. "What?" He shrugged as if to show he didn't really care. He could taste the salacious details on the tip of his tongue, and he wanted to savor them one delicious morsel at a time. "So she was fired for a little indiscretion? Big deal, this is *Italia*. I'm sure Mr. Conroy wouldn't think it warranted firing." He began to dial again.

"There's more," she said hastily, and then paused, as if unsure what to do. "There was another member of the staff that was let go as well."

Oh, this is getting very interesting. His cock stirred at the thought of Monique and several lovers. The girl was really dirty. He loved that. "Another employee?"

She nodded. "She was let go as well."

"A woman!" he exclaimed, then quickly regretted his unbridled enthusiasm.

"Shh..." Teresa said, shushing him and leaning closer as if to confide more.

Eager, Luc leaned closer.

"Deanna, one of the assistants to the director for food and beverage, she was, well...she was watching *Signor* Amatus and *Signorina* Le Bres when I found them...up on the terrace...doing things most inappropriate. And it wasn't the first time either. I'd walked in on them earlier in the day in her office and, Monique is voyeuristic it seems, according to Deanna. She likes watching others. Apparently Deanna says Monique watched her and Donovan when they were intimate." Teresa shook her head disapprovingly and sat back in her chair. Her face flamed red and she exhaled as if a weight had been lifted off her shoulders.

"Well, that does explain a lot." He was careful not to reveal his delight at what a truly superb minx Monique was and how his cock thickened at the thought of her watching some man with a woman. Had Monique been naked? He could just imagine those luscious curves of hers begging for a good plundering.

"You cannot tell a soul," Stiles said, almost conspiratorially.

"Of course." He rose from the chair. "Thank you for telling me. That makes things much clearer."

"And please, Luc, don't breathe a word of this to Mr. Conroy. We will get you a replacement art curator this week. I'll be in touch."

Luc only nodded as he exited the office with a wide grin.

Well, well, well. If little Miss Monique Le Bres didn't turn out to be just as sinfully sexy as he'd thought when he'd first met her. That, plus brains. What an enchanting combination. He couldn't dial J fast enough and tell him to reinstate Monique's employment immediately. Alessandro would be damned if he'd let a sultry goddess like her slip away. She was a prize catch and he'd almost stood by while her talents had been squandered elsewhere.

Chapter Ten

The shrill ring of her cell phone from her purse as Monique, with her cumbersome luggage, navigated the precariously narrow stone sidewalks that edged the canal. The midday sun was stifling as she paused, fumbling for her phone in her overstuffed handbag. She dug through all the last-minute items she'd shoved into it.

Glancing at the call display before answering, she saw it was Totally Five Star. *No fucking way am I answering that.* They could go screw themselves if Stiles was going to reprimand and embarrass her more than she already had, or ask for the freebies back that she'd stuffed into her luggage. That yummy hotel robe for one thing. Not so free, but she was damned well going to take a souvenir of her brief stay at the über-plush hotel. Who knew when she'd have the chance to stay at such a luxurious retreat again? Monique left the call unanswered and continued on.

She had no clue where she was going, just as far from that damn hotel as she could get. Beads of sweat trickled down her brow as she searched canal after canal for the *pensione* Marie said her brother ran. It was cheap and with the only money in her wallet the small stash Maria had given her, Monique had to make it last a few nights until she could figure out what to do—and how she could afford a plane ride to anywhere.

Blowing her bangs off her forehead with one exacerbated breath, she halted, her luggage crashing onto the cobblestones behind her. A shaded café beckoned with its low, overhanging awning. The café's quaint patio provided shelter from the warmth and a cold Coca-Cola if she dared spare the exorbitant euros necessary for it.

Dragging her belongings behind her, Monique crossed the canal bridge and plunked herself down under the respite of the café awning. She did have to admit that Venice was gorgeous, even in her foul-tempered state. She quickly ordered a Coke and guzzled the refreshment the minute it arrived—the crisp taste of something familiar. She drained the glass and topped up the drink with what was left in the bottle then squeezed the slice of lemon into it and dunked it into the remaining cola for good measure. She lifted the drink to her lips and froze.

That's him. The man who had shown up as she'd been packing up her office, the man sent to supervise her, obviously unaware she'd been canned.

Monique studied the tablecloth intently then cocked an eye upward to see if he'd passed.

"Monique, there you are," he exclaimed as if he'd lost a puppy and had just found it.

"Oh," she said slowly. She met his gaze as he came over to her table and leaned one hand on the tablecloth with familiarity.

"I was looking for you. Actually, we all were. Why didn't you answer your phone?"

Monique just stared at him with no idea what he was talking about. Who was looking for her and why?

He smiled and she noted he was more handsome than she'd realized. She raised her eyebrows when he pulled out a chair across from her and sat as if he had every right. *The nerve. Who does he think he is?*

"So what are you doing here?" he asked, leaning over the table toward her. His brown eyes glinted in the sunlight that streaked thought the weathered awning.

"I...I was just having a Coke." Immediately, she felt stupid stating the obvious as she tipped the empty bottle, playing with it nervously. His intense gaze made her uncomfortable. He still wore that tacky shirt and those dreadful chinos, but somehow he managed to be...to be...dammit—hunky. His wide shoulders and the tilt of his strong jaw reminded her of the man in the camel hair overcoat. Now, after the events of the last twenty-four hours, that seemed a lifetime away.

His eyes sparked with a knowing look, making her feel as if he could read her mind.

"I see that. Well, anyway, you should be getting back to the hotel. Lots to do. Better get cracking, as you Americans say."

His English was impeccable, as was his Italian, but she definitely detected a French accent as he spoke. Very continental. Damn, wasn't that what had gotten her into the mess with Donovan in the first place? She wasn't going to let this Luc Umbere get the better of her with his snazzy French accent. The sooner she set him straight that she was none of his concern, the better.

"But I've been..." She loathed to say the word 'fired', although she was pretty sure he'd found that out from that nasty Teresa Stiles. "I don't work there anymore."

"Yes, you do. Effective immediately, you are the *Curatore d'Arte*. That is what they were calling to tell you. You'd know that if you'd answered your damn phone."

Her surprise was difficult to conceal, her mind reeling. She had her job back? But why? Couldn't they find anyone? And why didn't he just do her bloody job if he'd been sent to supervise her?

She shifted in her seat, her eyes locked on him in challenge. "And what if I don't want to be *Curatore d'Arte* at the Totally Five Star?"

"It wasn't an invitation, Monique." There was something sensual about the way he said her name with a real honest-to-goodness French accent. It was the way she'd imagined her new name being pronounced all those years ago in trailer thirty-one.

He paused, seemingly surprised she wasn't jumping at the bait to take her old job back. "Not a request. It's an order."

Her appreciation of his accent vanished as she gasped at his tone. "You can't order me back to work."

He pushed his chair away and rose from the table as he dug for his wallet in his pocket. He placed a few euros on the table. "You're done here. Now, back to the hotel," he said, grabbing her luggage. He didn't wait for her to follow as he headed off down the narrow canal sidewalk.

Fuming, Monique just sat there, watching him walk away with her suitcases. As he carried on farther into the distance, she bolted up from her seat, snatched her purse and threw her napkin onto the table. Dammit to hell, she had her job back. There was no time to be a complete fool, so she hightailed it away from the café, her heels clicking as she went. She hoped she remembered the way back to the hotel.

With his long legs, the unnerving man with the French accent was well ahead of her, even with the impediment of her luggage. Aware there was no chance of catching her bossy supervisor, she ducked into an entryway for some shade and scrounged through her purse for her phone.

After pressing voicemail, she listened in surprise to the message that had been left by none other than Claudia Bauer, the personal assistant to James Conroy.

"We understand there has been some mix-up at the hotel and we are very sorry to hear you have departed from Totally Five Star Venice." There was static then some muffled noises in the background, forcing Monique to strain even harder to hear the words over the background noise of the canal. "Please, Miss Le Bres, return as soon as possible so you may resume your full duties of art curator for the Totally Five Star Venice. Mr. Conroy is counting on you to make the hotel his flagship in the chain. If there is anything I can do to assist, please do not hesitate to call me personally."

Monique was so stunned she listened to the message twice. There was no mention of the indiscretion she'd been fired for, or any mention of Teresa Stiles for that matter. Very puzzling. It was as if nothing had happened at all.

Was she just supposed to return to the hotel and pretend it never happened? That was going to be very difficult, especially if Donovan had been reinstated too. The moment she saw Donovan, Monique knew she'd ring his neck. Monique tucked the phone back into her purse.

With no money to speak of and stranded in Venice, she had no other choice than to return to accept the reinstatement. She'd be an idiot not to, but the job she'd coveted for months before she'd landed it now seemed to lack the appeal it once had. Up for a new challenge, Monique rallied, reminding herself it wasn't such a long way back to that dust-filled trailer park. She had a chance now to rise above the ashes like a phoenix, and damn right, she would. She'd wipe any smug looks Teresa Stiles gave her off the woman's face. She slung her purse over her shoulder and strode back to the hotel, only getting lost twice due to identical-looking canals. *This place is maddening and enchanting all at the same time. Sort of like that Luc Umbere.*

* * * *

Alessandro couldn't help looking over his shoulder in disbelief that Monique wasn't following him back to the hotel. That impertinent little wench. He had half a mind to put her over his knee and give her a good spanking for being so ungrateful. His groin throbbed when he thought about that round little ass under his hands. He flexed his fingers and traced along his palm, thinking of just how much fun he could have with that sexy minx if she'd just get her adorable bottom back to the hotel. He hefted the suitcases in his hand, giving up on the damn rolling wheels that only made the cobblestone sidewalks more challenging than usual. As he trudged along, he wondered just what in the hell she had in her luggage. Gratefully reaching the hotel, he scooted in the revolving doors, glad for the blast of cooler air that greeted him.

"*Signor*, please let me assist with your bags." A young bellhop appeared out of nowhere and took the bags from his grasp. "And your name?"

"Uh," he said, unsure what to do with Monique's bags. What if she didn't show up? He smiled. Then she'd have no clothes to wear. No bra. No panties. His cock twitched in delight as he visualized her nude. "Uh, these are *Signorina* Le Bres'. *Camera d'albergo, por favore.*" He told the bellhop to place the bags in her room. Then he remembered the attaché. "And this one in her office, *por favore.*"

The boy nodded and Luc gave him a hefty tip before remembering he wasn't Alessandro. Luc was an employee of the hotel, he would never tip like that.

Tapping his foot, he stood watching the comings and goings of the guests, thinking this was a colossal waste of time, just as the revolving door swept in the divine Miss Le Bres. Her face looked flushed from the heat, her blouse sticking to her buxom chest.

"Ah, *Signorina* Le Bres," he said, stepping toward her. He tried to conceal his pleasure at her return.

"Where are my bags?" She looked around him in annoyance.

"Already taken upstairs to your room. So now we are ready to get back to work." He sensed her reluctance. As she glanced nervously over her shoulder and toward the reception desk, she obviously was expecting someone, maybe that man with whom she'd been found *in flagrante delicto*.

Wait, there had been a woman involved as well as a man.

Monique shifted her weight from side to side on her sexy high heels, chomping at the bit, for what, he did not know. Him? He should be so lucky. No, the cold look in her eyes wasn't for him.

"Let's go to the office so we can review those plans for the rococo acquisitions," he said, trying to steal her attention from whatever was distracting her. "Then we will have a drink later," he ventured, catching her incredulous stare. "There is an exhibit of late baroque at the Medici Gallery. It would be prefect for us to attend and get more inspiration for the hotel's collection."

"I don't need a drink," the sexy American uttered. She turned on her heels and abruptly ended the conversation as she headed for the elevator.

Oh, so she wants to play it that way, does she?

Chapter Eleven

A smug smile of satisfaction cracked Monique's face when she stepped into the elevator. Luc caught up to her and hopped in. How quickly the tables had changed. She punched the second floor button. The elevator zipped quickly upward, so she only had a brief moment to glance at him and catch his nod as the doors dinged open.

Hesitantly, she exited with Luc right behind her. Damn, she hoped he didn't hover over her all the time. He was taking this supervising thing a little too literally if he thought he was going to follow her everywhere she went.

Heading for her office, she was surprised to find the door open. Somehow she'd expected they'd have it all sealed up. She stepped inside, noting it was exactly as she'd left it only a few hours ago. Then she saw her attaché on the desk beside the work binder she'd left behind with all her access codes. It seemed that someone hadn't wanted her to waste a moment getting back to the job at hand.

"I'll let you settle yourself," he told her. "I'll be back in an hour and we can go for a drink then to the exhibit." It was a statement, not a question. He left before she could answer.

Alone in the office, she thought it was some kind of hoax or something that she was back where she'd started. She went to her desk and opened the binder. The codes had all been updated. Someone had been very busy reinstating her. She looked at her watch. Four o'clock. They'd done all this in just over two hours. And they'd obviously anticipated she'd be back. With nowhere to go and no money, why wouldn't she return? She hated to be grateful to Teresa Stiles or whoever had reinstated her. The hell with them. She'd prove she was worth her weight in gold by making the best art collection she could. Quickly, she emptied out the contents of her attaché, fired up the computer and entered the tedious new list of access codes.

After an hour, Monique rested her head on her hands for a moment before picking up her carefully crafted list of appointments she'd had to cancel before she'd left. Just as she begun to dial, Marie came in with a wide smile on her face.

"*Signorina* Le Bres, I am so pleased you are back." The maid put the steaming pot of *caffè* and some biscotti down.

"Marie, it's good to be back," she said, actually meaning it. "Oh, and I have your money." Monique handed it back to her and expressed her appreciation for a helping hand.

Marie took the money and tucked in into her ample bosom. "You're a lucky woman, *Signorina* Le Bres. Someone must have put a good word in for you."

Monique snorted. "Teresa Stiles, no doubt."

"Oh no, it wasn't *Signorina* Stiles, the order came straight from James Conroy himself. Sargent Stiles in a foul mood, stay clear."

"Oh?" It both shocked and delighted Monique that Teresa Stiles was peeved. "And Donovan?" Monique ventured tentatively, wondering if he'd been reinstated.

Luc Umbere tapped on the open door, interrupting Monique's inquiry. His tall frame filled the space, making the room seem suddenly very small.

"She won't be needing *caffè*." Luc admonished the maid as he entered. "We're just about to go for a drink."

"*Si, signor*," Marie said obediently. She picked up the tray and partially closed the door behind her, leaving a stunned Monique to stare at Luc.

Monique put her hands on her hips in defiance. "That was uncalled for."

"I said I would come back in and hour and check on how you're doing. Then we'd discuss your plans for the work." He looked at his watch then back at her. "And it has been an hour."

Monique tapped her foot in annoyance.

"Bring your things, don't forget your agenda," he commanded.

Monique didn't move. She tried to think what smart thing she could say to this domineering man.

"Come on, *Signorina* Le Bres, don't keep me waiting. I want to hear more about rococo — over a martini, of course." He flashed a devilish smile that belied his irritatingly obstinate tone before he turned to exit, motioning for her to join him.

She didn't know if it was the look in his eye that made her acquiesce, or the fact that a martini after the day she'd had sounded awfully good. Monique snatched her notes off the desk and popped them into her attaché, then reached for her purse to join him as he stood in the doorway.

"Ladies first," he commented with a cocky grin.

"Thank you," she said as innocuously as she could. She stepped past him into the hall, very aware of his male scent—fresh, piny with a hint of musk. She loved that smell despite herself.

He closed the door behind her and smiled with satisfaction. "Now for that martini I promised you."

She led the way to the elevator, imagining his gaze on her ass the whole time she made the short walk. Coming up beside her, he pressed the elevator button.

They waited in silence. She couldn't think of a single thing to say. Secretly, she stole glances of him. His dark eyes reminded her of espresso. She diverted her gaze to her shoes, her heart beating so loudly she feared he'd hear it. The elevator descended from the fifth floor. *Please don't let it be Donovan.*

Finally, the doors dinged open and Monique practically jumped inside, eager to get away from their uncomfortable silence. Her stomach immediately sank as she spotted Teresa Stiles standing in the corner with her lips pursed. There was no way to escape with Luc behind her, so she joined Teresa without so much as a nod. He reached over her shoulder and pressed the lobby button.

The short ride down was bearable only because it took less than thirty seconds from start to finish. The moment the doors opened on the main floor, Monique bolted.

Monique turned back to see what was holding Luc up and smacked into Teresa, who was exiting right behind her.

"You must have friends in very high places," she snarled.

Monique wondered who had put a good word in for her. Surely not her boss back in Kansas. She hoped beyond hope that reports of her ill-fated deeds at the Totally Five Star Venice hadn't reached that far. If that were the case, then everyone knew about her indiscretions. *Fuck.* She needed that drink.

"What?" Luc asked, joining her. "Is something wrong?" He barely touched her as he led her to wherever they were going. "Come, you'll feel better after a drink."

She followed him as if on autopilot. He guided her through the crowds milling about the lobby to the piano bar sequestered behind those gauzy sheers she so admired.

"Sit." He motioned for her to be seated at a booth in the corner, then he strode to the bar.

Monique sat. Her mind still boggled, trying to figure out how she had gotten her job back.

She couldn't help but stare at Luc as he ordered their drinks at the bar. Tall and muscled, even she could see his athletic build in his poorly cut clothes. Her gaze lingered on his ass. It was sexy, that was for sure. *No, no, no.* He was her supervisor and she had to do better than she had with her last one. As if somehow sensing she was watching him, he looked back at her over his shoulder and gave her a sexy grin. Monique's cheeks burned as she cracked a weak smile and then became very busy playing with the cocktail coaster on the table.

Luc returned carrying two martinis carefully, so as not to spill them. Just as he started to put hers down, the drink almost slopped over the edge. He took a quick sip to keep the liquid from overflowing. The wet gin and vermouth lingered on his lips, glossy and tempting. He gave her the one he hadn't sipped from, placing it in front of her and then sat across from her with his martini. He said nothing, just looked at her and held his martini up.

"*À de nouveaux commencements.*" He toasted to new beginnings.

"You speak French," she said, trying not to sound impressed.

"*Za nove početke,*" he proclaimed. "Also Croatian. *Til nye begyndelser,*" he added. "That's Danish." He was more charming than boastful. "They all mean the same thing, *Mademoiselle* Le Bres — to new beginnings."

"Any other languages?" She decided to test the boastful linguist at his own game, hoping he didn't challenge her precarious command of Italian.

"*Para novos começosa,*" he uttered with one eyebrow raised for effect.

"Easy, I know that one," she exclaimed, proud of herself. "It's Spanish."

"Not so fast." His tone was playful.

Her pulse quickened.

"Portuguese."

"That was a trick," she said with a little pout. She knew she was flirting, but damn this man was not at all what she'd thought with him rattling off languages as easily as breathing. She couldn't help imagining just what other hidden skills he might possess, imaging him going down on her. Squeezing her legs together, she did her best to extinguish that image before it got the better of her.

"How do you know so many languages?" she asked.

He held his glass to hers. "Let's just call it an occupational hazard of the art world. *Di nuovi inizi,*" he toasted in Italian.

At least she understood that one. *"Di nuovi inizi,"* she agreed, clinking her glass to his. A quiver of excitement whipped through her, their gazes unwavering.

Nervously, she looked down at the tabletop then back up at Luc. She touched her glass to his. "To new beginnings."

"And now, about your work..." he said enthusiastically, shattering the tenderness of the moment. "Tell me more about your plans for the hotel collection. And don't leave anything out. I want to hear all about it, especially your rococo theme. Don't forget I have two tickets for us to attend that showing tonight at the Medici."

"Oh, right," she said, surprised he had tickets. It was well known in the art world that the Medici exhibit was by private invitation only. Maybe this Luc Umbere did know his art after all and had connections in the art world. He seemed a much better supervisor than that boy toy Donovan. Much more useful for helping her make her mark in the art world and far less lecherous, it seemed. Her face flamed hot and she quickly took a drink of her martini—too big a gulp—as the fiery gin went down fast.

He didn't conceal his amusement when her eyes filled with tears from the potent martini.

"Yes, you'll enjoy the exhibit. I'm sure you will. But for now..." His gestured for her list.

"Oh, right." Business, not pleasure, she reminded herself as she quickly opened her attaché and fished out the list. Before handing it over, she paused, wondering if her new supervisor would think she was too ambitious. Some of the works were well outside her budget, but she possessed good negotiating skills and had hoped to get some real buys for the hotel.

She handed Luc the list and he sat back in silence, reading it. Nervous, she sipped her drink, hoping it would calm her as he took his sweet time. Other than a few grunts of approval—at least she hoped it was approval—he said nothing, his brow furrowed as he read on. He reached for his drink and, after taking a sip, followed by another, he placed both the drink and the list on the tabletop.

"I'm impressed. It seems you're not just a beautiful face after all…" His gaze met hers.

She gulped, trying to suppress the flush of attraction as she looked into those beautiful brown eyes of his and saw her reflection in them. She wondered how she must look to him. As good as he looked to her? She hoped so.

He commented on her list. "I especially like that you've selected several of Giuseppe Bonito, an interesting choice. A Neopolitan. They have been undervalued recently and would be a great investment if you can get one at a reasonably fair price. You know they're in the catalog for the auction to be held at the end of the week."

"I know, that's just what I thought." The words came out fast, a little too eager for his approval, so Monique quickly played her response down, trying to dampen her enthusiasm. "Of course, there are many opportunities in the market right now. I'll just have to see what works out."

"You mean *we'll* have to see what works out. We're a team, remember?"

She chewed her bottom lip, the tang of the martini on her tongue only fueling the flush of desire that coursed through her. He was quite the mystery and she was beginning to love his surprises, discovering one after the other. Who would have guessed that those boring, old clothes belied a sophisticated, intelligent and downright sexy man underneath?

"Are you sure you're okay working with me?" He pressed on, possibly mistaking her silence for reticence. "No problems you want to talk about with me being your supervisor?" he asked.

"No." Her voice cracked, forcing her to gulp her drink for relief. *Dammit, he must know something about Donovan and me.* That was the last thing she needed.

"Good." He sat back comfortably in his chair. "You grilled me about my accent, Monique. Do I detect a twang in that accent of yours?"

Her cheeks grew hot. That damn Midwestern accent followed her around worse than the scraggy dogs in her old cesspool of a trailer park.

"What would you like to know, Luc?" She gave no hint that he'd put her ill at ease with his comment, reminding her just where she'd come from. "I can call you Luc, can't I? Now that we're a team," she said slyly.

He smiled widely when he laughed. *"Touché."* He toasted as he took a long sip of his drink. "I think you and I will make a fine team. *We* both want the same things."

Did he mean to have sex—*wild sex*—because that was just what she was thinking whenever he flashed that devilish smile at her. Or did he mean to procure to the best art collection they could? She observed the way he stroked the stem of his martini glass, sending a flutter of arousal between her thighs. In an effort to cling to some control, she crossed her legs tighter.

Chapter Twelve

One martini led to another then another. Monique's head spun. At least she assumed it was the booze and not the way Luc looked at her as she supplied him with the basic bio he'd requested. Nothing too personal, no hint of the trailer trash life she'd fled and her relentless climb up the ladder of success.

"And you went to school at Kent State, a long way from Kansas..."

"Umm." She reflected on her first step up the ladder that had led to her new life. "Yes, scholarships all the way."

"Bright," he observed.

"Ambitious," she corrected, never one to take compliments well.

"Both," he agreed.

It left her feeling uncomfortable at having revealed too much about her true self to this man she'd only just met—so un-Monique. She was accustomed to hiding behind a thick emotional wall of steel, asking what she needed and moving on, eye always on the prize, and never letting anyone in. But the way she was with Luc unsettled her. And he intrigued her.

"Impressive," was all he said. He reached across and gently touched her hand as she took the last sip of her drink and placed the empty glass back onto the table. His gaze lingered on her lips, tempting her.

Vowing not to give in to the simmering attraction she felt, she allowed her hand to touch his just a moment longer before whisking it away.

He only chuckled. "Oh yes, very impressive."

His expression was hard to read. Bemusement? Admiration? She couldn't quite tell.

"Shall we?" he asked, signing the check. He then pushed back his chair.

Her jaw dropped. "You've got the wrong idea, Luc, if you think I'm going to fall into your bed."

His loud, deep laughter filled the bar. Several other patrons glanced at them as Monique tried to hide her embarrassment.

"I meant are we ready to go to that gallery I was telling you about and look at the rococo items that I mentioned."

Her cheeks burned so hot she was sure they would burst into flames. She stared up at him, feeling utterly ridiculous—and angry. He'd played into her desires. Furious with herself, she threw down her napkin and hopped up from her chair—almost forgetting to grab her attaché.

"Ready then?" he asked. "For the gallery, not bed," he whispered.

He reached out and pulled her to him, his erection evident.

She gulped and nodded. He released her and led the way out of the bar.

Mortified with her *faux pas*, she berated herself for even contemplating breaking her newly formed rules about not having sex with her colleagues, let alone her supervisor... Gathering her resolve and the last shreds of her self-respect after that scene in the bar, Monique walked quietly beside him through the lobby and onto the crowded sidewalks.

* * * *

The sun dipped into the horizon. It cast a dusky hue onto the buildings, making their doorways and sunken windows appear even more secretive than usual. Monique wobbled on her stilettos, reminded immediately of the lesson she'd learned two days before when she'd snapped her heel. Tonight it wasn't just her poor choice of footwear to blame for her stumbling. She was sure booze and the uneven pavers conspired against her too. Luc quickly grabbed her hand in his strong grip.

"*Stai bene?*" He asked if she was okay.

Monique gasped. It was so familiar...'*Stai Bene*' were the same words her mystery man had uttered when he'd rescued her. The words still rang in her ears, as did the depth of his blue eyes that had sent her even more off balance. Tempted by the recollection, Monique snuck a glance at Luc, double-checking. Shit, the booze really was taking its toll on her. Her mystery man was a blond-haired, goatee-wearing, debonair vision. Gone as quickly as he'd arrived in one swish of his camel hair coat. But this man, Luc, the brown-eyed devil that he was, was very much there in the flesh as she walked hand in hand with him along the canal, his strength keeping her steady as she caught her shoe yet again.

"I'll have to carry you if you can't keep up," he said with a sparkle in his eye.

She looked over at him in surprise.

"You wouldn't mind that, now would you?" he teased, running his thumb on her palm.

She quivered in anticipation. "I am perfectly able to walk by myself, thank you," she said as firmly as she could.

"Fine." He let go. The instant release set her off balance and she stepped a little too close to the edge of the canal, teetering dangerously near to the water below.

His arm quickly went around her waist, the only thing that saved her as the momentum of her body sent her attaché plunging into the canal with a splash.

"Oh, no!" With Luc right beside her, his grasp still around her waist, she tried to go after the briefcase, kneeling on her hands and knees beside the canal. His grip remained tight as she realized the briefcase was long gone in the murky water.

"At least it wasn't a family heirloom," he commented.

She laughed. "It don't think it was even real leather." She was too embarrassed to confess that she'd just bought it online from some liquidation retailer for her new job. Genuine pleather. She'd been so excited about her big break in Venice she'd wanted to look the part when she arrived. And now the blasted attaché was at the bottom of the canal.

The hard cobbles hurt Monique's knees and she righted herself, grateful for Luc's steadying hands. She got her bearings and glanced once more in the direction of the lost case then proceeded onward. "I think I have everything I need on the computer, except that list of contacts I was going to call first thing in the morning. Shit." She'd have to start all over again.

"Don't fret, the works I am about to show you will be much better than anything on that list."

"I hope so or I'll be out of my job—again."

He only smiled and let out a short laugh then pulled her closer. "I'll make very sure you don't lose your job again."

"I doubt you could do anything about it," Monique said matter-of-factly. She tried to ignore how good he felt, her body pressed close to his as he wrapped his arm protectively around her shoulder. The scent of his shirt, crisp and clean, mixed with a hint of musk made her want him to do more to her than just help her keep her job. But rules were rules and she knew better than to get tangled up again with her boss.

Chapter Thirteen

The rambling Medici gallery was silent, except for the sound of their footsteps on the stone floors. Unlike galleries in America, this one was typical of Italy. Settled in an ancient stone building, smelling of damp from the canal it was built upon, the gallery's small unpaned windows offered openings for slivers of moonlight. Without air-conditioning, the small islets of windows let the air flow along with the thick stone walls that kept the gallery cool.

It lacked high-tech lighting with only a few halogens placed here and there, highlighting the paintings on display, making the vacuous stone rooms dark and ominous. Monique followed Luc through the first few rooms. She stopped to admire the massive, evocative François Boucher on the far wall of the third exhibit. So seductive, so sensual. With every brushstroke, the artist had captured the essence of rococo. It reminded Monique just why art history had first captured her imagination in her younger years—the promise of escape to a world where people lived lives so differently from hers. She was transported every time she looked into one of the masterpieces.

"You like that one." Luc made her aware he was observing her, as she had been lost for a moment.

Monique only murmured. She'd been to many galleries, studied countless works of art, but the rococo and baroque always made her heart beat faster, as if she could reach out and touch the flesh of the women, the pudgy babies, depicted so lifelike as cherubs. The soft hue of the artist's deft touch was nothing short of a mere miracle to her.

"It's very beautiful, indeed, but not quite within our budget," he commented.

Talk of a budget brought her back to reality, clearing away some of the buzz of the martini.

She wasn't there to ogle the art. She was there to *shop* for art and this painting was definitely not in her budget. Or *their* budget, as Luc kept reminding her. They were a team. *Some team.* He was too commanding to be a team player. She was quite sure if she lost her focus and gave in to her desires of the moment, this would not end well.

He led the way out of the room. "Come. I have something else I think you'll like."

"Oh, you've been here before, obviously," she said with surprise as she followed him into the adjoining room. She squinted to adjust to the dim lighting.

"It's one of my favorite galleries. The acquisitions manager is a good friend of a friend of mine, so we should be able to work out some very favorable acquisitions. Now tell me, what do you think of this one?"

Monique stood stunned by the small, exquisite painting in the center of the room, set on an easel because of its petite size in comparison to the other, wall-sized murals.

Speechless, she stepped closer. "It is so...so..." The words escaped her as she studied the image of a woman dressed in aristocratic finery with one stockinged leg revealed, a very risqué pose for the time. Just out of her view to the far side of the canvas was her suitor. He watched from beside a tree with a distinct glint in his eye at the prospect of the provocative woman.

"What?" Luc prompted Monique, stepping closer.

Monique fought the urge to reach out and touch the canvas, the fleshy tenderness of the woman's leg, the perfect rendering of rose-hued cheeks of her suitor.

"Scandalous!" Monique blurted. She then laughed heartily, seeing the artist had placed the suitor's hand precariously close to his crotch, near his concealed button fly, but definitely discernable to the trained eye.

"*Si molte scandaloso,*" Luc confirmed. "And the title is The Scandal of Madame Louisville. She was the king's niece."

"Oh dear, that *is* scandalous! It's a wonder the artist didn't lose his head for that."

"Quite the contrary. The king had a bawdy sense of humor, it seems, and he liked it very much. It's said to have had his approval."

"You do know about art," she said with astonishment, looking up at Luc. The deep glow in his brown, espresso eyes reflecting her face.

"You seem surprised."

"I am." Monique was self-conscious when he let his gaze linger on her. Studying the painting more, she noted the bodice of the dress revealed the hint of a dusky nipple blooming from Madame's low-cut neckline. Wisps of white lace were meant to conceal this from the casual observer, but on closer inspection, Monique clearly saw what the artist had wanted her to see. The subject's areola and the tip of her nipple, blush with arousal, peeked up from behind the lace.

"You don't miss anything, do you, Monique?" Luc touched her shoulder, making her tense at the intimacy of his touch as he moved it slightly lower. "The nipple is visible, hence the suitor's arousal."

Monique gasped as she looked again and saw that Luc was right. There was a distinct flare to the suitor's pants where his cock lay. The artist knew this and was playing with the subject.

"The nipple is too tempting for the suitor," Luc observed as he traced small, light circles with his fingertips on her upper arm.

Monique quivered as they stood so close. Alone in the dim room, the light illuminated only the painting.

"So rosy, tender and delicious."

His raspy voice made Monique's pussy moist. He inched his fingers closer to the rise of her breast. Luc's fingertips were inches from the bare flesh of her cleavage. His breath was hot and tempting as he leaned in closer. Unable to speak or breathe, consumed with desire, she ached to be held in his embrace. At any moment, she was quite sure she'd sink to her knees and let him do whatever he wanted to her.

"Yes, too tempting," he whispered, his warm breath igniting a fire along her skin.

Abruptly he stepped away.

The air suddenly turned chilly and vacant around her as he turned on his heels. "There's more to see in the next room. Better put that one on our list for sure."

Stunned by his departure from the room and a bit angry at herself for getting caught up in the moment, thinking he was coming on to her, she studied the canvas again. Not about to be pulled when he yanked her chain, Monique purposely took her sweet time examining the painting, making a note on her phone to check the margins and signature of the work before acquiring it for Totally Five Star. It was a 'must have', that was for sure. *Oh, and I need to know the price, of course.* She added that pesky little detail to her notes.

"I'm waiting…"

Luc's stern tone from the doorway forced her look up from her phone and stuff it into her purse. Damn, he looked good standing there in the dark room, the moonlight gilding the stern but seductive look on his face. His jaw was set, as was the inquiring arc of his eyebrow. Her resolve ebbed away further as she looked at those brown eyes—dark, almost sinister, if they weren't so dammed alluring in the dim light.

Silently, she moved away from the painting, reluctant to appear obedient and follow his orders, but with no other exit other than the one they'd entered earlier, she was forced to follow him. And besides, it turned her on whenever he went all alpha. And how she'd loved those pants when he pressed closer to her, his more than obvious erection taunting her—tempting her.

He made no attempt to move out of her way as she entered the narrow hall connecting the two exhibits.

"Excuse me." She slipped past him, very aware of how he made her feel when they were so close.

"Certainly," he said, his tone revealing his slight amusement as she looked up at him.

Monique knew she should be annoyed at being his play toy. She'd had enough of that with Donovan and look how that had ended. But this guy was different somehow.

He followed her into the next room. "Right this way. There is another gem we might consider acquiring for the hotel."

"Let me look for myself." Her tone was defiant. She purposely hid her smile of satisfaction at trying to reclaim the upper hand as she moved toward several paintings on display.

The room housed a series of works by another rococo artist, one lesser-known, but slowly gaining popularity among art circles. The works weren't oils, but three individual nude sketches. She studied them attentively. The soft, shell-like curves of the female form, so perfectly rococo, so beautifully depicted. There was nothing else in the works but each singular nude, the same model for all three. Monique was a gambling woman and wagered that the model was probably the artist's lover.

"Tell me what you think," Luc said from a few feet behind her, as if giving her space to assess the works.

"Oh, now you want my opinion. Only a moment ago you were ordering me around."

"Monique," he said, stepping right behind her, his tone surprisingly reassuring. "I think you can handle it, am I right?" he asked suggestively. His deep, steady breath was the only sound in the room as she held hers when his hand slipped along her shoulder, tracing a gentle pattern on her arm.

"It's very good," she said, remembering to breathe and deliberately ignoring his question. "These are going up in value at a rapid rate and to have three in a series, I would think, would be an impressive acquisition for the hotel."

"It is," he said, his touch alternating between light and then firm.

Monique looked up at him as he placed both hands on her shoulders, aligning his body to hers.

His touch became more suggestive when he dragged his fingers, one by one, slowly but firmly, down her arms and back up again. Each flicker of his fingertips sent a wave of arousal deep between her legs. The prospect of what it would be like to have him make love to her, to take her, right there in the gallery made her panties moist.

"Do you think they are the same model?" he asked, negating whatever space was left between them as he pressed closer.

"Yes," she said with a small gulp.

"Good, then we agree..." His trailed into a whisper.

Agree with what? With the painting or to giving in to you and having you fuck me senseless right now? She wanted to scream her consent for him to touch her any way he saw fit. Instead, she stilled her wild thoughts as best as she could. "You can tell by the curve of the breasts," she stated, finally finding her professional opinion. "That this is the same woman, and that little mole by her right nipple confirms it."

He exhaled a slow, deep breath, now slipping his hands onto her waist. She could feel his heartbeat between them as his palms came to rest on the curves of her hips.

"I hadn't noticed that," he said. His breath was hot on her neck as he nudged her long hair, his lips so close to her skin she felt she would burn up with desire. With want. With need. "Those nipples are divine, the way the artist has paid such attention to each one, it's as if we can feel the weight of those breasts with each stoke of his charcoal." He slid his hands upward.

Speechless, Monique bit her bottom lip when he moved his hands over her hips, toward her breasts. She reached up, instinctively halting them. Although she craved his touch, she knew better. He wrapped his fingers around hers, their entwined hands resting on her décolletage. The rise and fall of each uneven breath she took caused his hands to fall slightly lower.

It was too much. He circled her hands against the round slopes of her breasts, making her pulse grow uneven as she touched herself at his command. Her arousal got the better of her as she fantasized about him fucking her from behind until she screamed in surrender. How could she resist him? She wanted him so badly she could just imagine his erection within rubbing distance of her ass. All she had to do was wiggle her hips and she was sure she would feel his hard cock on her buttocks.

Her panties grew wetter at the thought. Unable to move, just standing there, her fingers tight within his, his broad arms wrapped around her, cocooning her from the outside world, she tipped her head back to look up at him.

His dark brown eyes sparked with approval. He wanted her as much as she wanted him. She could see it, feel it in his grasp, knew she was losing all control as he dragged his palms higher with hers tucked in them. Onto the rounds of her breasts, her nipples tightening under her fingertips as he opened his grip, moving her fingers over her erect buds through the fabric of her bra. Her body quivered from him controlling each delicious move. He orchestrated her touching her breasts, pleasuring herself, making her lean her weight against him, giving up, feeling his hard cock nudge her buttocks.

Footsteps on the stone floor brought Monique back from the brink of surrender. Immediately her eyes flashed open, and she snatched her hands from Luc's just as an elderly docent strolled into the room, seeming surprised to see them there.

"*Scusi,*" the gentleman exclaimed.

"Sold!" Monique burst out, eager to cover up just what she and Luc had been doing.

Luc chuckled, breaking the ice. "My, the woman does know what she wants. Sold it is, then," he said to the man.

"Of course, I'll have to check the margins," Monique interjected, looking at the docent then at Luc. "I have to go over everything before I bid on anything at the auction or sign any contracts for the hotel, but I definitely do think these sketches are perfect."

"*Molte bene,*" the elderly docent nodded. "*Bueno note.*"

They bid him good night and he disappeared as quickly as he had appeared.

Monique stepped away from Luc, using the incident to break the tension between them and gather her wits.

"They are lovely," she said, looking back at the paintings before starting to head into the next room. "I'd be sure to add those to my list and go over the details before I purchase them."

"Ah," Luc corrected her, his hand in the air. "Before *you* purchase them?"

"*We,*" she said playfully.

"That's much better. And don't worry about lineage or margins. I can look after all that for you. It's what I'm here for."

Funny, I thought you were here to drive me out of my mind with want.

Chapter Fourteen

Monique strolled briskly a few steps ahead of Luc Umbere, purposely keeping her distance after the close call of seduction. She wrestled with her conflicting emotions.

Monique looked at the final selection of paintings before the gallery closed.

She busily double-checked her list on her phone, feeling lost without her attaché. She made triple sure she had what she needed before leaving the gallery with Luc leading the way. She had to admit, despite the brief dalliance of passion, they'd made good progress tonight with a handful of potential purchases, and since Luc had agreed to check the margins and lineage of each one, it freed up her time to meet with other vendors.

Stepping out into the night alongside Luc, Monique was surprised to find it wasn't much darker outside than it had been inside, given the low lighting of the old gallery. The moist air kissed her as she hugged her arms tightly, trying to shed the damp as they walked along the canal.

"You must be starving. I know the perfect place," he offered.

Oh. Dinner alone with him. Something told her it wasn't a good idea. She knew damn well she'd wind up in his bed, and she couldn't risk that kind of exposure again. *Can't trust myself alone with him is more like it.* Steeling herself, she held her ground — albeit very shaky ground.

"I'm okay. Kind of tired after my big day back at work. I can get something at the hotel."

"Of course. In that case, we can eat in your room." It wasn't a question but a statement. This man was very good at saying what he wanted and not giving her an out.

"Uh, that wasn't quite what I meant."

"We could eat at mine, but it's farther away."

"Aren't you staying at the hotel?"

"No. No accommodation was included in my contract, so I have to stay somewhere more reasonable."

"Oh, I just assumed you'd be staying at the hotel."

"So, dinner in your room, then..." He ignored her query and placed his arm around her waist as they walked side by side.

She stopped and turned to face him, his hand still on her waist.

In the soft twilight, he looked so handsome, the streetlight illuminating his strong jaw and the soft creases of his smile. It caught her off guard before she rallied her rapidly retreating reserves against his charms.

"Luc," she started, thinking how best to turn him down. "I just don't think it's a good idea if we...if we..."

"If we what?" he asked coyly and pulled her closer. She didn't resist as she looked up at him.

"If we...if we go to my room. It's not a good idea."

"It *is* a good idea."

"No it's not," she said, feeling foolish for bantering with him in his embrace. She fought the urge to reach up and touch his jaw, to trace the outline of the cleft in his chin. To taste his lips. Fuck, she was no good at resisting this man.

"Come to my room, then. We'll dine at my hotel. It's farther for you to walk, but it will be well worth it." His flashed a super sexy smile at her as he moved his hands over her hips and cupped her buttocks to him.

"Luc," she exclaimed just as his lips met hers.

His lips were soft and searching as he embraced her, the waft of musk and the sense of rippling male muscle under his shirt made her want him even more. He gripped her ass hard as she kissed him back. Lost to the moment, she craved him more than anything. She glided her hands along his broad back, down to his waist as they explored each other's mouths with abandon.

"Someone will see us," she finally murmured, vaguely aware of the fact that they were in public, not far from the prying eyes of the hotel.

He gave a deep rumble from his chest as his lips met hers, then he lifted her slightly so her feet barely touched the ground. Swiftly, he moved her farther from the canal to the nearest building.

He pressed her into the dark alcove, and Monique opened her eyes when her back touched rough stone. He pulled one of her legs up to him, wrapping it around his waist as he pinned her against the wall. Luc kneaded the almost bare flesh of her ass against the hard stone front of the building. Her jaw dropped open when his fingers slipped between her legs, grazing her mound through her sheer panties. She nearly begged for more. He teased her slit through the fabric. Kissing her neck, he then moved along her collarbone and down her cleavage, his raw hunger matching hers. He moved the panties to one side and slipped a finger into her wetness.

She cried out at the sensation, clawing at his back in pure pleasure. Luc stroked her channel and slowly dragged his finger back out, slick along her folds, before touching her sensitive clit. It trembled and throbbed with appreciation, and her whole body shook when he expertly caressed her bud. She bit into his shoulder to stifle her groans. He repeated the motion, making her world spin as he finger-fucked her. She came hard, clinging to him and arching against his every move, lost in the sensation.

Luc did not give her a chance to recover. He stroked her G-spot, and she bucked against him, panting and calling out despite trying to be quiet when her second orgasm consumed her. He flicked her sensitized nub again. She was unable to conceal her cries as she crested again and shouted out his name.

"Oh, Luc, yes, yes..." She collapsed into the intense release, glancing to see if anyone had overheard her shouts of pleasure.

He gave a satisfied grin, his fingers still between her legs, and offered one last little pat to her clit before removing his hands, her skirt falling back into place. She became aware of his body pressed against hers, the embarrassed flush of what she had done, what he had done. Suddenly very shy and unsure, she placed her hands between them, making a little space as she looked up at him.

"The lady definitely knows what she wants," he said.

"I didn't mean for that to happen." She smoothed her skirt, further widening the space between them, and looked around to see a couple walk by. Shit, anyone could have seen them, tucked into the alcove but certainly not out of view. Images of her skirt hiked up and Luc using his fingers to pleasure her made her aware of how reckless she'd been, but also aroused at the same time.

"Well, I did," he said with a satisfied chuckle. "You are completely irresistible." He placed his arm over her head to brace himself against the wall and lowered his lips to hers. He made it clear she wasn't getting away any time soon. Damn, why did it have to feel so good when he forced her to accept that she wanted him?

"This *can't* happen again." She stalled the imminent kiss. But she knew damn well she wanted more of this hunky boss of hers. Who in their right mind could resist a finger-fuck like that?

"What a shame. We were just getting started," he said.

"I can't afford to lose my job." She looked anxiously over his shoulder. "I'd be out on the street again."

"You *are* out on the street." His lips met hers in a slow and seductive kiss as he nibbled on her bottom lip before pulling away. "Very well, then, if that's what you want, I won't bother you anymore."

How dare he give up so easily? Sure, she'd said it wasn't a good idea, but when he kissed her like that, she was open to giving it a chance. To give in to his lush, searching caresses.

"I've got to get back to the hotel. It's late." She turned quickly from him before he could see her disappointment. Testing him, she waited for him to reach out and stop her, but he didn't.

She knew it was foolish to hope he'd stop her. Monique kept walking but not very quickly, giving him one last chance.

"It's not safe at night," he called out finally as she picked up her pace. A few heavy strides later, he appeared next to her. "At least let me walk you back to the hotel."

"Very gentlemanly," she said sarcastically, sounding bitchier than she'd meant. It was just that him being a gentleman was precisely what she didn't want from him. Oh, how he could already wrap her around his little finger. He was driving her mad with the promise of just how good things could be. But she was scared to let herself fall for another man like her last lover back in Kansas, who would not only jeopardize her pride but also ruin her career.

Luc said nothing. The silence taunted her as they walked, this time with more space between them than before—but this was different. The playing field had changed. He'd felt her up, and she'd loved every minute of it when she came hard against his hand. There had been no concealing her delight when he'd been pleasuring her. He'd had her right where he'd wanted her. He must know that it put him in the driver's seat. As much as Monique hated these types of games, she always seemed to find herself in them. It went with the territory, she reminded herself. If you want to play with the boys, you're going to get hurt. And she sure did love playing with the boys. *Especially irresistibly sexy men like Luc who aren't at all easy to read.* It intrigued and thrilled her.

Desperate to regain the upper hand, Monique said nothing. It was a good thing her domineeringly dashing supervisor had been with her as she'd missed a few turns along the way and he'd gently corrected her, motioning in the right direction. All those damn baroque buildings looked the same, and the canals were barely discernable in the low light. She did her best not to wobble on her heels and hoped the hotel would appear soon.

They rounded a corner and the Totally Five Star Venice entrance greeted her. Thank goodness. That walk of silence had tormented her. She'd thought of all the things she could say to him, but didn't know where to begin. She was so confused. The sooner she got up to her room – alone – the better.

"Home sweet home." She broke the ice, ready to spring through the front, eager to escape being tempted by him.

"So it is," he said with a mischievous gleam in his eyes. "Seeing as you've refused my offer for dinner, I'll see you tomorrow. We will continue going over the acquisitions."

Monique nodded, remembering what she was really there for – her job.

"Goodnight, Monique, it's been a pleasure," he said, taking her hand in his. He held it up to his lips before kissing it, his own hand lingering for a moment near his nose. He inhaled. "*Un vero piacere.*"

The translation made her knees weak. *A true pleasure*. The man had no idea just how much pleasure and torment his affections were giving her.

"*Piacere mio,*" he whispered.

As she nearly ran through the front doors, needing immediate relief from the wave of desire that had filled her when Luc had lifted his hand to his nose and inhaled, Monique's cheeks felt like they were on fire. *Fuck*. The man was too much. She'd never be able to resist him if he kept that up.

Determined not to turn back and look out of the front doors, she headed for the elevator. But her will was too weak. She snuck a glance out of the corner of her eye and saw him still standing outside. *Double fuck.* She was in deep trouble. It was official. His broad shoulders undid her. The man was totally irresistible.

* * * *

Luc turned on his heels and carried on the minute he saw her slip into the elevator. Enchanting. Intoxicating. Overwhelming. He'd resisted fucking the daylights out of her there along the canal, his cock hard and throbbing when he'd slid his finger into her tight, wet hole. He'd been sure he'd come if he hadn't bitten down on his tongue to keep from blowing his wad. Patience — that was what he needed with that little vixen. Coming on too strong was the wrong course of action with her. She was hot as a hell and keen for sexual adventures, judging from her recent *faux pas* at the hotel with the staff, but he'd have to tread carefully if he was to win her into his bed. The last thing he wanted was to scare her off. There was too much at stake. The millions he could make off the art they were acquiring and the fact he *had* to have her. She was simply irresistible to him, and the fact she was reluctant to give into her passions was even more of a turn-on.

Chapter Fifteen

Monique peered out from under her covers. Someone was honking loudly and she resisted the urge to throw something out the window at the persistent driver. Finally, she fully regained consciousness and realized it was a boat horn. No cars, of course, in Venice. After dragging herself out of the divinely comfortable hotel bed, she walked over to an open window.

The canal looked more like an international shipping channel with the early morning vendors going every which way, their gondolas and small barges overburdened with produce and deliveries. The boats were so low in the water that she marveled they didn't sink. The sun was just rising over the Santa Mara Della Luce, its tiled domes appearing almost golden and quite a sight, even for the sleep-deprived Monique. She glanced at the clock on the nightstand and saw it was only six in the morning. It felt more like the middle of the night, thanks to her internal clock still being off-kilter.

Deciding to seize the day, Monique strolled past last night's dinner tray, half touched on the coffee table in the living room. She hadn't had much of an appetite after the exhausting yet exhilarating scene with Luc by the canal. Instantly, Monique's nipples stiffened at her memory of just how Luc had pressed her up against that stone wall, hiked her skirt up and given her just what she'd needed. Then he'd left her feeling frustrated by her own mixed signals when all she really wanted was to give in to the promise of more intimate pleasures. *Dammit. Why have I been so weak, allowing myself to get caught wanting more? Not just wanting. Needing. That was even worse.*

She'd have to do better today. Resist his charms and keep things business as usual. Not that there was business as usual at the Totally Five Star. Every day was more bizarre than the last.

Grabbing a piece of half-eaten bread from the dinner tray, she then nibbled on the stale toast as she headed for the shower. Monique was dying for an espresso. Hopefully, Marie would bring the caffé sooner than the usual ten a.m. Anything to keep Monique's focus on the task at hand—curating the best collection for the hotel she could. And keeping Luc at arm's length. Cock's length was more like it. Monique chortled as she stepped into the shower.

* * * *

An hour later, Monique was at her desk, busily going through last night's art selections and bemoaning the loss of her attaché as she entered the information from her notes into the computer. Luckily for her, she'd had a flash drive tucked safely in her purse and most of her information was salvageable. Just not her paper notes, something she loved to keep, never quite trusting a computer.

Marie arrived with breakfast and piping-hot coffee.

"So early, *Signorina* Monique," the friendly maid exclaimed as she placed the tray in the usual place.

Monique nodded. "I wanted to get a head start on the day."

"*Molto bene*. So how was your *appuntamento con il, Signor Umbere?*"

"It wasn't a date." Monique shifted awkwardly in her chair.

Marie pressed down firmly on the French press then poured her a steaming cup of the dark liquid. She brought it over to her desk.

"But it was fine. Thank you, Marie, for asking."

Marie stood looking at her as Monique took a big sip of the strong coffee and offered a satisfied murmur.

"He is very good-looking, *Signor* Luc," Marie commented, seemingly lost in her thoughts as a smile lifted the corners of her lips. "Despite his odd taste in clothes. But then I was always a sucker for brown-eyed men. My Alfredo had brown eyes, full of life...and lust."

Marie roared with a spirited zest that surprised Monique.

"Back in Romania, we have an expression, *ma faci sa visez in culori.*"

"I don't speak Romanian," Monique replied. "What does it mean?"

"You make me dream in color."

"Oh," Monique exclaimed. "Very apropos."

"What is apropos mean?"

"You nailed it, Marie, whatever it was you said. That's what apropos means. The literal translation is appropriate, as in correct. Oh, I do like that saying though... You make me dream in color," she repeated, laughing along with Marie. "I may have to learn Romanian."

"*Sì, Signorina*, you just may have to," the maid said, chuckling as she started to leave.

"Wait, Marie," Monique called out.

When she did, Monique leaned over her desk for Marie to come even closer, as if cautious that someone was listening. Monique couldn't be too careful after her rough start to her dream job. "Do you know if Donovan was reinstated at the hotel?" She almost whispered.

"No, *Signorina* Monique." The maid shook her head. "He no longer works here. *Scomparso*. Vanished."

"Oh," Monique said with surprise. She had been quite sure if she was rehired then so was Donovan. "And what about that girl, his girlfriend?" Monique probed as casually as she could.

Again, Marie shook her head. "No, poor girl said something about having to go back to Russia." Marie shuddered and crossed herself, lowering her gaze as she did.

Monique felt very glum indeed as she closed the door behind her. She knew it wasn't that damn girl's fault they'd been caught then fired, even though it was the girl who had led Monique to succumb to Donovan's advances. Vanity had made her do it. Monique was well aware that she was a grown woman and no one made Monique do anything she didn't want to. Luc Umbere could attest to that, she snickered inside. *Oh la la*, what she could have gotten up to last night with that sexy man if only she'd allowed herself the risk. Monique chuckled before sipping the hot caffé.

* * * *

Luc couldn't keep Monique off his mind as he sat in his three-star hotel room, a dozen piazzas away from the Totally Five Star Venice. He chewed on the end of his pen, entranced by his recollection of last night. How deliciously sensual that woman was, how she smelled and tasted when she finally surrendered to his touch. His fingers still buzzed with his memory of her soft flesh and her hard little nub under his thumb, the way he'd sent her into orgasm at his command. His cock stiffened under his robe at the memory.

In no hurry to stop the daydream, he let his mind wander. It was good to be out of those awful Dockers and that tacky shirt and wear his silk robe. He was much more comfortable as Alessandro than Luc. He relished the solitude of being himself within the confines of his hotel room. But when he put those contacts in, combed his hair to one side and slipped into the mundane clothes, he became Luc. That was whom Monique surrendered to. But deep down in his gut he knew it was really Alessandro she craved and had succumbed to. It thrilled him that she didn't have a clue he was the man from the street. He'd done a good job whisking away that day before she'd had time to remember him. But oh, did he ever remember her.

The prospect of seeing his charge again made his body ache for more of that hot, little slit. He knew Monique wanted it. After all, she had bedded her previous supervisor, from all accounts, and she seemed to enjoy being watched from Ms. Stiles' reports. Monique was no prude, that was for certain. He'd make sure he bedded her, and soon.

But playtime would have to wait. For now, he must go over the auction files again, cull the selection he'd made from his personal collections and decide which works were best suited for the upcoming sale. After he had that nailed down, he'd contact his bidders and give them their orders. It was as easy as taking candy from a baby.

The formula was quite a simple one, but had provided Alessandro with a new zest for art collecting. His old way of buying and selling art had become mundane over the past few years. His interest had waned. That was until he'd begun riding the adrenaline rush of a much more risky art game. Running up the prices of his items at auction, using his own bidders to up his lots, until some sucker bought them. The result—Alessandro walked away with a handsome profit and the thrill of total control.

Maybe that's why Monique intrigued him so much. She challenged him. She was not at all what she appeared on the outside. Strikingly sexy with a Midwestern twang, he could have easily filed her in the 'not worthy of his time' category. But under that beautiful shell was a woman with fire inside her. A hard edge he bet meant a past more interesting than her exterior revealed. And she was bright—that he could tell from her quick wit and ability to match him at every turn. All that plus a keen eye for art. He *had* to have her. The heady concoction of lust and longing egged him on. Not to mention that she held forty million euros of J's to spend however she wanted, under Luc's supervision, he reminded himself.

He stopped and reflected. Was he so evil he would rip his friend J off by driving up the auction and making the hotel pay exorbitant prices for works owned by him? No, he wasn't that evil. But the sexy curator from Kansas with the come-fuck-me way about her would be very useful as a decoy at the auction to distract his own bidders from doing what they did best—making him a fortune. All while he could observe, incognito, as Luc.

Monique's bidding would give him the legitimacy he much needed, an added edge to his usual tactics. Alessandro rubbed his hands together in anticipation. He could make more in this one night than he ever had. As long as the sexy goddess didn't bid on any of his works up for sale, and he'd make damn sure she didn't. He didn't need to rip the hotel off or his friend off, just the general, fickle art community.

The promise of money flooding his coffers delighted him, and the thrill of the chase was more than half the fun. Well aware money didn't buy everything, he knew what he really wanted wasn't for sale—Monique Le Bres' unwavering desire for him to fuck her like she'd never been fucked before. He'd have to earn it. He reached down and touched his cock, stroking it while imagining Monique's hot, wet mouth wrapped around his shaft. He groaned and leaned back in his chair, his release exploding as he pictured the luscious chestnut-haired beauty abandoning all control at his command yet again.

* * * *

Monique worked away all morning, hardly lifting her fingers from her keyboard. She barely noticed when there was a knock at her open door then someone stepped in, the intrusion forcing her to her lift her head suddenly.

"Ouch," she exclaimed as she her neck kinked when looked up at the visitor in her doorway.

Teresa Stiles stood there, sour-faced as ever. "I just came to see if you've settled in—again."

Monique rubbed at the sore spot in her neck. "Yes, fine, everything is fine." She hoped this wasn't going to be a prolonged conversation. She didn't feel like having to express her gratefulness to the uppity Ms. Stiles for getting her job back.

"And you've met *Signor* Umbere, I take it?" Teresa glanced around the room, surveying it the way a drill sergeant inspected his troops.

"Yes." Monique tried to keep the image of Luc's hand up her skirt at bay.

"Umph," was all Teresa said. She turned her back to her then paused in the doorway. "You're damn lucky to have your job back, *Signorina* Le Bres. I didn't realize you had friends in such high places." She glanced over her shoulder and smiled stiffly before she exited.

What the hell was that about? What friends in what high places?

"*Signorina* Stiles?" Monique called out after her.

"Yes?" Cautiously, Teresa stepped back into the doorway, the same stiff smile on her face.

"What did you mean about friends in high places?"

Teresa pursed her lips, revealing her obvious annoyance. "Well, whoever it is that put in a good word for you has the ear of Mr. Conroy, that's all I can say." She huffed with disapproval and departed, slithering back under whatever rock she'd come from.

Puzzled, Monique just stared at the empty doorway. Did Teresa really think Monique had some secret 'in at the top' with James Conroy? Was it Donovan? Did he feel guilty? Did he even have the ear of James Conroy? She highly doubted that. What about Donovan's young lover—the Russian? Did she have some connections to Conroy, enough to reinstate Monique? No way. The girl was fresh out of hotel school and besides, why would she feel bad about Monique's job? Monique had enjoyed watching Donovan making love to the woman in the hall. She couldn't possibly be aware it was pure pride that had driven Monique to allow Donovan to kiss her on the terrace just because the girl had been watching. No, it didn't make sense that she'd put in a good word for Monique, even if she was certainly pretty enough to gain Mr. Conroy's attention and bend his ear. The whole ordeal was messed up.

Grateful for however she got her job back, Monique vowed a silent pledge not to let Mr. Conroy down.

* * * *

Working away through lunch, Monique didn't even poke at the delicious-looking *salade niçoise* that Marie had quietly left for her while she was on the phone. A tiresome but necessary phone call to some long-winded art dealers. No one could fault her for not doing her due diligence for the auction and double-checking her lists to make sure all pieces were accounted for.

After she hung up with the last call, she checked her watch and looked at the vacant doorway, hoping to see Luc appear any moment. Glancing at her watch again, she stifled her irritation that he wasn't there yet. It wasn't as if he'd said what time he was coming in today, and she hated that she was actually annoyed he wasn't there. That she looked forward to seeing him. That he had that effect on her. One brief, sensuous encounter in his arms and she was putty in his hands. At least that's what it felt like — that she wanted to be in those muscled arms of his as he thrust his thick cock into her. She shushed her imagination and reminded herself that behavior like that was exactly how she'd lost her job. Now that she had a second chance, she couldn't screw up. *Memo to self—do not screw your supervisor. No matter how tempting he is.*

Turning her attention back to the tasks at hand, she poured herself a cup of cold coffee from the carafe and added some cream and a hefty spoonful of sugar, knowing she shouldn't. She couldn't resist. She would be hovering around pleasantly plump and she needed to get to the gym and start working out again. There was too much to do to worry about that right now, and Luc didn't exactly seem to mind the extra bit of flesh on her ass and the fullness of her breasts. She smirked and dumped a second spoonful of sugar into the *caffè* and sipped it. *Umm. Perfect.* The gym would have to wait.

Picking up her phase two acquisition notes from her desk, she carried them and her cup over to the windows—even if she had to work today and didn't have time for gazing at the goings-on of canal life. Placing the cup down onto the window ledge, she couldn't help but linger. Her papers still in hand, she scanned her plan for the second installment of art she had listed and took a sip. Hopefully Luc would approve the acquisitions—there was nothing she hated more than having to answer to a supervisor. Then again, she did have forty million euros at her disposal, so she could understand James Conroy requiring some sort of supervision. Thank God, he'd sent Luc. Donovan had definitely not been up to the task. He'd thought rococo was a man. Sputtering espresso, Monique laughed at the recollection.

Luc's appearance in the doorway made her jump as she dabbed the dribbles of coffee from her chin.

"Here, let me," he said, coming swiftly to her. He took a napkin off the nearby tray. Tipping her head upward with one hand, he wiped the liquid from her chin with the other.

She felt helpless in his embrace. He tossed the napkin aside, but his thumb remained on her lip, sending thrills of delight through her as she looked up at him.

Oh God, I have no resolve against this man.

"Better," was all he said.

"Better," she agreed.

"What was so funny? I saw you laughing as I came in. Alone. In the window."

"Oh, nothing." She whisked her hand to dismiss the thought. The last thing she needed was him knowing she'd been comparing him to Donovan and that Luc came out well ahead.

"In that case, how about we go over what you've been up to? Tell me your progress on the auction selections."

"Sure," she said.

She slipped back behind her desk as he sat in the chair across from her, crossed his legs and leaned back comfortably, as if he was going to be there for a while. Her heart skipped a beat as he rested his chin on his hand and rubbed it ponderously. Those hands, those fingers. She tightened her thighs together, hoping to extinguish the fire he was lighting inside her, her pussy thrumming as he licked his lips and locked his eyes on hers.

"Well?" he prompted with a smirk.

He must be a mind reader, too. She squeezed her thighs closer.

"Uh, here, I made this short list." She passed him the sheet of paper. "Did you check out the margins and the lineages?"

He nodded without looking up from the list. "I have someone working on it for me. For us," he added and looked up to meet her gaze. He threw the piece of paper down onto the desk and stood. "I have a much better idea. Let's get out of this stuffy office, away from the hotel."

She gulped as he filled the room with his presence, making her think deliciously dirty thoughts about just what he might have in mind.

"I have a place I'd like to show you. I'm quite sure you'll like it. A little island." He stepped closer to the window and pointed to somewhere in the distance. "Come on, get your things. Let's go. We can talk about the auction on the way there. Much more civilized than you holed away in here when Venice in the springtime beckons."

Monique just sat there, not sure what to do. She had a pretty good hunch that if she went with him, the last thing they'd do would be to discuss the auction.

He waited for her. How unusual. He had made it quite clear what he expected her to do, but now it was as if he was offering an escape from the hotel to do just what she wanted. To give in to her attraction to him. For her to make the choice to join him. His cocky look made her suspect he knew what she wanted him to do to her.

"How can I resist?" she replied. "Springtime in Venice and all," she repeated his phrase, loving the way he'd said it, with his French spin.

Luc smiled, reached for her hand then pulled her to her feet. "There, that's better. Now grab your things and let's get going. The sun will be going down soon, and it's best to see the island at sunset."

Monique reached for her purse, her other hand still in his as she stuffed her notes inside. Impatiently, he led the way out of the office, giving her a little pat on the ass that made her squirm with delight.

Chapter Sixteen

The milky green water lapped against the sleek wooden hull of the launch as Luc slowly steered the boat away from the dock. Monique watched him deftly navigate the perilous moorings of dozens of gondolas and barges in the canal. He dodged one of the canal ferries when he pulled the throttle back and headed to open water.

What a sight. Luc with his carefully parted hair was now a carefree hot mess. Dark brown hair tousled, his sun-kissed skin glistening when he glanced back over his shoulder at Monique. His shirt billowing in the wind. His eyes hidden by sunglasses.

Oh, damn, he is so sexy like this.

In total command, he pushed the throttle down so hard it pressed Monique back into her seat. The motor vibrated through her bottom, making her clutch the side of the boat while they whipped across the light chop of the water.

Venice slipped away, dreamlike, in the distance, becoming a mystical place the faster they sped toward open water. Monique was taken with the beauty of the disappearing city. Barely a glimmer, afloat amidst the ocean. A Neptune of sorts. All that was visible now were the spires of the tallest buildings as the city was lost in the late day fog.

A Turner painting. That's exactly what it reminded her of as she looked up at Luc then all around at the marshy land they were leaving behind. The sun began to sink, sending a warm ember flickering over the sea. Monique inhaled the scent of ocean, acrid and musty. Luc hit a few waves, and she bounced hard in her seat. He looked back at her when he hit another wave, and she screamed out in surprise, clinging to her seat for safety. He only laughed and held the throttle firmly, jumping from wave to wave, careening farther into the sea.

Where they were going, she had no idea. Some island, he'd said, but she'd be damned if she could see anything out in the hazy end of day. Her gaze settled happily on Luc's broad back, imagining his muscled form underneath. She pondered how such a dorky-looking man as he'd been when she'd first met him had turned out to be such a stud. *The clothes.* That was it. Everything else, his mannerisms, his speech, his stature and those sultry brown eyes all shouted Type A stud, mixed with an air of sophistication that she found intriguing. Almost like he came from money. She snorted, glad he couldn't hear her over the roar of the motor. Trust her to sniff out old money. Raised in a rusty, old trailer in a dust bowl, she had a nose for affluence. She craved it. And she knew it when she found it. But to hell with affluence. This man was way too seductive for her to care if he had two pennies to rub together.

For now, far from the confines of the hotel and from Teresa Stiles' prying eyes, Monique was alone with this divine man. A recipe for a whole lot of trouble. And dammit if she didn't look forward to every second of it.

The tilt of Monique's chin and the wide smile when she guffawed about something—probably the giant wave Alessandro hit head-on instead of slicing at an angle like he was supposed to—made his loins ache for Monique. The innocence with which she'd accepted his offer to come on the 'friend's boat' to some island astounded him. She was an unusual mix of temperaments. A chip on her shoulder half the time, and the rest of the time she was so sensuous and ripe. As ready to be plucked as if she were a ruby red plum just falling from the tree into his hand. He imagined just how delicious all of her would taste, from those precious tits of hers to that round little rump and that silky slit.

Bam. He nailed another wave head-on. *Better concentrate, Alessandro.* Turning his head to double-check Monique was fine, he reminded himself that it was *his* boat after all. Usually he had a driver shuttle him back and forth from his secluded island home to his private dock. But he was not Alessandro when he was with Monique. He had to remind himself to omit any reference that the boat he was driving was his, and to avoid any hint that the house they were slipping away to was his. He was Luc. As far as Monique knew. His pulse raced at the thought of taking her to his island, his home, his art collection, all without her knowing it was his. With any luck, he'd win her into his bed. His cock stiffened as he tried to focus on the route to the island. He could just make out its shape in the distance.

* * * *

The sun slipped into the Adriatic, sending a foggy, mauve haze on the water. Luc docked with impressive efficiency. It seemed she could add boating skills to her already growing list of things he did well. He hopped out to secure the lines. Monique stepped out from the boat, stretching as she placed one foot on the wharf, the other still inside the vessel, the gentle rocking making her unstable. Luc quickly finished with the lines and went to her aid.

Once she landed successfully with both feet on the dock, she looked up at the impressive villa before her. It seemed the only home on the island from the look of things, its rosy plaster walls and ornate façade a hint of the luxury that might lurk behind the vine-covered stone wall that surrounded it.

"And who lives here?" she asked inquisitively.

Luc led her by the hand up the stone stairway that reached an arched entrance in the stone wall. "A friend."

"A friend with deep pockets," she said under her breath. She assessed the immense beauty of the place as they carried on through the impressive stone arch and continued up a series of very steep stairs to the villa above. Pausing at the wrought iron entrance, Luc motioned for her to go ahead. She nodded and walked past him. She continually gaped at the beauty of the villa's courtyard with its tranquil fountains and manicured topiaries that led the way to a huge set of double wooden doors. Oxidized copper door handles were set in the middle of each massive door, Venetian style. Oh, she did love Italy. All her life, she'd dreamed of coming here, of studying the great masters, and now here she was in a real, live grand villa with a real, live hunk.

As she followed Luc through the front doors, she was taken aback that he'd just walked right in to the villa. "Aren't you going to ring the bell?" she asked.

"Oh, no, my friend isn't here right now. He's away in...in Paris. He said we'd have the place to ourselves." He slipped his arm around her waist as he spoke.

Her eyes widened in anticipation.

They weren't actually inside the villa yet. The doorway they'd just gone through led to another courtyard, this one ringed on all four sides by balconies overlooking the courtyard below. Elaborate architectural balustrades framed the villa's inward-facing walls. Monique could just make out doors at the far end of the courtyard. Those immense doors must lead to rooms she could only imagine, given the grandeur of what she'd observed so far.

Luc nudged her. "Come, there's something I want to show you. I think you'll be quite impressed." He kept his hand around her waist then cupped her hip with his hand, making her quite aware things could get very intimate now that they were far from the prying eyes of the hotel. She wondered if that's what he'd been planning all along. She sure hoped it was.

Testing the waters, Monique glanced around. "Isn't there any staff here?" She looked back over her shoulder as Luc walked them across to the other side of the courtyard, toward a set of large wooden doors, both intricately carved. Their detail became more evident with every step they took.

"Yes, but they are very discreet. I doubt you'll even see them."

Her pulse thrummed at the way he said discreet, almost with a hiss. And the fact that whoever's home this was, was so very rich their staff was *discreet*. Oh, she really was in fancy-pants territory now.

Luc released his hold on her hip and opened the wooden door. It hinged on a pivot and the moment it was open, Monique stood in awe. Speechless. Amazed.

The opaque Adriatic lay straight ahead through a massive stone-walled room with no doors or windows to protect it from the elements or the sea. Just open air and the most spectacular view she could have ever imagined.

The gentle slap of waves meeting the edge of the floor and a waft of the salty sea air made her inhale deeply. Dizzying in its grandeur, she took a moment to adjust. It was so rich, so ethereal, that she had to stand and take it all in.

"Quite extraordinary," she exclaimed as she followed Luc across the intricate gold and cream mosaic-tiled floor. She took in the groupings of couches, occasional chairs and amazing statuaries that were down one small step and into the main area. She realized this must be the living room, although a place this size probably had several living rooms.

Barely able to keep her jaw from hitting the floor, she eyed the impressive art collection that flanked the room. If she hadn't known better, she'd think she was in a museum. Whoever owned this home had an astute eye for art and a seriously sinful checkbook, by the look of the paintings. Monique did her best to conceal her stupefaction when she was just sure she spotted a Caravaggio then a Rubens then the very distinctive Warhol on the far side of the room. But that couldn't be. Those were worth *many, many* millions. But then again, this villa wasn't exactly low-rent, she reminded herself.

"You like Warhol?" he asked, catching her ogling the painting at the far end of the room.

"I like Picasso better, but I sure wouldn't mind having a Warhol of my own. Your friend...he must be quite the collector."

Luc laughed and she faltered. How silly of her to assume this was a man's home? This could be a woman's home just as easily. Perhaps a lover of Luc's? A jealous twinge taunted her as she frowned at the prospect.

"Yes, he enjoys collecting beautiful things. It's like sport for him. The thrill of the chase, the feel of his teeth sinking into a rare find."

Monique's pulse quickened. How erotic when Luc described collecting art that way, like an animal stalking its prey.

"Drink?" he asked.

He strolled over to the far side of the room, leaving her gawking before following his lead. Watching him move across that grand room was an even more enjoyable view than the art collection. She made note of how his wide shoulders narrowed to that ass of his. Oh, how she'd love to...to...well, to do exactly what she knew she shouldn't. But then again, when had Monique Le Bres ever done anything she should?

"What would you like?" he asked. "I have everything here — I mean, he does." He looked up at her and quickly started getting ice from a bucket and plunked it into two crystal glasses. The ice hitting the glass echoed throughout the room, adding to the cavernous feel of the place.

"Anything's fine, G and T, scotch on the rocks. Whatever's easy."

"Whatever's easy?" he said with a cocky glance. "Scotch on the rocks it is," he affirmed, pouring the dark liquid into deeply etched crystal glasses. He then came around the bar to hand her the drink.

The crystal was heavier than it looked. She rolled the rounded base of the glass around in her hand, admiring its heft. *This must be the really good stuff from Ireland.* Waterford, that was it. She'd seen it in a high-end magazine she'd thumbed through on her long flight from Kansas to Venice.

Oh, how she did love luxury. She felt right at home here in this villa with this sexy man. It was as close to a dream come true as she could ever imagine when she sipped the scotch and smiled up at Luc.

"Are you hungry?" he asked.

He narrowed his gaze and made her tremble with rogue thoughts.

He had no idea just how hungry she was. And just how badly she'd been fighting her arousal the whole time they were back at the hotel. Ever since he'd plunked himself down across from her at that café and told her she had her job back. Ordered her back to work, no less.

"What were you thinking?" She played along, curious where this would lead. Was he actually asking her if she was hungry or suggesting something else? She could only hope it was the latter. Food could wait.

"I think you're hungry...but it can wait. Come," he said as if reading her mind. Taking her free hand in his, he led her into the middle of the room then onto the Carrara marble grand terrace that was at sea level. The last few steps disappeared into the sea as it lapped over the edge of the white marble, making it wet and shiny in the dim, early evening light. How completely intoxicating, this villa that led right into the sea. And the millions of dollars of rare art surrounding them. There was no security in sight, but she knew a collection like this must have a very sophisticated protection system. She wouldn't be surprised if they were being watched at that very moment, even though it appeared it was just the two of them.

Monique sipped her drink as Luc lingered barely behind her, his body so close she could feel the vibration between them.

She licked her lips, tasting the scotch, and inhaled with relief as he wrapped his arms around her, cocooning her in his embrace, his drink still clutched in his hand.

"What do you think of this place?" he asked. His breath was hot on her neck with each word he spoke, making her shiver with anticipation.

She gulped. "It's beautiful...more than beautiful. It's magnificent."

"*You* are magnificent."

His lips barely grazed the flesh of her neck as she cocked her head to one side so he could nuzzle his five o'clock shadow against her skin.

"Luc." She murmured her approval.

He nipped and caressed her neck, sucking on her earring for a moment, sending a tingle right down between her thighs, her panties moistening.

"I don't know if we really should be doing this..." she said without much conviction. Monique was quickly losing her will to play it safe, to keep her job and not dabble in the affections of her boss.

He was undeterred. He did not release his grasp, but merely rested his hands on hers, their crystal glasses nestled together on her chest. His kisses became more tantalizing as he kissed his way down her neck and used their coupled hands to nudge the fabric of her blouse.

"I mean, you're my supervisor—" Her voice caught as his lips touched her skin, stoking the growing fire within her.

"But we're not at the hotel now, are we?" He squeezed his arms a little tighter around her.

She could feel his stiff cock against her ass. Such a turn-on.

"No," she agreed, struggling to keep her gaze focused on the darkened horizon. The subtle rhythm of the waves sloshing onto the marble floor made her melt into his embrace.

"And you're a beautiful, sensual woman…" He bit lightly on her neck before moving along to another spot. "And you cannot deny what you feel, what you need, Monique. The pleasures I can give you…"

Her pussy tingled as he spoke those words, aching for him to fill her most intimate place. To fuck her. At that very moment, she was willing to give it all up. Luc's touch was too tantalizing. *To hell with the hotel and with protocol.* She admitted to herself that she had no more resolve to resist this man who intrigued and seduced her like no other had before.

He kissed his way along her collarbone and then back up to the tender spot behind her ear, all while his arms held her captive. Gleefully captive.

"Your silence means yes." He pressed his cock against her suggestively and he ran his hands eagerly against her breasts.

"Yes," she groaned out her approval.

Her body thrummed as he moved against her, rocking his hips to the rhythm of the sea, his hands and his scotch glass teasing her nipples, the cool glass then his hot touch. She wanted to beg him to take her. Right there. Right now.

He was driving her crazy, touching her while she still had her drink in her hands, their crystal glasses clinking together with their movements. Unable to move her arms in his, she arched back against his chest in pleasure and ran her high-heeled foot behind her, up along his calf, as he bit her lightly on her neck. Then he nipped his way down her collarbone. She kicked her shoe off and rubbed her foot farther up his leg.

He grunted as she wriggled her derrière against him, his erection pressing hard on her buttocks. Scotch splashed on her shirt. Not that she cared.

"Oh no, better get you out of that," he tisked.

She murmured her enjoyment while she kept on rubbing slow circles over his cock pressed to her ass, driving her wild, along with his kisses down her neck and shoulders.

He smiled and his lips met hers, wet and needy. Kissing furiously, biting, nipping, nibbling. She craved him. Yearned for him and his cock buried deep inside her.

"Here," he murmured mid-kiss, clutching his drink as he grabbed hers and took it from her.

She looked up in surprise as he flung the glasses out to sea — they landed with a splash.

Turning her around into his arms, he kissed her like she'd never been kissed before. Hard and hungry, he crushed his body to hers, roaming his hands greedily over her curves, tugging at her clothing as she did the same, drawing his shirt from his waist, eagerly finding bare, muscled flesh. The waves sloshed against the marble, the occasional one spilling onto the floor, soaking her feet as she kneaded her hands along his broad back, pulling him to her as he undid her zipper.

He slipped her pants off her hips then threw them over his shoulder.

With a satisfied grunt, he grabbed her by the ass and hoisted her up to him. Their lips were locked while she wrapped her legs around him as he dug his fingers into the soft flesh of her bottom.

Monique opened her eyes as he swooped her up into his arms. He was carrying her in his strong hold up the few stairs leading back into the vast room. The ocean was fading into the night as she looked behind her.

They vacated the grand room. She clung to him as he turned left and went down a low ceilinged, limestone-walled hallway, lit only by lanterns. As he turned to navigate another narrow passage, he was careful not to bang her knees on the rough stone walls as she caught a glimpse over her shoulder.

"That's not a—a Monet?" she asked.

He stopped and looked back at what she was looking at.

"In fact it is. Good eye, Monique." He squeezed her ass a little tighter and gave her a kiss before hefting her higher on him.

"Shit! A Monet here—a real one?" she asked.

"Shh, you've such a dirty mouth, and I know just what to do with it." He kissed the words from her lips as he resumed walking, their bodies entwined, his breathing heavy with the exertion of his efforts combined with the kiss that nearly took her breath away.

He paused at the stairway then, without reservation, he took the stairs two at a time, his lips never leaving hers as he carried her up the ornately carved, stone staircase. Not seeming to tire, Luc exhaled as they reached the top and headed for a doorway at the far end of the hall.

"You really know your way around here," she observed as he elbowed the door open and shut it behind them with his foot.

"I'd really like to know my way around you," he said with a devilish smile. He carried her across the room. A bedroom with a giant four-poster bed — something that looked like it was out of a castle — stood in the middle.

He paused. Then he kissed her, biting tenderly at her lip before throwing her down onto the bed. She squealed and he growled then jumped right beside her, wasting no time rolling on top of her.

Chapter Seventeen

"I'm going to take my time fucking you," he growled at the beauty splayed out on his bed. Her brunette locks fanned on the bedcovers like a fan, her face rosy with excitement. And those tits. *Holy fuck, those tits.* He wanted to bury his cock in them and come all over her. His balls tightened as he gazed down at her.

Monique licked her lips. He couldn't tell if she was nervous or just being oh so provocative, something she did to perfection. Not caring about the cause, he pushed her already open blouse farther apart and reached for those luscious breasts, shoving the bra out of the way to expose her round globes. The removal of the lacy fabric revealed tawny nubs that more than met his approval as he leaned over her, his feet still on the floor, his mouth meeting one delicious nipple at a time. She groaned and wriggled under him as he sucked and teased her perfectly erect buds. She clawed at his shirt, trying to pull it over his head to no avail and only interfering with his sucking.

He reached up for her hands as they clutched his shirt over his head. He took her wrists in his grasp, the fabric of his shirt falling from her grip as he pinned her down, her breasts rising with the action.

"That's more like it. Patience..." he murmured. He went back to sucking each nipple, slowly teasing her. She arched and bucked her appreciation under him, her breathing so quick and ragged he knew she was on the edge. This little vixen was so quick to come he'd have to slow her down. Take his time with her. Make her beg for it.

"Ahh..." Monique cried out when he bit tenderly on her nipple and gave a little tug before looking up at her. Her wrists still bound by him, the room ebbed away, her world coming apart with the deep rolling climax building inside her. She ached for release. He sucked again and bit lightly as she writhed in pleasure under him, unable to move her arms, loving the feel of surrender despite her usual desire to be in control at all times. But right now, she wanted him to do what he pleased with her. So far, everything he'd done had been explosively erotic.

Her breath caught when he tugged on one nipple once again then slid it in and out between his lips, giving it a flick as her whole body quivered in one electrified sensation. Luc let out a gentle laugh when she whimpered. With every tug, her nipple throbbed, swelling with pleasure between his teeth. She could hardly stand it. She ached for him to invade her, to slide hard and deep, filling the longing between her legs.

"Please..." Monique moaned. He released her when she groaned louder. She wriggled under him.

"Patience..."

"Fuck patience," she sputtered.

His eyes sparked with mischief. "I'd rather fuck you."

"You know what I mean." She ached for his cock.

"Okay, fair enough, let's get you out of the rest of these clothes."

"That's better," she said as he released her wrists. Able to bring her arms down, she quickly began undoing the rest of her blouse, eager to rid herself of the bra.

"Uh, uh, uh," he said. "Naughty girl. I'll do that." He swatted her hand away and slowly undid the remaining buttons on her blouse, using his fingers to tease her swollen buds, now so sensitive.

He flicked one nipple then the other and looked at her—waiting for her response. She bit her lip at the pleasure-pain sensation. She watched him as he did it again and smiled when he looked up at her.

"One more?" he teased, his lips barely grazing her nipple.

She was going to explode if he taunted her like that. "Oh, so you want it like that, do you?" She bucked her hips to press against his crotch and rub against his stiff erection.

"I want it every which way," he said, moving away. He quickly unfastened his pants, belt first then the fly. They were almost down to the floor in one movement, giving her an eyeful of the tent in his boxers.

"And the shirt…" she reminded him. She shimmied out of her pants, the silky fabric slithering to the floor, then she unhooked her bra.

He stripped, but the boxers remained. She threw her bra over her head and looked up at him.

"You are gorgeous." He took his time assessing her body, his gaze roaming over every curve.

She sucked in her stomach, conscious of the little tummy roll she never could flatten.

He seemed not to care. His attention lingered. "Panties off." He slid a finger inside them and gave the elastic band a little snap.

"Boxers off," she sparred back, loving this sexy game of control.

"Ladies first."

Purposefully, she hooked two fingers in each side of her panties, slid them off then kicked them away with a flourish. A groan escaped Luc as he watched her, then he pulled his boxers off, his cock springing free. He gave the boxers a toss with his foot, sending them somewhere in the far corner of the room. But Monique didn't care about anything at that moment except his thick, beautiful cock. Just wanted to slide it into her mouth, slow and easy. She trembled at the thought as he moved even closer, her eyes on the prize. She licked her lips and looked up at him.

"Later," he said, as if reading her mind. "I want to taste that pussy of yours." He lowered himself and pushed her gently back down onto the bed.

She sank into the down comforter. He nudged between her knees, spreading her thighs farther apart, leaving her completely exposed as he kneeled before her pussy. She quivered with anticipation. He placed his hands on her inner thighs and pressed them wider apart, exposing her folds.

"There," was all he said as his hot breath thrilled her slit. He gently licked her clit. She gasped when he slid a hand under her ass and lifted her, making it natural for her to place her legs on his shoulders. He moaned something when he circled her clit with the tip of his tongue and delved deeper into her folds.

"And what have we here?" he asked. "*La fica*," he murmured in Italian. "Such a beautiful pussy."

She writhed with anticipation. He stroked his hands over her buttocks and pulled her to him to bury his face between her thighs.

"*La fica.*" The words tumbled from her mouth.

He slowly licked the sensitive skin so close to her crease then used his hands to allow his tongue easy access to her slit.

He paused and looked up at her, a satisfied smile on his face. "*Si*, you learn Italian very quickly. Pussy is *la fica.*"

Luc inhaled and nuzzled farther into her folds, caressing her clit as she cried out in submission to the exquisite pleasure he was giving her. She trembled and grabbed hold of his shoulders, the tip of his tongue finding her special spot.

"Oh, Luc," she gulped as he pushed her so close to the edge of an orgasm.

He paused, making her crazed for more.

"*Ti piace*? You like?" The glint in his eyes confirmed he knew just how much pleasure he was giving her.

"Umm..." she murmured.

He teased her with the tip of his tongue, darting it in and out of her crease. Monique watched him before closing her eyes in complete surrender to the intensity of the climax that was building deep inside her. Wriggling with pleasure, she shook as he lapped at her clit then circled it with his tongue, forcing her over the edge.

She panted and moaned her release for all to hear.

Collapsing, she welcomed his body when he slid back up her. Bearing a wide grin on his face, he licked her juices from his lips. "*Delizioso*," he proclaimed.

"Oh, God, you Italian men will be the death of me," she said then kissed him, the sweet taste of her musk mingling on her tongue.

"*Non italiano,*" he stated, "*Non sto Italian. Sono Frances.* I am French." He paused and pulled away as if waiting for her approval. "*Bene?*"

"*Molto bene,*" she said. With a deep laugh, she kissed him back, not caring at the moment if he was Icelandic or what the hell he was.

He nibbled along her neck and down her shoulder then tweaked her nipple. Her breasts had become so sensitive from the orgasm that his kiss wicked down to her core.

Unable to stand the intense pleasure of his tongue, she shook and groaned at each flick, her juices wetting her even more than before. She met his motion, moving her hips so he could delve deeper.

He gripped her ass and squeezed as she gave in to the overwhelming sensations. He sucked on her clit and she rocketed out of control. She yelled out his name and shuddered in climax once again.

"Umm," he said soothingly, lapping slow, long licks along her slit.

She squirmed when he hit her sensitive spot.

"It seems someone likes to come," he said.

"I do," she panted out.

Luc teased, unrelenting in his sucking. She cried out in relief as the wave of pleasure taunted her a second time. A heavy pulsing in her pussy grew with each lick of his tongue.

"Come, again. I know you can." The sounds of pleasure escaped him when he bit ever so lightly on her little hooded bud nestled in her slit, shattering her into a million pieces. She reaching out for him and crested her release.

He chuckled and pulled his hands from her buttocks. "Much better." He stood from his kneeling position, her juices glistening on his mouth when he looked down at her. He thumbed her nipples one at a time, then he ran his hand over her torso, tracing lightly just before her mound.

She snatched at his hand, stopping him. "I want you *in* me," she said in a throaty command that she barely recognized.

"Oh, you do?" he teased back. He ran his thigh along hers, his cock still out of her reach when she tried to move her hands lower to stoke it.

"I do."

"In here?" He ran his fingers down her mound and into her slippery folds.

She trembled with delight. "Deep, deep, in there," she urged him.

After sitting up, she pulled him to her and buried her face in his rock-hard stomach. She gripped his ass and then lowered her face to the curls at that base of his gorgeous dick.

"Just a sec," he said, easily moving from her hold.

She watched him search his pants on the floor and produce a condom.

"Prepared?" she snickered. He'd known full well that she'd wanted him all along. He had led her on — and she'd loved it.

"Always." He rolled it over his thick erection, her eyes widening while he smoothed the sheer latex and stroked himself a couple of times before coming toward her.

She gladly lay back and spread her legs, eager for him to enter her — to fill her completely.

"You make me want to come just seeing you like that. Your luscious wet cunt ready for me, plump and ripe..." He nudged her legs wider apart and stood over her. Pausing, he adjusted his stance so his cock was in perfect alignment with her slit. He leaned over her, and their lips met just as he teased her clit with his cockhead.

"Oh, oh, oh," she whimpered with their lips locked.

With a thrust, he plunged deep inside her. His sudden invasion stretched her. She grabbed at his wide back, wanting him harder and deeper insider her. He pumped into her, and she welcomed each long stroke hitting her special spot, making her ache all over again for release.

"You're so fucking tight," he cried out, thrusting faster.

She met his rhythm, his cock pulsing while she clung to him and bit his shoulder. He pushed her to the brink one more time. Her channel clenched, their breathing jagged as he drove deep and hard into her. Shuddering, she came, holding him tightly when he grunted his release. She wrapped her arms around him, breathless and panting.

"And to think I thought you brought me out here to show me the island," she teased when he rolled off her. They lay with arms and legs entangled in the fluffy duvet, cradling each other in their post-fuck bliss.

"I did bring you to see the island. There is amazing art here I wanted to share with you — I mean show you," he said, shifting to face her. "But you are so irresistible that I couldn't help myself." He kissed her, her honey still on his lips as he slipped his tongue into her mouth and tasted her more deeply before releasing her. "Now what's your excuse?" he asked cockily.

"My excuse?"

"For making me fuck you like that," he prompted her.

"Oh, yes. Well, I guess I'll have to plead innocence."

"I don't think so," he scoffed, pulling her to him. "You're a very sexual woman, you know what you like and you're not afraid to go after it. I like that."

She hummed her agreement. "I'm glad you like it. Not everyone thinks it's a virtue to be so uninhibited."

He grabbed her ass and squeezed. "Fools."

Chapter Eighteen

Monique rested her head on Luc's chest and stroked the indentation between his pecs. She gazed out at the black night. She had been so consumed when Luc had carried her into the bedroom that she'd barely noticed the open wrap-around windows, their shutters thrown back to let in the night air. This really was quite a villa. Luckily, her stud had friends in such high places. It sure beat getting caught back at the hotel or having to go to his room, which he'd referred to as a grade B motel, nothing as luxurious as the Totally Five Star or this splendid island retreat in the middle of the Adriatic.

"What are you thinking?" He brushed the tendrils of hair from her face, still damp from their lovemaking.

She laughed softly and looked up at him, arching her neck to make eye contact. "Just how lucky it is that you have such friends in high places, that we can be alone in a place like this."

"Far from the hotel..." He trailed his hands over her shoulder and down her back until he found what he seemed to be looking for. Cupping one of her ass cheeks in his hand, he pulled her closer to him.

"Exactly." She meandered her touch down his chest and across his hard abs. The man must work out a million times a day. Something even better than his muscled chest caught her attention. His cock stood at attention as she grazed his groin, twining her fingers through his curls at the base of his shaft.

"Now you kiss me," he commanded as he released her. "Suck my *cazzo*."

"Of course, *tuo cazzo*," she said with a slow smile. Lowering her head then gently kissing her way south, she followed the path she'd made with her hand along his chest, stomach then his groin. He mumbled some sort of appreciation when she reached the base of his cock, her breath heavy on his shaft as she inhaled the scent of their lovemaking. She then blew on his length, stroking him thoroughly as she lowered her lips to take his cock into her mouth. She slunk down his body, licking her lips with desire, then she rubbed the head with her thumb. The slick pre-cum allowed her to easily run her hands along his length and back up to the slit on his cockhead.

His breathing was ragged. He ran his fingers through her hair carelessly, guiding her face to him, still guiding her head as she parted her lips and welcomed him into her mouth.

"*Il dolce Gesù*," he groaned. 'Sweet Jesus' the moment she took him deep into her mouth.

He pressed her lips farther onto his cock when she relaxed her throat muscles and stroked his full length with her tongue. His dick pulsed and quivered in her mouth as she grabbed his buttocks and drew him even harder to her as she sucked him.

"Holy..." His words careened with a primal grunt when she flicked her tongue over the head of his cock.

She sensed how close he was to coming. One more flick and she felt the pulse of his cock on her tongue when he moaned and tensed, filling her mouth with his cream.

A deep suck of air from Luc's chest told her he loved her efforts when she swirled and licked every inch of his ramrod shaft. Moving her down along his body for better access, she then rose up onto her heels, his hand still on her ass. Her pussy quivered when he came close to her mound, his fingers now near her slit when she took his cock deep into her mouth, as far as she could, then sucked back up to his tip.

"Good God, woman," he growled.

Monique wrapped her mouth around the head of his dick, making a tight seal before she did it again.

His hoarse whisper and the stiffening of his entire body told he loved it. And she was only just getting started...

His cock felt like it was going to explode in immense release when Luc fisted Monique's hair. He tried to hang on to every precious second of ecstasy while this wildcat moved up and down his rod, licking and sucking until he thought he would go insane. Slow and tormenting, she rubbed her body along his thigh each time she took him deep into her hot, wet mouth. Aching for more of her, he slipped his hand from her ass to her cunt and flicked her erect clit, surprised at how hard and throbbing it was. He tapped lightly on her bud and felt her mouth contract in pleasure tighter around his shaft. She altered her pace with her tongue when he circled her clit with his finger then dipped into her hot little channel. His balls tightened the moment his finger was deep inside her, feeling her quiver at his command when he massaged her special spot just inside her channel, her legs immediately trembling with response. She moved her tongue faster along his shaft. Unable to control himself much longer, he gave her one last finger-fuck and pulled his cock from her mouth.

"Behind," he ordered and pulled her up to him. He flipped her over, then he positioned her on all fours.

She watched him over her shoulder. That look on her face, the expression of a woman begging for more, made it very hard not to shoot his wad all over her creamy ass. Control. He needed control.

Steadying his desire, he assessed her perfectly shaped rump and stroked her ass cheeks when she cocked her hips from side to side. She gave him a provocative glance and one last luscious lick of her lips before turning her head back to face the headboard. As if to say, 'go ahead and do what you know we both want you to do'.

His cock stiffened and throbbed at the thought as he rubbed it against her derrière while sliding his fingers between her ass cheeks. She quivered slightly, but kept her head down. He continued his exploration along her cleft and then into her wet slit.

Her outer lips were swollen from all their lovemaking. Her erect little clit still stood at attention. He fingered it before delving two fingers deep inside her. She moaned in pleasure, grabbing the sheets. He teased his cock along her ass again, his fingers inside her pussy, feeling her tighten and release when he stroked her then pressed his dick against her bottom. Wrapping his other hand around her, he held in position while he tested the waters, massaging his throbbing cock against her ass cheeks while he teased her dripping slit.

This woman was insatiable. But would she like anal? He loved the thought of giving it up the ass to this ripe beauty. She was adventuresome — he knew that from what Teresa had told him. But just how much, he wasn't sure. He was about to find out.

Trembling with immense waves of pleasure, Monique tried to stay on all fours while Luc taunted her with his thick erection — unrelenting with his other hand in his attention to her clit and inner passage. Bucking against him, she looked back, wondering if he was going to do what she hoped he would do. He slid two fingers into her pussy and pressed his cock even closer to her rear entrance.

Monique made small circles of encouragement with her hips. She heard him moan, deep and guttural.

"I hope you've brought some lube with you," she said. "And more condoms."

"I'll get some." He stroked her back soothingly before rolling off the bed.

Monique watched in surprise when he disappeared out of view. She could hear his footsteps as he walked away then a ray of light streaked across the room from him hitting the light switch wherever he had gone. Rustling and the sound of a drawer opening and closing were the only things she heard before the light went out. She heard his footsteps draw close to the bed. In the dim light, Monique could barely make out the packet of condoms he threw down onto the bedside table before climbing back onto the bed to join her.

"Now, where were we?" he asked, repositioning her.

"Here," she said playfully and wriggled her hips at him.

He rolled on a condom.

"I can hardly wait," he answered hoarsely and reached past her head for the lube.

"Where did you get that?" she asked in surprise.

He squirted the wetness onto her ass crack, his slippery fingers warming the liquid.

A moment later, she gasped. Luc held her hip with one hand to steady her as he slid one slick-lubed finger into her rear hole. He waited for her to relax before he went farther. "You're tight everywhere," he growled. He nudged his cock against the back of her thigh and crest of her rump while he stroked her anal passage with one finger. She trembled, sure he could feel her entire body quiver. He reached his other hand around to caress her breasts.

Turned on but also nervous, she arched her neck back at him and was rewarded with him bending over for a kiss. Soothed by the move, by him exploring her mouth, she didn't mind when he went further. He added another finger to her rear entrance, making her exclaim at the invasion.

"*Tutto bene*?" He asked if she was okay as their lips parted.

She was panting and breathless and could hardly speak when he continued squeezing her ass cheeks roughly.

"*Si*," she said, hoping he wouldn't make her say what she wanted. *I need him to fuck me up the ass.*

Seemingly satisfied with her affirmation, he removed his fingers then nudged her anus with the tip of his cock.

"Yes, please. Do it," she begged.

He pressed a little farther, one hand on her hip, the other guiding his shaft into her rear passage.

"Christ, you're so fucking tight," he moaned, continuing, slowly and evenly.

She curled her toes. "And you're so fucking big, *il tuo grande cazzo*," she cried out when he filled her.

He pumped slowly into her, each deliberate stroke filling her with the ache for more.

Holding her steady, Luc increased his strokes — longer, deeper, until she could barely take it anymore. His cock throbbed in her ass, his balls tight against her slit. He reached around and placed one hand on her mound while he kept thrusting into her ass, teasing her clit with his fingers then dipping them deep between her folds, finger-fucking her in tandem with his cock up her ass. She succumbed to the overwhelming sensation of him filling her in two places. Her moans were jagged and met his heavy breathing when he leaned over her, his hot breath on her neck as he pushed her to edge of insanity again, forcing her scream out in surrender when the pleasure wave crashed over her. Shaking in climax, her whole body tensed when she came like she never had before. He grunted and pumped harder. She knew he was so close. Biting into bit into her shoulder, he let out a stifled groan and shuddered. He came, filling her rear hole.

* * * *

The light switching on woke Luc from a deep sleep. Even before he cracked his eyes open, he was well aware of the offender responsible for waking him from a glorious slumber. She leaned across his body, her breasts grazing his chin and shielding his eyes from her view. *Shit.* He'd forgotten that he'd taken out his contacts before he'd fallen asleep and was now blue-eyed Alessandro — not brown-eyed Luc.

"What time is it?" Monique asked, her tone frantic.

He placed his hands on her round ass cheeks and pulled her to him playfully. He kept his eyes closed, not only because of the damn missing contacts, but also because it was blissful to drink in the scent of her when he nuzzled her tits.

"I don't give a damn what time it is, you woke me, you saucy wench."

"I can't be here overnight," she said, apparently still fumbling on the night table for his watch, which he'd wisely taken off when he'd bedded her the first time that evening.

He sucked on her tit and pulled the nipple gently with his teeth, feeling her wriggle in response. "No one's going to notice you're gone," he said soothingly, not caring about anything when he had this sexy woman in his bed.

"It's two a.m., Luc," she exclaimed, obviously having found his watch. "What about your friend? It's the middle of the night, so won't he wonder what's going on his bed if he comes home?"

Luc tried to conceal his satisfaction at the irony that *his friend* was in his bed at that very moment. He'd almost blown it when he'd gone and gotten that condom and lube, eagerly fetching it from his bathroom drawer, forgetting it wasn't supposed to be *his* bathroom, *his* villa. His enthusiasm to fuck her up the ass had almost shattered his cover. Luckily, the little vixen had been so eager to receive him she hadn't noticed. But now the contacts. That was trickier. He couldn't let on it was his bed. His bedroom, his villa. Damn, this was harder than he'd thought it would be. He resumed sucking on her pert tits, aware that she was becoming aroused as her hot, wet pussy stroked his growing erection.

"If you're sure it's okay," she said.

Eyes shut, he felt her place his watch back on the nightstand, then reach to turn off the light, bending farther forward, her heavy breasts now smothering his face. God, he was in heaven. His cock twitched and throbbed when she moved her wet slit along him and she hit the light switch.

"What?" she exclaimed.

It jolted him out of his bliss between her breasts.

Luc quickly looked up to see her holding the white notepad he kept next to his bed. *Fuck.* He'd thought he had thought of everything. He'd missed one small detail.

Tucking his face back into her breasts, he didn't have a clue how to handle this. Well, there were worse fates than hiding your face in a beautiful woman's bosom.

"Alessandro Bonnard. From the Residence of Alessandro Bonnard." She read the name on the notepad with obvious awe — twice.

Once was more than enough for him as he quickly whirled through several options.

Option one — *Truth. Not a chance.*

Option two — *Pretend he didn't hear her and keep kissing those lush titties of hers.* Lame, but it might be worth a try. He so did love those titties, and he didn't want anything to come between him and the pleasure of the sexy minx on top of him.

Option three — *Lie. Bingo.*

"Turn off the light," he murmured, squeezing her ass cheeks suggestively. Then he sucked on her other nipple.

She squealed in delight. She wriggled her hips excitedly when he flicked his tongue around one pert nipple.

"You're not telling me this is Alessandro Bonnard's villa?" Her tone was excited, and not just from him sucking on her breast. "Not *the* Alessandro Bonnard. Renowned art collector. That's your friend?" She laughed and then arched backward, pressing her slit against his cock.

His cock responded by swelling even more.

"Umm," was all he murmured.

"I don't believe it." Monique moved her hips suggestively, rocking on his dick.

He reached up with his eyes shut and drew her to him, silencing her with kiss.

He felt her turn off the light as they kissed, but before the room went black, he saw the twinkle of intrigue and lust in her eye. Good thing she couldn't see his smile in the darkness. His secret was safe and he was about to have amazing sex for the third time with a woman whose sexual appetite rivaled his.

What more could a world-renowned art dealer want in one day?

Slowly and steadily, Monique stroked her pussy over Luc's thick shaft. She enjoyed the sound of his low grunts with each movement.

"You like this?" She moaned, her clit meeting the tip of his cockhead. She swirled her hips from side to side, giving him a nice little tickle with her erect nub.

He grunted and showed his approval when he squeezed her hands tighter in his, moving his hips to match her rhythm, pressing his cock to her clit just as she gave in to a wave of orgasm, her juices slickening his shaft.

"Your hot, little cunt, *piccola fica calda*," he snarled.

She gasped her pleasure at him talking dirty to her. Most men were afraid to say cunt for fear of offending the woman, but she loved it.

"I want you in my hot, little cunt, *piccolo fica calda*," she replied. She cocked her hips hard against him.

His balls contracted in response. She was so wet and ready that his shaft almost slipped inside her. He stopped moving and released her hands.

"Condom," he said.

Monique gladly reached across to the night table, fumbling in the dark until she found one. The scratch of the notepad made her oh so aware she was fucking this devilishly handsome man in a world famous art collector's bed. A wet dream for an art history postgrad with a penchant for upward mobility. But right now, the only upward mobility Monique desired was his stiff rod filling her.

She ripped the foil package with her teeth and scooted lower down his body. Slowly, with expert precision, she rolled the condom over his beautiful shaft, giving a squeeze when she was done. His cock throbbed, and she smiled to herself. The man was the best lover she'd ever had. And she'd had plenty, but this one made her wild.

Her grip was firm on his cock while she straddled his thigh, making sure her pussy rubbed on his knee, pleasuring both of them. He sucked his breath in when she stroked his rod, slow and deliberate — wriggling her hips to massage her clit on his knee. His knee was wet with her arousal.

Monique kept the pace, aware he was getting close to coming. She could feel him throbbing in her grip.

"Ready for my hot, little cunt?" she teased, rolling off his leg.

"On all fours," he said, taking control again. "It's a better angle for getting in that wet snatch of yours."

The coarse words practically made her come right there as she eagerly got on all fours and backed herself up to the edge of the bed where he now stood. He adjusted her slightly and sucked in a deep breath when he dragged his tip on her slit then dipped into her hole. He gripped her ass and pushed hard and deep into her passage.

"Oh." She clawed at the bedsheets.

"Hot cunt." He panted, pumping into her.

"Harder," she cried out. Her whole body moved forward when he banged into her with such force she rose up on her toes, wanting him deeper, harder, fuller. "I'm going to come," she called out with urgency.

He slid a finger into her ass. She shattered into the immense climax of his dick buried deep in her and his finger up her ass. Clenching and releasing, she could feel his closeness when he gripped her hip harder with one hand and came along with her, their deep grunts of pleasure filling the room.

Chapter Nineteen

Day broke, and Monique squinted out from her pillow. *Ummm.* She felt the space beside her, where Luc had been moments before he'd gotten up, most likely to pee. She snuggled lazily in the warm spot he'd left, her mind reeling with last night's lovemaking. It had been carnal, edgy, but also sensual and sensitive—an odd combo to find in a lover. She grinned from ear to ear and caressed her face with his pillow, inhaling the scent of him, imagining just what fun they could get up to together, except he was technically her supervisor. Now that was a bit of a problem. Look what had happened with Donovan. But she wasn't at the hotel, now was she? Her inner vixen argued with her common sense. No rules here at this palace on the sea. In this stranger's bed. Wait. Not a stranger per se—the bed of Alessandro Bonnard, a world-renowned art collector. A billionaire who her lover, Luc, was friends with. *It doesn't get any better than this, now does it?* The minute she got back to the hotel, she was going to Google everything she could find on the notoriously elusive art collector.

"What are you giggling about?" Luc jumped into bed with her then wrapped his arms around her tightly.

She inhaled the clean scent of shaving foam. His smooth jaw told her he'd already shaved. "You showered without me?" she said with a purposefully pouty tone.

"Had to. Can't lie about all day." He nuzzled against her and gave her a kiss. "As much as I'd like to spend all day in bed with you, we've got to get ready for the auction tonight," he said with a smile.

Monique looked into those deep brown eyes of his that sparkled amber in the morning light. "I know." She threw her head back, remembering that it was auction day and there was a lot she had to do to get ready for it. Lists to double-check. Phone calls to make. "I'd better get back to the hotel."

He squeezed her closer. "Not before you have breakfast, you won't. I was a terrible host. I never even fed you last night."

"But you made sure I didn't go hungry..." Stroking her thigh along his, she felt his cock hardening between them. The man was insatiable. "Screw breakfast," she said and rolled on top of him, straddling him.

"You're my kind of woman, Monique Le Bres," Luc said. He placed his hands on her hips and brought her down to meet his lips.

His throbbing erection slid perfectly between her legs, as she hovered above him, sliding her slit along his length, loving the feel of his cock—naked, no condom. Her pussy was so sensitive from last night's sessions that she felt every nerve in her body was more alert, more heightened than she would have thought possible. His wide smile confirmed that he was enjoying this as much as she was.

She wriggled her hips in small circles to put extra pressure on his shaft. He rewarded her with a wider smile and a flicker of his eyes as he reached up to cradle her breasts in his hands, his cock surging between her swollen folds.

"Not so fast..." she teased, brushing his hands away. She put them back over his head. The movement caused her to her lean forward along the length of his torso, her hands still on his wrists. He surprised her by sucking one of her nipples into his mouth.

"Hey," she exclaimed, taken aback by the tenderness of her nipples.

He suckled and bit lightly. She held his arms over his head, seeming to immobilize him, except for his mouth. Enjoying this, she continued massaging his cock. Closing her eyes, she kept with her rhythm, first rubbing, then rising as she reached the tip of his cock, then nestling herself on him to do it all again. The intensity of his sucking increased each time she bore her hips down on him, bracing herself over him, loving the way they were moving together, desiring more than anything for his cockhead to dip into her wet folds unfettered by the condom. No matter how sheer they were, she ached for the heat of his naked cock.

"Better get a condom," he gasped.

She slid her clit over and over along his shaft. Her nipple slipped from his mouth.

"Oh, I don't want to... I know we have to...but I love the feel of you on my bare flesh."

He tried to move his arms, but she shook her head and pressed them back in place with all her strength.

He only laughed. "So you think you're strong enough to pin me down, do you?" he challenged. Immediately, he broke her hold and surprised her by pulling her down to him and kissing her full on the lips as his cock throbbed between her legs. With his newfound freedom, he grabbed to each side of her ass and parted her cheeks, reminding her of last night's anal play. Of how totally unhinged she'd been at his hands when he'd plowed deep into her anus. She murmured when Luc squeezed her butt harder, stretching her cheeks, allowing her slit to open farther, exposing more flesh to him. She quivered against him.

He quickly slid his fingers further between her mound and his cock. Stroking her pussy with expert precision, he obliterated any soreness inside her, and she matched the rhythm of his touch. Her pussy grew wetter when he rubbed her swollen bud, forcing her to give in to him once again when he teased her to the edge of ecstasy and back.

"I can't," she panted.

He pressed his thumb on her nub. She squeezed her inner walls against the deep urge mounting inside her, the ebb and flow of intense pleasure beckoning her.

"You can. Come for me with that tight, little cunt of yours." He paddled his palm rapidly on her clit, then he squeezed it the moment she dissolved into the climax, unable to fight it any longer. Coming hard and deep, she fisted her hands through his hair, their tongues entwined. She groaned into his mouth. Her body clenched, her muscles rippling with release.

Catching her breath, she straddled him and tried to pin his hands back down. She was, determined to regain the upper hand — if she could. He frowned.

"No fair," he scolded at her attempt to restrain him. But the flicker in his eyes showed he was anything but displeased.

"My turn now. I'm in charge." She knew it was just a matter of time before he overpowered her, turned her over and fucked her any way he pleased. Every way he pleased seemed to be just what she ached for as well. But for now, she could pretend she was in charge—as long as he'd let her.

He chuckled throatily. "Okay, then…" He raised his hips to tease her slit and opened it with his dick while nipping at her lips, kissing her fully before stopping. "You can do whatever you like to me, then."

"Really?" She thought of all the options of just what might blow her mind. "I can think of a thing or two."

"Be my guest, you sexy temptress," he challenged her. "Whatever you want to do, whatever makes you come all over me—that's what I want."

Smiling, she kissed him and quickly released his hands.

"Where are you going?" he asked, disappointed.

She scooted off him, giving one last caress against her wet slit before she turned herself around and straddled him in the opposite direction with her back to him. She heard a murmur of surprise then approval as she hovered directly above his groin, her legs over him like riding bareback backward. He cupped her breasts and squeezed when she rocked on her hips and wriggled her ass.

The hum of their want filled the room.

He ran his hands along her back and over her hips, grabbing her bottom. She felt a new rush of arousal wash over her when he slid his fingers between her crease. She rose slightly, allowing him to find what he was looking for—her clit. She shivered in delight, rocking against his touch, guiding her hips and his hand to just the right spot.

"Oh…" Her voice trembled. She enjoyed his fingers patting her clit rapidly until she moved her hips just enough to make it difficult for him to reach her clit.

"No fair," he groaned.

Monique lowered herself onto his hips, allowing no room for his hand. Slowly, she ran her pussy along his cock.

"Okay, fair..." He sighed with obvious approval, hic cock growing even more erect against her wetness. "Whatever the lady wants."

"I want to feel every inch of you, without a condom..." she said.

She shifted her hips back, leaning her weight forward and downward so she touched every inch of his cock. Tipping her hips even farther back, so her clit just grazed his balls, she was able to go even farther forward, low over his legs, running her hands up and down his thighs but still so close to him she could feel him clench under her.

"Monique." He whispered the words between his lips.

Again, she repeated the slow movement. He responded eagerly, spreading her ass cheeks to open her slit. Quivering with each move, she stroked his length with her slit and then lingered over his balls. He groaned. His balls tightened under her when she teased them with her clit.

"I love the feel of your cock, so hard and big," she uttered.

"Uhh." He groaned his enjoyment.

She paused, knowing it sent him wild by his stuttered breathing and the strength of how he grabbed her ass cheeks. His fingers dug into her, so close to her rear hole it made her crazy as she continued. Each glorious stroke more intense than the last. The heat of his shaft throbbing, pulsing, with each movement she made.

Lowering herself further, she tipped her ass up just as he pressed his thumb against her rectum. She came over his shaft, her juices wetting his length as she bore down. He slipped his thumb inside her anus while she circled her clit on his shaft. He pressed into her rear hole and she began to thrust, unable to contain her climax from taking over. She begged for more, aware words were escaping her lips that were nothing short of a plea. He lifted his hips so his balls were pressed tight to his base when she lowered her folds over him, rubbing over his length as he moaned approval. Rocking backward against the invasion of his fingers in her ass, a wave of release swept over her, making her come hard against his cock while he kept finger-fucking her rear hole.

"I'm coming again," was all she could say as she rubbed and panted, bearing down on his length. She ducked her head down, shoving her ass straight up into the air against his hand. Monique took his cock deep into her mouth. It was too much for him. He exploded his immediate release, his hot cum dripping from her face.

"That was amazing," she said dreamily, tasting his salty juices on her lips.

"Amazing," he agreed.

It had been such a turn-on, riding him backward with no condom, just flesh to flesh, his balls had clenched against her when she'd caressed her clit over his shaft and balls. She'd had to be careful not to ram his unsheathed cock into her at the end when that second wave of ecstasy overwhelmed her. He'd surprised her by fingering her ass. So exquisite was the sensation that all she could think to do was to suck his cock hard when they'd both come together in ultimate release.

"I'll never get out of here at this rate." She panted as they recovered their breathing, once again lying in the tangle of sheets. Resting her head on his chest, she looked out at the blue sky meeting the blue water and sighed. "I wish I didn't have to go…"

"I do too." He ran his hands along the curve of her buttocks, tempting her with the pleasures he'd bestowed last night.

"Come on," she said, forcing herself to roll away from him. It was harder than she thought when he reached out and tried to pull her back to him. "Later tonight?" She hoped that she could stick to their deal if he did. If not, her red-hot lover would have her back in the sack any second and she knew she really should get back to the hotel. After all, as much as she'd like to spend the day being bedded by her supervisor, she had just gotten her job back.

"Deal," he said.

She rose to collect her clothes.

"But tonight I'd like to try something more adventuresome."

She widened her eyes at his tone while she tried to find where the hell her panties had got to. "Adventuresome?" she hesitated to ask, having the distinct feeling she was opening Pandora's box.

"A little bondage," he suggested, cocking one beautiful brown eye at her.

She gulped. As open-minded sexually as she considered herself to be, bondage was uncharted territory for her. But then who better to initiate her than this dashing Frenchman who was pals with the Who's Who of the art world? He was much more sophisticated than she was and Monique was more than a little tempted by the prospect.

He smiled encouragingly. "I'll take it slow." He rolled closer to her and reached out from the bed.

"For now, I need to find my clothes, Luc," she said, trying to dress to conceal her flutter of nerves and excitement.

Luc only smiled. "Downstairs, remember?" he asked coyly.

Oh yes, she remembered. "They're scattered around the living room. What if your friend, Mr. Bonnard, comes home and finds my panties in the middle of his living room? I'll be mortified."

"He's in Paris, I told you." Luc rolled onto his back and laughed. "And besides, I know he'd love your panties as much as I do." He smirked and pulled the sheets back, revealing his erect cock like a prized statue.

She eyed his very impressive, thick shaft from the base to the perfect-shaped head. *God love men like Luc Umbere.* Shameless in his appreciation of all things sexual. Finally, she'd met someone as lustful and crazy for sex as she was.

Monique picked up one of the pillows and threw it at him. "You're too much. I've got to get out of here before you seduce me again." She laughed joyfully and grabbed one of the sheets off the bed. She wrapped it around her, leaving a very nude Luc to come after her as she made her way out of the bedroom to find her clothes.

"Monique," he called out. He caught up with her in the hall, catching the trailing end of the sheet and giving it a good yank. He pulled her into his arms, as if he'd planned it all along in perfect choreography. "I have half a mind to take you right now, tie you up with this sheet so you don't get away."

His lips met hers with such force that she couldn't resist. She linked her hands around his neck and kissed him back, hard and deep.

"Later. Tonight. After the auction," she said at the end of the breathtaking kiss.

"I'll hold you to it," he said.

He pushed her up against the wall, the cold plaster hitting her barely covered ass.

Chapter Twenty

As they cut across the lagoon and along the busy waterways, Monique couldn't suppress a smirk that she'd been so royally pleasured by Luc Umbere, far from the watchful eye of the hotel and that mean-spirited Teresa Stiles. No one would find out about her night of illicit decadence at the hands of her relentless lover. Unless, of course, Luc spilled the beans, but he seemed to be circumspect, respecting her need for privacy by taking her to his friend's villa. Oh, and what a friend. Did he actually rub shoulders with the likes of Alessandro Bonnard, the reclusive art collector who moved markets with his acquisitions and sales of art? She smiled. Luc cut the motor and tipped his head toward her when they pulled up canal side not far from the hotel.

They were two lovers sharing a secret. The notion thrilled her. It made her want him to turn that boat around and head straight back to the sanctuary of the villa on that remote island. But she knew better. Work called and she had to practice some discipline after all.

Besides, Luc had insinuated their next foray would be bondage. The thought tantalized her.

He slowed the motor and hopped out just as a couple of gondoliers stopped to lend a hand and tied one of the lines to the wharf. Stern line, she thought it was. Not much boating experience growing up in Kansas.

"I'm afraid, Cinderella, it is pumpkin time," he said and smiled down at her in the boat, extending his hand.

"Are you saying I'm about to turn into the ugly housemaid?" she scolded. She slipped her hand into his and let him assist her up and over the ledge of the boat onto terra firma.

"Not at all." He patted her ass as she started to step away before he halted her with his grasp, almost toppling her over had he not caught her in his strong embrace. "Nothing could be further from the truth my beautiful and most adventuresome vixen…"

His words faded as his lips met hers in a thorough kiss that left her speechless and barely aware they were in a public place kissing. This man was going to get the best of her if she didn't watch it.

"Luc, not here," she reprimanded once she caught her breath. But she didn't move to release herself from his grip as she spotted the gondoliers walking away to the far side of the wharf.

"Of course not," he said and let her go. "Later. You promised, tonight, after the auction. I will do what I want to you."

His low growl sent a direct flush of heat between her legs.

"I am a woman of my word. I'll see you later — at the auction." She smiled back at him, trying hard to keep the upper hand but well aware she'd lost that game

twelve hours ago when he'd wooed her into bed —
again and again.

"See you there. I'll meet you out front. Have your
list ready."

"I will." She hurried away, afraid if she stayed a
moment longer she'd be in his arms again or down in
the hull of that boat doing just what she wanted to
with him.

* * * *

True to her pledge to herself, the first thing Monique
did when she returned to the hotel was hurry to her
office and fire up the iMac. Her hands almost shook
with excitement. She was about the find out all about
the man whose luxurious home she had enjoyed. And
it wasn't only the home she'd enjoyed. There was also
the toe-curling, most erotic and tantalizing sex she'd
ever had. And there was more to come if Luc kept his
promise about the bondage later that night.

With anticipation, she typed in Alessandro
Bonnard's name. Her pulse raced as fast as her mind.
She'd heard about him in art circles, but he was very
circumspect, barely ever seen in public but well
known for moving the art markets with any
acquisition he made.

Immediately, pages and pages came up on
Alessandro Bonnard. Monique scrolled through the
entries, all the usual. There were no photos of the
man, but plenty of images of his staggering art
collection. Carrying on, she searched Wikipedia,
which provided a very short bio and gave the facts she
already knew, followed by an extensive list of art
acquisitions and sales.

The next two pages of entries were all about his philanthropic work. Apparently, Luc's friend was not just ridiculously rich but also *very* generous. Monique scanned the entries for a mention of the palatial Venetian villa, but there was none. Disappointed that there was not a word about the grand villa where she'd spent such a fabulous night with her talented lover, she searched for Alessandro Bonnard and residences.

A list an arm long came up, everything from yachts in Barbados to homes in Geneva, London, Tokyo and Paris to name a few. Intrigued, she kept searching, finally finding one obscure reference of a new acquisition of a Venetian home linked to some more philanthropic work in Italy. Clicking on the listing, Monique stopped immediately and peered at the screen.

She gasped.

There before her was a grainy photo of Alessandro Bonnard. A little out of focus, obviously taken by paparazzi. He was exiting a children's hospital in Rome after making a sizable donation to a new cancer wing.

"Holy shit!" Monique exclaimed loud enough that she looked up at her empty office to see if anyone had heard her. She ducked her head back down at the screen.

Alessandro Bonnard was my rescuer.

The man in the *Calle Obertege* the day she'd first arrived in Venice. The man who had extended his hand to her. The man in the debonair camel hair overcoat. The man with the goatee. She stared, trying to see his deep blue eyes, but the picture was too grainy. The picture became larger when she used the zoom button but it was even grainier than before.

Monique was anxious to tell Luc that she had actually met his friend in person. She scanned quickly, looking for more images to make doubly sure that the man in the photo was the vanishing man with the deep blue eyes from the *Calle Ostreghe*.

Deciding philanthropy and children's hospitals were the key to finding more about Bonnard, Monique widened the search and found several news articles and a few photos—all black and white—and none with good resolution.

They weren't going to be much use in confirming that he was one hundred percent the man she'd met in the street. Flicking through the images, one caught her attention—Bonnard stepping into a car, his face sheltered from the camera. His profile made her stop. Looking at the photo, she realized he was wearing a hat that covered his hair except for a small fringe around his jaw. He was wearing thin-framed glasses, same as in the other photo. There was something very familiar about the man. Peering closer, she looked at the photo and if she didn't know better, she'd say it was Luc's profile, Luc's jaw.

Oh, now that's ridiculous. She'd barely met the man and now she was comparing him to her Luc.

She searched as quickly as she could under Luc Umbere's name and Alessandro Bonnard. Nothing. Were they brothers? Was that possible? Twins, perhaps? One blond, the other brunet? That would explain the similarities in the shape and tilt of the jaw. She gave head a shake. The photos were terrible, not accurate images of the reclusive billionaire by any means. It was a huge coincidence that the biggest art tycoon in the world had swept her off her broken heel into the safety of his fleeting grasp. That was that. Damn, if she'd known who he was that day in the *calle*, she would have loved to have asked him for advice—he was the perfect source for her new job. Surely an art connoisseur such as he would have a tip or two for her. Well, not all was lost. Alessandro Bonnard was friends with Luc. That was something.

The sooner Monique met up with Luc at the auction, the better. She couldn't wait to tell him about her anonymous encounter with the mysterious man her first day in Venice and how it was his good friend.

* * * *

The rest of the workday was a complete struggle for Monique to stay focused on the task at hand, completing the acquisition list for the auction all the while plagued by questions about Luc Umbere and Alessandro Bonnard. Something deep inside her niggled. Visions of her mysterious rescuer in the camel coat and Luc twined together, tempting her with fantasy. Tandem visions of Luc and her mystery man making love to her caused Monique to shiver with delight. Oh God, she was never going to be able to focus on the auction tonight with all this Bonnard business going on.

Marie appeared in the doorway and jolted Monique from her daydreams of art curator grandeur intermingled with images Luc and his friend doing whatever the hell they wanted to her. *Including the bondage he mentioned.*

"Oh!" Monique exclaimed.

"I am sorry, *Signorina* Monique, I didn't mean to startle you."

"Oh no, it's fine, Marie. I was lost in thought."

The maid nodded and placed a tray laden with a delicious-looking meal on the table near the window.

Some sort of seafood salad by the looks of it—exotic and tempting. She eyed the fresh baked *pane* and *burro*, so melt in your mouth good, and the pot of steaming *caffé*.

"Perfect," Monique said, getting up from behind the desk.

"I bet you're hungry, no breakfast," Marie stated. She didn't make eye contact with Monique, instead fussing with the chilled bowl of rich and creamy yellow butter curls.

"I did have breakfast," Monique, corrected her. "Just not here," she confided with an irrepressible smile.

Marie looked up and cracked a grin, her blue eyes sparkling with mischief. "I thought as much. Your bed was not slept in." She raised her eyebrows in satisfaction and crossed her arms across her ample bosom as if waiting for details.

Monique quickly spat out her rehearsed excuse should anyone ask where she was last night.

"I was working late last night, trying to get ready for the auction." It was almost true, wasn't it? They had talked about art while he'd carried up to the bedroom of his friend's multimillion dollar refuge, before Luc had thrown her down on the bed and fucked her like no one had before.

Her face reddened as Marie said nothing, just studied her, making Monique's cheeks burn hotter.

"I must say you look very well rested today—radiant I'd say—but then that's not my place." Marie winked at Monique and turned away.

"Don't tell anyone, Marie?" she pleaded, aware her job would be on the line again.

Marie stopped in her tracks then turned back to her. "Of course not. Just be careful. I mean, because of what happened last time." The woman leaned closer and whispered, "It's not that new young lad, Richard, or whatever his name is? The new quality control manager?"

"No, definitely not," Monique said, grateful that Marie didn't seem to suspect it was Luc after all.

"Good," Marie said. "He is not up to snuff. But that new supervisor of yours, what's his name…" She smiled cheekily at Monique. "The good-looking one…"

"*Signor* Umbere."

"*Signor* Umbere, now he's very tempting, isn't he?"

"No idea," Monique said a little too quickly, her cheeks so hot she could use them to light a fire.

Marie laughed and shook her finger at her playfully. "I should have known it was *Signor* Umbere."

"Oh, don't tell anyone," Monique begged.

"Wouldn't dream of it, dear. Wish a man like him fancied me. I'd make sure my bed was put to good use."

You and me both. Monique waved a friendly goodbye to Marie, still laughing at the older woman's moxie and hoping she truly would keep her mouth shut.

Chapter Twenty-One

Barely able to suppress his thoughts from wandering back to the evening of wooing Monique to his bed, Luc tried to gather his wits for the impending auction that night.

He paced around his small hotel room. There was a great deal at stake tonight. As Alessandro, he planned to sell almost thirty million euros of art if the market and his shills worked the way he had calculated. But then, he never miscalculated, did he? He was a mastermind art collector, operating now under the well-veneered guise of art director of the Totally Five Star Venice. And having Monique at the auction pursuing her own agenda for the hotel acquisitions gave his evening a new legitimacy as her supervisor and J's envoy.

Monique would be acquiring works for the hotel — but definitely none of his. Alessandro would make sure of that when he coached her on what to buy and for how much. He'd been surprised when she'd confessed last night that she didn't have much auction experience. She seemed to have plenty of experience otherwise—in the bedroom and in just about every other room of his house. That sexy minx would no doubt distract the other bidders with her come-fuck-me sexiness. His shills could easily drum up the bids on the art he hoped to move. Meanwhile, Monique would get her coveted pieces. James Conroy would be very pleased. And Luc would do his job overseeing Monique, all while Alessandro made a cool twenty million euros profit. What could be better?

His cock stirred in his pants, straining the fabric, a reminder of just what could be better than stealing money right under the noses of the high and mighty in the art world—having Monique's gorgeous, round bottom under his palm, feeling her quiver and quake as he pleasured her the way he ached to. The very thought of the taut silk ties he would use to bind her, to immobilize her while he showed her the heights of ecstasy she could only imagine, made him smile. He'd seen the glint in her eye when he'd brought up something 'more adventuresome'. Fear mixed with curiosity when he'd pinned her up against his bedroom wall and whispered just how he'd planned to make love to her later that night after the auction. When she'd bit her lip and had looked up at him wide-eyed, he'd used all his self-restraint to resist having his way with her right then. He hoped absence would make her heart grow fonder and her legs open even wider for him. Oh, he could hardly wait.

He removed his contacts then ran his hands through his hair, ruffling it. He opened his laptop, ready to finalize his plans for tonight.

After calling a few of his contacts and making his final game plan, he leaned back into the desk chair by the window and gazed out at the piazza below. The Venetians sipping their *caffè* or glasses of vino in the late-day sun with not a care in the world. Luc watched on, admiring the fine architecture, the hint of the sun's yellow haze as it moved behind the nearby basilica. A few noisy tourists caught his eye as they snapped photos on the steps of the ornate marble fountain in the center of the stairs. Oh, it was a marvelous city, Venice, and one of his favorite places to spend time. Now that Monique was here, the city was definitely his most favorite. That woman made him lose his mind with desire. Not something good for his business plan, he reprimanded himself as he turned back to the laptop. Move the goods first then focus on giving Monique the night of her life—and his too—if he played his cards right.

* * * *

Standing next to the easel that displayed in bold letters that the auction was set to start at eight that evening, Monique waited anxiously in the foyer of the *Museo Civico Correr*. She glanced at her watch then around for Luc, wondering just what was keeping him. They'd agreed to meet half an hour ago to make sure they got good seats and so that he could brief her on auction protocol. She could barely contain her excitement at telling Luc that his friend was none other than a man she'd meet the first day she'd been in town. She was sure that would blow Luc's mind, as it did hers. Maybe Luc would put in a good word with Bonnard for her—who knew when one might need the favors of a magnate like him. He probably wouldn't even remember her, the way he'd practically fled after making sure she was okay. She guessed she was wrong about him having a wife. The Internet had confirmed he was single, with a few sightings of

Alessandro in the company of some very famous actresses and celebrities. Oh, to think she had slept in his bed. She laughed. Not that there had been much sleeping with the talented Luc Umbere kissing every last inch of her.

Fidgeting with her purse strap over her shoulder, her hands trembled. Monique hated to admit to Luc that she was a neophyte to fancy-pants auctions like this one. She needed some coaching so she could be sure she bid correctly on her selected items and that it would secure her up-and-coming place in the art world. But the words just tumbled out easily last night in Luc's capable embrace. She felt she could tell him almost anything—an unsettling feeling for her. Monique was used to guarding her emotions and only using men for her sexual pleasure. Venturing to trust a man…well, that was virgin territory for her.

Luc had assured her that he would help her at the auction. After all, it was the job he'd been hired to do. Monique smirked, remembering he'd said that right before he'd flipped her over on her front and thoroughly explored her backside. Oh, she could barely wait for tonight, tempted and nervous at the same time by his suggestion of bondage.

Looking around the now-crowded lobby, she noticed that auction goers were filing into the grand room behind her. She shuffled nervously, thinking that this would all go terribly wrong if Luc didn't show up. She wanted to nail this auction with aplomb and imagined how Mr. Conroy would herald her achievements if she snagged the works on her list. With Luc's tutelage, and maybe his connections to Bonnard, tonight's success would launch her from mid-rate art curator to world-class, all with one flick of her paddle…or card…or whatever the hell it was the bidders held up during the auction. She'd only seen it on TV.

The sooner Luc got there and briefed her, the better.

The bell rang and a gentleman announced, "*Dieci minuti.*" Ten minutes until the auction. Just as she swore nervously under her breath, Monique smiled with relief when Luc strode in wearing a suit and tie. A well-cut suit and tie, not his usual run-of-the-mill style.

My, my, my. The brown-eyed devil was quite the looker when he was all dressed up. She couldn't help but notice — with a hint of jealously — that several young women eyed him up and down as he walked toward her. She stared, imagining he was wearing the camel hair coat and that his eyes were blue and his hair blond. *It's official, I must be going mad.*

"Monique." He took her hands in his and kissed her deeply, much too deeply for a public place.

"Not now, Luc," she said.

"Later," he murmured seductively as he slid his hand around her waist and gave a slight squeeze. "Shall we?"

Before she could answer, he ushered her toward the door that led to the grand auction hall.

"Wait, I have something I have to tell you, something you'll *never* believe," she said with urgency.

"It can wait. We're going to be late, my saucy little vixen."

Unable to contain her enthusiasm, she stopped in her tracks, bringing them both to a conjoined halt. "Luc, I was looking up Alessandro Bonnard on the Internet." The words tumbled from her lips. "Your friend, the one whose villa we…we…" Monique's cheeks burned hot as a few auction goers passed close enough to make her whisper instead. "And you'll never believe this but—"

Luc interrupted her, practically sweeping her up off her feet as he moved them through the doorway to the auction "Googling him? You can't be serious." His tone was stern and reprimanding.

Suddenly she felt ridiculous—a country bumpkin in Venice. Carried away with dreams of grandeur.

Of course it was crazy, and Luc wouldn't be impressed that she had met Bonnard in person. He was Luc's friend. After all, he probably saw him all the time. She scolded herself for being so easily impressed and looked up at Luc as he released her once they were inside the grand hall.

He said nothing. He scanned the room but did not look at her. She could tell he wasn't pleased. That was the last thing she wanted on the night of her big auction. She followed his gaze slowly around the room and saw it was filled to capacity, give or take a few vacant seats. What if they couldn't sit together? She didn't want to be on her own during this. There was too much at stake with James Conroy's money.

"You *are* going to tell me how it's done, right?" she reminded him.

He took her hand and led her to a row that had two vacancies.

"I don't have a clue," she confided under her breath. The air was stuffy and the mood ominous with Luc's hand still planted on her waist.

"You have your list and your limits, just follow them. You'll be fine," he said to her, his tone softening as he took two bidding cards from an usher handing them out. "Here." He motioned for Monique to head to the two empty seats. Scooting past the already seated bidders, Monique was embarrassed as she stepped on more than a few toes.

Luc was close behind her, seemingly undeterred, his hand resting on her ass as if to steady her. He gave a little pat on her bottom just as they reached the two vacant seats. Well, at least he was over his apparent dissatisfaction with her Googling Alessandro Bonnard. She'd be sure to broach that subject much more carefully. Maybe she wouldn't even tell Luc that she'd thought Bonnard was the man who saved her from a fall. Would it would piss Luc off? Maybe even make him jealous. Damn, she didn't know much about her sexy supervisor other than he had an extensive knowledge of fine art and he was a demon in the sack. A trickle of arousal and nervousness wicked through her when she reached for the card, her hand shaking. Was it the excitement of the auction or the look in his eye that reminded her of what he had planned for later?

Luc kept his grip on the card, seating himself next to her. He leaned closer and whispered, "Remember, stick to your list and your bids. You'll do just fine." He glanced up to the front of the room then all around as if searching for someone.

"I thought it was *we*," she stammered.

The auctioneer approached the lectern and the crowd hushed.

She looked at Luc for reassurance but his gaze remained fixed straight ahead. Dammit. She needed his help. She didn't dare fuck this up.

Before she could give it another moment's thought, the auction was off and roaring. Paintings, sculptures, jewelry was produced on cue by the auction assistants, while Monique scanned her catalog, making sure she knew which lots she was to bid on. Fellow bidders eagerly flicked cards.

The auctioneer expertly kept pace with the bids until the rap of his hammer and the defiant, "*Sold!*"

Excitement hung heavily in the air, the scent of acquisition, the thrill of the hunt, as the bidders competed relentlessly for their coveted items. Monique scanned her list again, grateful that her items hadn't come up yet. It gave her more time to fortify her resolve against these much more savvy buyers.

The crowd immediately fell silent as an assistant pushed a display cart to center stage. A palpable sense of awe blanketed the room as the Rodin sculpture was rolled into place. Monique would recognize that piece anywhere, as did the rest of the crowd. She shivered with excitement at just what high bids this Rodin would bring—well out of her range for the hotel—but still, to be sitting so close to the famous sculpture, and at an auction no less. Who would have thought she'd propel herself from the dust bowl trailer park to the auction houses of Venice?

Through the swoosh of her rapid heartbeat, she couldn't hear the auctioneer announce the name and the owner of the Rodin. Luc squeezed Monique's thigh and smiled at her. He, too, must be excited. She smiled back and anxiously waited to see just who would bet on such a piece. Monique scanned the room, curious to see if she shared the same airspace as a multimillionaire art collector who could dig into his or her pockets and produce the kind of coinage this sculpture was going to bring.

Bidders immediately rallied with their clients represented over their phones, signaling to the auctioneer they were ready. The auctioneer struck the hammer and started the bidding. Hot and heavy, the pace quickened as Luc's hand inched slowly up Monique's thigh, dangerously close to making her lose concentration. Monique brushed his hand away, aware they were in public, as she tried to keep up with the goings-on all around her. Having none of it, Luc rested his hand on her thigh again then nudged just under her program and crossed hands, out of the watchful eyes of any overseers. He began making small circles on her thigh, teasing her as she gave him a little smirk.

The crowd erupted in a roar as the pool of bidders fell off, one by one, the price tag too steep for their pockets. The bidding was now reduced to a two opponents. A blonde woman, who Monique could only see from the back, her hair in a beautiful chignon, very Grace Kelly, and a bearded Asian man with horn-rimmed, tortoiseshell glasses, seated on the far side of the room. Both bidders had their phones glued to their ears as the two adversaries chased the price of the Rodin higher and higher. Then silence.

The auctioneer repeated the previous bid. Another pause, the auctioneer held his hammer in the air ready to strike.

The woman flipped her bidding card again, and the audience murmured their surprise.

Everyone's attention went to the Asian man to see if he would raise her bid.

"Who is that?" Monique whispered to Luc. She watched as if she were at Wimbledon, her focus moving from bidder to bidder.

Luc said nothing. He kept his hand moving upward along her thigh. She grew moist and so horny for him as she squirmed in her seat, his hand slipping ever so discreetly under her skirt. Shit, she would cry out if he kept this up.

She flinched with pleasure, so turned-on by the tension of the battle for the Rodin and Luc's unrelenting attention to her soft, sensitive skin through her panties. Monique uncrossed her legs and parted them slightly, eager for more.

The bidding continued. She forced herself to focus, despite the pleasure Luc was giving her. Another outburst erupted from the crowd as the bidding zoomed higher, well out of the suggested sale price. The woman pressed on, the Asian matching her bid for bid.

"I wonder who that is on the other end of that line?" Monique muttered under her breath.

Luc grazed his fingertips on her clit through her panties. She twitched in delight. Her program fell to the floor noisily along with her bidding paddle. Luc quickly removed his hand from between her legs when Monique reached for the things that had fallen under the neighboring chair.

"Here," the woman next to her said. She stretched down to retrieve the fallen items from under her seat. Handing them back to Monique, she smiled politely and whispered, "It's very exciting, isn't it? Alessandro Bonnard could be one of the bidders—imagine that. No wonder that man on the phone is getting a run for his money."

"He's here?" Monique gasped and turned to look at Luc to see his reaction. Disappointed that Luc gave no sign of interest about the infamous art collector's presence, Monique craned her neck in all directions to see if she could find the man in the photo.

"No, he's not here." The woman nudged her.

Monique looked over her at her again.

"The man never shows in public, doesn't have to. He sends his bidders. That little fellow on the phone could be his, but I don't think so, because he's losing from the looks of things." She winked at Monique as if it was some kind of inside joke.

Monique obliged with a knowing nod back. No way did she want this woman thinking she was an outsider.

The Asian bid again. All eyes went to back to the blonde bidder. More silence, followed by a final call from the auctioneer. The blonde woman shook her head.

The auction hammer slammed down, and the auctioneer called out the bidding was over for the Rodin.

"See? He got it," the woman next to Monique exclaimed. "Maybe he *is* Bonnard's errand boy after all."

"Well for that price, he can have it," Monique told the woman, as if she was a seasoned auction goer rather than a fine art auction virgin.

Luc squeezed her leg. *Was he trying to shush her?*

"What?" she asked Luc in a hushed whisper. Not waiting for an answer before she excitedly relayed what her neighbor had just told her, she added, "That woman said it was Alessandro Bonnard bidding on the other end of the line. Imagine that. I wonder what she'd think if we told her what we did last night in your friend Alessandro's bed."

"Don't miss the upcoming bids," was all he said, seemingly ignoring her exciting announcement. He kept his eyes on the auction podium. "The lot you want is coming up soon." Luc pointed to her catalog.

Oh, shit. She'd been so excited she'd almost forgotten she was there to bid.

Chapter Twenty-Two

Monique eyed the next work being wheeled onto the auction stage, a divine-looking marble sculpture, late baroque period. She was well aware it wasn't on her list, but damn, it would be perfect for the sculpture garden on the rooftop. Flipping through her catalog to the line item as fast as she could, she perched on the edge of her seat, almost breathless as she nervously glanced at Luc.

"I think I should try for this one."

"No." He shook his head and placed his hand across her lap, closing the catalog.

"I think it would be perfect, late baroque. There's enough money for it." She pleaded her case when the bidding began. "You'll see."

Tentatively, she put her paddle up, then yanked it away from Luc's grasp when he tried stopping her. Never one to be told what to do, Monique charged on, holding the paddle even higher.

The auctioneer nodded in her direction, acknowledging Monique's bid before carrying off with the rapid-fire nodding as the room became animated once again. The bidding quickly jumped from five to ten million euros as the Asian man on the phone and several others bid it with enthusiasm. When price rocketed higher, Monique was unable to commit more money for the hotel and reluctantly let her paddle rest in her hands and the sculpture went to the highest bidder — this time the blonde woman.

Afraid to glance at Luc and see his expression of 'I told you so', Monique busied herself with flipping through the catalog. Luc reached out. This time it wasn't to stop her but to give an encouraging pat of affection. Lifting her head, she saw the look on his face. He wasn't mad at all. He smiled. Obviously, he didn't realize how much she'd wanted the piece. But there would be others.

Damn, the bidding had already starting for one of the lots she did want to bid on while she'd been going all gooey over Luc's apparent mood swing for the better. Shifting focus, she quickly turned to the items that were ones she'd agreed on with Luc to acquire.

Monique held her paddle straight up, this time with more conviction that her last bidding attempt. This lot was hers to win. She wanted it even more after losing the previous bidding.

The bidding for the collection of three rococo paintings quickly zoomed from four hundred thousand euros to one million nine hundred euros and was heading higher. Monique double-checked her notes, trying to keep her calm when she shot her paddle up again. The Asian man was at it again with the phone glued to his ear. He matched hers and any other bidders every time. Damn, at this rate, she'd never get the art she wanted for the hotel. Frustrated, she surrendered in defeat when the lot sold for three million euros, well above her budgeted acquisition price, and slumped back in her chair exhausted from the stress of the bidding.

"There will be another chance," Luc encouraged, pointing to the next lot then her notes next to the item line. "Try for that one."

The woman next to her leaned over. "Too bad, love, better luck next time. Hard when Alessandro is the ringleader." She politely excused herself and scooted out of the aisle.

"That does it, I don't care if he's your friend or not," Monique huffed at Luc. It pissed her off that Bonnard was consistently beating her and everyone else. As dashing as he might have been in the street that day, this was business. And she was never going to get impress Conroy if she didn't show some guts and go toe to toe with the Asian man and whoever else here was Bonnard's lapdog.

Seizing the moment as soon as the bidding started on a rococo painting and accompanying sculpture, Monique shot her paddle upward. Defiant against defeat to Bonnard, she wanted this. She *needed* this. Monique matched the others bid for bid, and the prices ratcheted upward, making her heart skip a beat and her head whirl when the bidding passed the two million euro mark.

Luc's watchful eye was on her when he patted her leg as if to slow her down. He obviously didn't know Monique Le Bres well enough. "You might have to let this one go."

"Not on your life," she snapped back under her breath. Monique wanted the damn oil and sculpture no matter what. Outbidding the crowd, Monique was the leader at three million. Sweat prickled on her brow. The Asian bid again and she was once again in the chase from behind for the art. He *must* be

Alessandro Bonnard's man. Monique forced her hand up again just as Luc placed his hand out to stop her. She ratcheted it free and stuck her paddle up again.

Three million six hundred euros, the auctioneer boomed. "Going once…"

Tapping her foot feverously, she held her breath. She was going to get it, yes, she was.

"Going twice…" The auctioneer looked at the crowd, especially at the Asian then Monique for any motion.

The man flinched.

He raised his paddle.

"Four million euros." The auctioneer bellowed as the man outbid her.

"Shit," she cursed under her breath. She saw several heads turn back to her. Protocol be damned, she wanted this. Thrusting her hand up again. And again.

"Five million euros," the auctioneer pronounced dramatically and nodded to Monique.

Silence filled the room.

"*Sold* for five million euro."

"I got it!" Monique squealed with as much restraint as she could muster. She nudged Luc, her smile cheek to cheek and her excitement uncontainable as the crowd quickly went onto the next lot. "I *got* it," she said, her paddle now safely stowed on her lap. "Isn't it wonderful?"

Luc didn't smile. Didn't crack any emotion.

Oh, so that's how this goes. He's playing it cool, not wanting to gloat in front of the other bidders that I've won the bid. For five fucking million euros. Holy shit. He could keep stone-faced all he wanted. She'd beaten Alessandro Bonnard at the bidding. Monica Le Bres was officially one of the 'in' crowd of the art world.

Her auction cherry officially popped. And she'd loved every luscious minute of it.

She held her hand up again to bid on the next lot. Luc placed his hand out and stopped her. The auctioneer looked confused and paused before quickly picking up the bids of the crowd.

"But I want that one. It's on my list," she said. Had he lost his ever-loving mind? She was losing money on these items while he was playing games.

"Take it easy," he said.

She pulled the paddle out from under his hands and shot it up again, eagerly bidding on a new lot.

She looked nervously at him, wondering if he was going to get all cranky, but he just stared straight ahead, expressionless. The thrill of the chase had her adrenaline pumping. Monique kept up with the bidders, eventually coming down to her and the Asian man and one elderly woman in a tweed suit. Another five million later and Monique had the cat in the bag as she crossed out the next lot she'd acquired from her list.

Unable to refrain from gloating at how she well she was doing, she nudged Luc conspiratorially. He remained seemingly unimpressed as she tried for his approval, at least to share her enthusiasm.

"I'm a natural at this," she teased him, hoping for some good humor. Instead, she was met by his deadpan expression.

"Budget," he snarled.

She continued bidding on the next lot, determined to get the art she wanted and hold her own against the infamous Bonnard.

"There," she exclaimed, winning the next lot, not able to conceal her delight as she tried to cajole Luc with her enthusiasm. "Take that, Alessandro

Bonnard," she muttered to him. She sat out the next lot, one that she wasn't interested in.

He frowned in obvious frustration. "You don't even know it's him bidding."

"Don't get pissed because he's your friend. You're supposed to have my interests at heart—*our interests*." She squeezed his thigh as he'd done to her and leaned over very close. "For the hotel of course." she said.

Someone behind her uttered, "Hush."

Luc looked over his shoulder and said nothing. He met Monique's smile with his. Relief filled her when his brown eyes flashed with familiar delight. "Haven't you had enough for one night?" he whispered, his breath hot on her neck.

It sent a thrill right through her as he placed his hand over hers, pressing the paddle hard onto her lap.

"Mmm," she purred, getting his drift. The many delightful ways to use that paddle other than for bidding filled her thoughts. "What did you have in mind?"

"Come with me." Luc took her hand and led her out of the row, causing quite a commotion when they stumbled over the other bidders waiting for the next lot. "And make sure you have your paddle," he said sternly, looking back at her. But the spark in his eyes belied his tone as he stepped out of the row and placed his hand on her back to direct her up the aisle and out of the auction.

Chapter Twenty-Three

Luc's long strides were no match for Monique's much smaller steps as she lagged behind him. The click-clack of her heels on the wood floor echoed as he attempted to wrangle his outrage, fueled by guilt, before they got into the lobby. He must be careful not to give any clue away of just how enraged he was that things had gotten so out of hand at the auction. Definitely not what he had planned. Dammit, he reminded himself it wasn't Monique's fault that she'd been caught up in one of his bidding wars over his art—Alessandro's art. And how was Akito to know not to bid higher until some sucker in the crowd bought it hook line and sinker and made Alessandro a rich man? *A very rich man indeed.* The little wench wasn't supposed to bid on those paintings and win, but Christ, that's just what she had done. And now James Conroy owned more than one of Alessandro's paintings at an astronomically inflated cost. Good thing his friend J had deep pockets. But Alessandro didn't make his money by ripping off his friends or lovers. His items up for auction were supposed to be bought by some unsuspecting loser.

"Luc, wait up..." Monique called out, nearly breathless.

He strode through the lobby and out into the crowded walkway in front of the auction house. More unsuspecting bidders lined up, waiting to come in and be fleeced by his shills. Shit, they were so good at it they'd fleeced the last person he'd wanted them to. Who'd have known the vixen would be so headstrong? So tenaciously lustful in her pursuit of what she wanted. He should have known from how she was in the bedroom that she'd never be one to let what she wanted to get away. That characteristic would bode well for him later tonight when he took her back to his villa again. An encouraging thought after a shitty start to the evening.

He stopped and took a deep breath before he turned to face Monique.

Damn, she'd been a nosy wench Googling him. What if she'd found out *he was* Alessandro Bonnard? Then what? His cover would be blown. Fuck. It wasn't bad enough that he had just ripped off his friend J, but now the woman who blew his mind as well as his body was onto him. Or was she? He'd have to take his chances and see just what she knew.

His tortured mind eased at her wide-eyed smile of delight that would charm any man when she jumped up and down on her four-inch heels.

"I can't believe I got those pieces, can you?" she said, not waiting for an answer. She clutched her auction paddle to her chest as she spun around in a mock pirouette. He would have liked to have directed his fury over the botched auction at her, but he couldn't be mad. Monique's glee was hard to rebuff.

"I mean, I never would've thought I'd beat Alessandro Bonnard at bidding, but I did—I mean, *we* did." She swooned against his chest, her auction conquest making her obviously giddy.

Luc tried to refrain from flinching at yet another mention of the famed Alessandro Bonnard.

"You did admirably well," was the most gracious thing he could think to say. His head spun with just how the hell he was going to get out of this with J.

"*We* did, but not bad for a newbie, an auction virgin," she cooed. She slid the paddle seductively down his chest then over her breasts, taunting him with her luscious innuendo.

"A virgin?" he asked, his interest piqued, as evidenced by the bulge in his pants that defied his foul temper. His dick had a mind of its own and right now, it wanted her—every hot, wet inch of her. "Somehow, I doubt that," he taunted back.

She shifted from side to side, moving the paddle over her curves and then upward along the bloom of her breasts and up her neck before she held the paddle to her lips.

"You don't know *everything* about me, Luc Umbere."

"And you don't know everything about me, Monique Le Bres," he sparred back, thinking just how little she did know about him. He doubted she'd like those facts once revealed.

She just smiled behind the paddle, her eyes flickering with impishness as she bit sexily on the edge of it.

"I can think of much better uses for that." He took it from her then pulled her hard against him and kissed her with fierceness he didn't know he possessed. His anger at the auction proceedings only fueled his desire to do something right—paddle the tight, little ass of the vixen in his arms until she cried out in surrender.

"Luc!" she exclaimed when he nipped at her lips. She looked back over her shoulder toward the auction house. "Don't we have to settle our bill?"

"It's on the Totally Five Star account. I took care of all that."

"Oh," she said, reminded he was a take-charge man in every way.

He wasted no time, running his hands over her body. The paddle dropped from his hand and he pushed his tongue deep into her mouth, invading her.

He scooted his hands up under her skirt and as she ground against his massive erection. She heard footsteps and the disapproving "tsk, tsk" of some passerby.

"Luc," she stammered, forcing her hand between them. "Not here." She anxiously glanced around.

"Come." He took her hand in his as he bent swiftly to pick up his paddle. He then led the way down the darkened canal way. "Back to the villa with you, then I can do whatever I want to you."

He said it with a Machiavellian laugh that made her quiver with excitement.

She knew full well what he had planned for her. Bondage and a paddle—she'd bet her right ass cheek on it. The thought of him overpowering her thrilled her as her pussy throbbed with arousal.

"Not the villa," she said, trying to keep her head on straight. Her lust made common sense difficult. "Bonnard is there, you heard the woman at the auction…" Monique bit her tongue and refrained from informing Luc that she had met his friend, if ever so briefly.

"Oh, right… Uh, then how about the hotel?"

"Better be yours. My suite maid, Marie, is already onto us."

"Mine it is," he said, resuming his lightning speed.

Monique once again struggled to keep pace in her shoes. "Dammit," she uttered, stumbling over a rogue stone.

"You're going to kill yourself in those heels. Here," he said, stopping to swoop her up into his arms. With a satisfied smirk, he carried her down the street. "Much better."

Unable to say much as she watched Venice go by, she could hardly believe he was carrying her all the way to his hotel room. He hefted her a little higher in his arms and gave a little squeeze to her ass.

"Are you sure you're okay?" she ventured.

"Never better," he said and nipped at her shoulder as she clung to his neck while he nearly sprinted over a bridge and down the other side.

"I don't want you all worn out when we get there…"

"No fear of that, I can assure you." He stopped in front of his hotel entrance and opened the door with the crook of his foot before carrying her through the lobby. Heads turned as he headed straight for the elevator. Definitely not the incognito entrance, but then, nothing this man seemed to do was low key.

With her arms wrapped around his neck and her auction paddle now clutched in her hands, the elevator door dinged open and Monique gasped.

"*Signorina* Le Bres." Donovan smiled as he stepped out of the elevator in the green hotel-issued employee's uniform. He moved sideways to allow Luc room to enter the elevator.

"Thank you. As you can see, my hands are full," Luc joked, oblivious to Monique's frozen expression.

"What floor?" Donovan asked.

Monique noted his nametag said Bellman. Shit, he really had gotten the boot and she was none too sorry for him.

"Three," Luc answered.

Donovan nodded and pressed the button for him, then he stepped out of the way, but not before pausing to flash what Monique considered a snicker.

"Good to see you again, *Signorina* Le Bres, *il piacere è tutto mio*," Donovan said.

How dare he say the pleasure is all his, the sly scoundrel. The doors shut as Monique fumed, barely aware of the elevator slowly beginning its ascent in the fashion of an aged hotel.

"I take it you know that fellow," Luc said.

Monique looked away, her cheeks flaming, only to see her reflection — and Luc's cocky smile — reflected in the mirrored panels.

"Yes, he's an acquaintance." She hoped they could leave it at that.

"I see, but wasn't that the same person who was your supervisor before I arrived? Coincidental that they would both be named Donovan."

She gulped. "Yes." Of course Luc who know who Donovan was. He'd been sent to assist him in overseeing the art curation — overseeing her. All he had to was read the damn nametag to put two and two together.

The doors dinged open.

Luc said nothing more. With Monique cradled in his arms, his cock stirred at just what he was going to do to her. And what a damned turn-on it was that they'd run into Donovan in the elevator—the source of vixen's reported indiscretion. Luc had noticed the young man brashly flirting with the hotel colleagues over the past few days, then when he'd first read the man's nametag, he could barely believe it was him. And a young woman had been involved, according to J's dragon lady, Teresa Stiles.

My, my, the temptress in his arms was a sexual creature, if he'd ever met one. But he couldn't help feeling protective too. The lusty look in the young man's eyes made Luc's blood boil.

Monique wriggled in his clutches as he opened the door to his small hotel room. The scent of her perfume and the way her long hair spilled onto his forearms caused him to forget all about decking Donovan.

The room was dark as they entered. Reaching one hand free from under her, he flicked a switch. The room brightened and she shifted impatiently in his grasp.

"Now, now, I'll put you down when I am good and ready."

"I'm not a possession."

He suspected she was purposely pushing his buttons. "You are to me tonight. Remember our deal?" His cock throbbed, the fabric of his pants stiff with his arousal as he carried her over to the alcove with the bed and stood there with her still in his arms. "Deal?"

"We'll see…"

"Oh, you want it like that, do you?"

He abruptly released her, tossing her into the middle of the bed. She bounced on the mattress as he dove on top of her, the paddle flying out of her hand then clattering to the floor.

Ripping at her clothing, he kissed her. She clawed back at him and then fumbled with his shirt all the while rubbing her torso against him.

Kissing and nipping his way down her neck, he undid a couple of buttons of her blouse, eager for those round tits of hers. She tugged her shirt open just enough for him to access a beautifully budded nipple.

"That's better," he said.

He sucked the peak between his lips.

The slow murmur of approval and the way she bucked underneath him where sure signs she was loving this as much as he was. She reached around him and tugged his jacket from his shoulders, then yanked his shirt from his pants.

"Need I remind you I am in charge?" he growled. He rolled off her and quickly tossed his jacket aside then the shirt, followed by undoing his pants. The finality of the clang of his belt buckle on the wood floor made Monique's eyes widen.

"Whatever you say." Her eyes sparkled.

He lay back down on top of her, moving his weight to one side so he could undo her blouse one button at a time, in search of her round, creamy breasts. He still hadn't come all over them, but then, the night was young.

Chapter Twenty-Four

The uneven hitch of her breathing was the only sound in the room as she lay spread eagle on Luc's hotel bed with only her panties remaining. Monique quivered with each maddeningly slow stroke of his fingers and the way he'd removed her clothing methodically, piece by piece. She ached for more of his touch and wriggled in overt appreciation of each caress.

Luc's touch lingered on the edge of her panties then trailed along the rim of her mound before dipping ever so slightly under the lace. She squirmed when he teased her by gently tugging at the lace fabric. He blew his hot breath on pussy. It was too much for her and she arched up at the exquisite sensation.

"No." He swatted her hand away as she reached up to pull him closer. "Patience, my Monique."

"I don't want to be patient," she panted.

He continued to delve into her panties, and she spread her legs wider. She met the resistance of his thighs, which prevented her from opening her legs for him like she craved. When his finger barely touched the crest of her slit, she knew the promise of his tongue was imminent.

Halting, he gazed up at her as she licked her lips in anticipation.

Saying nothing, he straddled her, completely naked, his thick cock standing at attention, bobbing and pressing against her body as he bent and kissed her on the lips.

"Turn over," he encouraged.

His gaze stayed on her when he moved to make room for her to roll over. Her pulse quickened as she did as she was instructed. She felt him lean over her and reach for something, his cock brushing against her buttocks. Then he retreated to straddle her thighs, this time kissing softly down her spine, then the sensation of something rough that followed the same path and stopped right on her ass.

Flat, firm, something rigid rested on her ass and it wasn't his cock – that was for sure. Small circles with the object gave her a clue as he caressed her bottom with what she knew must be the auction paddle. She flexed her feet in response to just what he might do with that paddle. Spank her? Would it hurt? Would she be able to take it? Would she like it?

"Ever been spanked?" he asked, his voice husky. He ran the paddle over each of her butt cheeks then gave her a light, little tap.

"No," she stated, her voice hesitant.

"And would you like me to spank you? I'd like to very much."

His hard cock replaced the paddle.

"I'd like to feel you quake beneath me as I paddle your beautiful little ass." He spanked her and pressed his hot, thick cock along her crease. His body weight lay heavily against her thighs as he spanked her once again.

Her pussy quivered with a deep ache she hadn't known the stinging of her skin would produce.

"Okay?" he asked. He ground hips against her, brushing the paddle on her buttocks before giving her another soft, little spank.

"Yes," Monique croaked. She wanted to beg him for another, anything to satisfy the deep longing inside her. "Another...please..." She heard his grunt of approval.

"Of course," he said, pulling her by one hip. "Rise, it will feel better." He positioned her in a low, downward dog pose then moved behind her on the bed.

She waited on all fours, her head and upper body pointed down toward the pillow, with her hips higher. He said nothing, just ran the paddle back and forth over her ass in a teasing manner. Then he struck her—one firm smack to her buttock. Monique cried out in surprise—and pain. Then white-hot flames prickled her skin as something deep inside her thrummed, vibrated, ached. He ran one hand around her hips, cupped her mound then smacked the paddle against her ass again. She groaned at the sensation. Heat and pressure from his palm teased her slit, and he paddled her again, this time firm and hard. She wanted more, she wanted his fingers inside her—and the paddle on her ass.

"Tell me what you want," he coaxed, squeezing her butt cheek before sliding one finger into her aching slit.

A guttural sound escaped her. Her whole body quivered when he left his finger inside her channel then spanked her again.

"Fuck," she cried out. Her pussy clenched around his finger, drawing it deeper inside her. She wanted more—more of him, more of whatever the hell he was making her feel.

"That's what you want? Fuck. Well, we'll get to that in due time but for now..."

He struck her again, this time sliding another finger into her channel, forcing her to buck against him as the ripples of a climax built deep in her groin. Craving more, she wriggled her ass and looked back at him.

His cock was at a right angle, hard as could be. She watched him raise the paddle and spank her again, this time he slipped his finger out of her passage and over her clit. Monique collapsed forward when the orgasm rolled over her, driving her down to the bed. She shuddered and rode the release.

"Good girl, but we're not done." He pulled her back up onto all fours. "Seeing as you're enjoying this so much, I think it's time I made sure you don't get away."

She glanced back at him anxiously, the haze of her orgasm fading as she realized he meant tying her up.

"You're okay with it, aren't you?"

"I don't know," she ventured, getting cold feet, but afraid her reluctance would insult him and that it would stop the pleasure he was giving her.

He smiled. "I think you'll like it, just like the paddle, which you seemed to enjoy even more than I did," he said, resting his hand on her ass.

Her bottom tingled under his touch, so sensitive from the spanking.

"But if you're not ready—if you don't want to—I won't restrain you. But just so you know, it does intensify your pleasure. I'll go very slowly. Tell me if you need me to stop. You can trust me."

Her throat constricted and tears welled in her eyes. She looked away, not wanting him to see the effect his words had on her. *Trust.* He'd asked her to trust him. *She trusted no one.* This was foreign territory for her. Very unsettling—and very tempting—at the same time.

"Go ahead..." she uttered, surprising herself. She felt his hands caress her bottom gently, dipping down to her wet folds, making her mad for more of him—for his cock, for his hand and his paddle.

"We need a safe word," he said, then left the bed to go over to the closet.

"A safe word?"

"Something you say in case you want me to stop—if it's too much."

"Oh," she said, embarrassed that she didn't know about safe words. "Monet," was all she said.

He laughed and grabbed some silk ties from his closet. "You never cease to amaze me, you wicked, little vixen. It's what I love most about you, I think." He strode back to the bed, the ties clenched in one hand. "Monet it is."

Did he just say he loved me, or was he just caught up in the moment?

Standing at the edge of the bed, he took one of her wrists at a time and pulled them gently behind her back, moving her torso to bend forward. He paused to adjust her pillow so she could rest her head comfortably. He bound her wrists together behind her back then tweaked her position. Placing her feet together, he adjusted her knees out farther, leaving her ass in the air. Her face was to the pillow with him right behind her. The soft silk of the fabric thrilled her as he then bound her ankles. Nestling himself behind her tied feet, he placed a hand on her back, holding her steady while he stroked her exposed slit. She shuddered when he teased her clit with his fingertip before dipping it inside her.

"So much better," he soothed.

His hand on her back comforted her, reassuring her as he pleasured her with his other hand. Her juices dripped and slicked his touch.

"Such a beautiful cunt," he whispered, bending down to kiss her buttocks.

He rubbed his chin over her rump. The sting of his stubble on her ass cheeks made her quiver for more as he fucked her with his fingers and bit her bottom.

Then the crack of the paddle followed, and she shouted out in complete surrender. He teased her clit and her body, her mind and soul yearning for more — for his cock buried deep inside her. He spanked her again, now pressing his fingers into her pussy, filling her in sync with each vibration of the paddling.

"More," Monique gasped, her words muffled as she bit into her lip. She clenched her fists against the all-consuming ecstasy that thrummed deep inside her.

"More or Monet?" he asked, immediately stopping.

"More. Fuck, more," she shouted, unable to contain her need. "Cock, please, fuck me now," she begged him again.

His hand left her back and she felt him shift his weight, then the rustle of a condom packet followed. In a moment, he returned and nudged the head of his big dick into her slick opening. Just what she'd asked for. Only she needed it *now*, faster, harder, and he was only teasing her with dipping the tip in. Her inner walls contracted with an urgent want.

"More," she begged. "More."

He slid deeper inside her, more like a wiggle than a stroke. Then he struck the back of her buttocks with the paddle. Everything ebbed away except the shattering feeling of coming apart, of her orgasm splitting her in two as she gave in and rode the crescendo. He spanked her again, the stroke of the paddle vibrating through her. He plunged his cock into her, paddling her ass as he did.

Nothing could have ever prepared her for the intensity of her orgasm, unable to move with her hands bound behind her, her feet tied together, and he fucked her—hard. White light turning to purple blinded her as she squeezed her eyes shut and felt the best orgasm of her life take her to places she'd never been before.

* * * *

The morning light scattered across Luc's small hotel room. The tattered carpeting and tired fabric on the upholstered chairs was now visible. Last night, Monique had been nervous, anxious really, about going back to his place, and what he'd had in store for her, so she hadn't even looked at his shabby hotel room. She'd been focused only on the conquest at the auction that had given her some much-needed courage. Well, that and his demanding appetite for all things sensual and sexual. She smirked when she entered the small living area in a silk robe.

Definitely not the hotel-issued robe, but then, she was learning all sorts of new things about this dashingly daring man who wielded an auction paddle like she'd never imagined possible—right across her ass. And oh, how she'd liked it—no, loved it. She'd surprised herself with the trust she'd placed in him when she'd agreed to let him do whatever he pleased while she was tied up on his bed.

"You're already dressed," he said with a frown. He took her in his arms. "Not planning on running off, are you?"

"No." She surrendered easily to the wonderful scent of him and his muscular body. "But I do have to get back to work sometime. After all, you're my boss. How would it look if I were late?"

"I can make you *very* late." He nipped at her lips and pulled her to his erection.

"I'm sure you can."

He moved his hands lower, just over her bottom, which was still tender from last night. When she'd slid her panties on this morning—while Luc had lain sound asleep like a god after a feast—even the delicate lace on her skin had forced her to wince.

She gasped when he patted her ass lightly, as if he was aware it was not only making her uncomfortable but turning her on at the same time.

"Tender?" he asked.

He ran his lips along her jawline, his teeth just grazing her skin. She flinched when he cupped her cheeks eagerly.

"Ummm." She enjoyed the mix of pleasure and pain and opened her mouth in a deep, low groan of acceptance.

"Now listen, before I head back to the Totally Five Star, I wanted to tell you something about your friend, Alessandro Bonnard." She gulped, realizing she was actually nervous about telling him she'd met his friend in the street, especially after Luc's reaction last night when she said she'd Googled Bonnard. Luc had seemed downright appalled that she'd done such a plebian thing. Of course, it was old news for Luc, rubbing shoulders with the rich and famous, but she was very new to the experience. At least now, after their extraordinary lovemaking, she could explain to him how she knew his friend and why she'd Googled him in the first place. Monique was almost positive Luc would understand. Maybe he'd even find it a funny coincidence.

"Ah." He placed his finger over her mouth to silence her. Then he quickly moved it from her lip, down her neck and to her breasts. His lips teased hers.

A knock at the door made her flash her eyes open and she looked at Luc.

"I ordered us some breakfast. I couldn't send you back to the hotel *totally* famished, now, could I?" he asked, his brown eyes sparkling with mischief.

"I'll get it," she said as he released her. "At least I'm dressed." She headed for the door, leaving Luc and his large erection on display in the middle of the room. "I'll have to tell you about your friend over breakfast. You'll never believe it..." she continued, glancing back to make sure he was decent.

His stiff cock was visible, pressing out from his robe. She motioned for him to cover up. He looked down then proudly opened his robe to reveal his erection in all its glory just as the person on the other side of the door knocked again.

"Luc!" She gasped, as if appalled, but she really couldn't wait to get her hands on that dick of his again — and to hell with telling him about his friend.

Monique double-checked that he'd covered himself up before she unhooked the latch on the door. Then she triple-checked that Luc was behaving before she opened the door.

A large tray laden with savory-smelling foods greeted her. The person behind the tray was barely visible. Monique ushered the maid into the room, then followed her. The maid placed the cumbersome tray on the table in front of Luc.

"Good morning, *Signor* Umbere," the woman said with a heavy eastern European accent. She turned toward Monique.

Monique's mouth opened, but no sound came out.

Donovan's young woman. The one I watched make out with Donovan as I touched myself in the hall.

"Oh, *Signorina* Le Bres." She looked at Luc quizzically then back at Monique. "It's you..." Her gaze seemed stuck between Luc and Monique as she just stood there, unable to say a word.

"You two know each other?" Luc offered.

Monique was quite sure she'd caught a suggestive tone to his voice.

"No," Monique said.

"Yes." The young woman ignored her and went about setting up the breakfast tray laden with baskets of *pane* and a delicious-looking egg concoction, probably a type of frittata. "*Caffè?*" she asked, motioning to the pot and looking at Luc for direction.

"Yes, please," he said, moving closer. "How do you two know each other?" he asked as she poured them their *caffès*.

"Totally Five Star," the young maid blurted out defensively.

She met Luc's gaze as he smiled widely at her then glanced back at Monique with a questioning lift of his eyebrow.

Luc cast a knowing smile at Monique.

"Maybe I do remember you," Monique chimed in, as nonchalantly as she could, anxious to get the damn girl out of there.

"I see," Luc said, his gaze wavering between her and Monique. "That will be all for now, thank you."

"I'll show you out," Monique said with relief. She was right on the blonde's heels. "Thank you for delivering the breakfast." Monique summoned her most professional demeanor then leaned in as she held the door open and under her breath said, "Don't say a word."

The girl turned back, her mouth open as if to speak.

Luc watched Monique escorting the maid to the door. That was odd. He couldn't hear what Monique said to her, but this must be the woman of Monique's indiscretion who Teresa Stiles had mentioned. Luc's cock twitched at the thought of Monique in a ménage with that young woman. And what a little savior the maid had been. Monique had just been about to bring up talk of Alessandro Bonnard again. Shit, he needed that like a hole in the head. Last night's art auction was sure to raise suspicion in the art world, as he'd moved more paintings than ever in one evening. He needed to lay low. Monique wasn't getting hurt, and his first priority was reversing last night's disastrous events. Maybe after that he could consider telling Monique his real identity.

His lover closed the door and stood there for a moment after the maid had departed, her right hand still on the doorknob. Turning toward her, Luc couldn't contain his smile.

"My, my, my, aren't we even more of a vixen than I'd thought?" he said with a hearty laugh.

Monique turned five shades of red. That alone told him what Stiles had reported was bang on the money.

"I don't know what you're talking about," Monique said casually. The way she chewed her bottom lip belied her light tone as she walked toward him, the shimmy of her hips as enticing as the wary look in her eyes.

"Oh, I think you do," he said. She attempted to pass by him, apparently hellbent on looking out of the window. He reached out and grabbed her by the arm.

He swiftly pulled her to him and his lips met her hot lips. Soft, womanly flesh connected with his hard, aroused body. The thought of Monique being involved with that woman — involved enough to get fired — made him throb with desire as he bit, licked and nibbled her.

"You kissed her," he whispered then rapidly shed her of her clothes.

She muttered a couple of words between breathless caresses. "I never..."

"Then what?" he taunted. Tugging her blouse from her, he reached for her round tits, loving their weight in his hands. He crushed them, cupped them, her nipples growing taut and erect under his touch.

"I watched...her and someone else...if you must know."

"And did you enjoy it?"

"I did." She confessed her dirty little secret.

He could tell she was turned on when she bit and nipped at his mouth, eager for more.

"Oh, you little scamp. I definitely have to put you over my knee for that."

Monique didn't need to speak, her body told the story as she moaned and slid along his body, his hands still on her breasts as she slunk down his torso then opened his robe. She greeted his cock with the tip of her tongue.

Her breasts fell from his grip as she wrapped her lips around the head of his dick, causing him shiver and shake with pleasure. She sank to her knees and ran her hands up and under his robe to grab his buttocks. Pulling him to her, she buried his cock deep into the hot wetness of her mouth.

"Fuck." He groaned.

She licked and sucked his length. Swirling her tongue in circles along his shaft, she tasted every inch of him before stopping to lick his balls.

His breathing was edgy and rough as he gripped her hair with his hands, guiding her head back and forth on his cock while he pumped in and out of her mouth. Her tight little lips made a slapping noise with each thrust.

"Show me how much you liked watching," he teased her, twining his fingers faster and harder through her locks.

She flicked her tongue in swirls around the base of his cock. Monique stopped and looked up at him when she gauged he was getting close. His gaze met hers, her mouth wet and shiny. "I like cock, specifically *your* cock, *tuo cazzo*," she purred.

Slowly, she traced the helmet of his dick, drawing a perfect outline with the point of her tongue, her other hand now on his shaft, stroking up and down as she focused her mouth on his tip.

"How about *la fica*? Do you like that? I know I do..." He growled when she thrust his cock deep to the back of her throat. He could feel her almost gag as she began fucking him with her mouth.

"Shit," he called out, barely able to stand as she sucked him hard, his cock pulsing, his balls so heavy with need. The need to come all over her tits. Her face.

He tipped his head back in delight.

"Tell me what you want..." Her voice was throaty and deep as she slowed her pace, gripping his cock hard, as if she knew just how close he was to exploding. "Tell me…"

"I want to come all over your face, your tits," he gasped.

She flicked his tip then brought her hand over this cockhead and back down again, following it with her tongue.

He trembled. He was so close. She watched his response when she rubbed his cock over the outside of her mouth, nipping and gently kissing it as her pink tongue darted out and touched his cockhead.

"Come all over me," she commanded.

She sucked long, deep strokes up and down his length, one hand gripping his buttocks, the other cupping his balls. Her hot, slick mouth was too much for him when she tightened her seal and moved her tongue in little circles under the tip of his dick. He spiraled into release. Opening her mouth, she pulled him from her lips, his milky cum splattering all over her face and throat when he shot his wad all over his brazen beauty.

"That's right," she said. She tried to lick his cum from the edges of her mouth while she smeared his cream on her throat, up and over the curve of her tits.

He watched her circle his cream around each nipple, her cheeks flushing with pleasure.

She smiled. "I told you I like cock."

"And I like cunt. You should try it sometime."

"Maybe I will," she said, slowly rising to meet him.

Her lips were shining with his juice when he kissed her, tasting his musk on her as she kissed him back fully. Oh, he had his hands full with this one – that was for sure. He was really falling for her. She had gotten under his skin in a way no woman ever had. Starting as Luc, he'd been more free than he ever had been as Alessandro, and now all he wanted to do was fuck this little minx all day long, but he'd have to tell her who he was soon and deal with the consequences.

Chapter Twenty-Five

The narrow passageways were crowded with tourists and locals alike when Monique hurried back to her office just before noon. She'd spent far longer in Luc's room than she'd meant to, especially after that unexpected appearance of Donovan's flame.

Whatever Luc had thought she and that girl had gotten up to seemed to turn him on. Monique couldn't believe she'd confessed to her moment of voyeurism. At least she hadn't divulged that she had been watched, too, by the young girl when she had succumbed to Donovan's advances. The only thing Monique had achieved was getting them all fired in the process. Damn, Luc probably knew that already. He was her boss, after all. But rather than scare Luc off, any knowledge he seemed to have of her indiscretions turned him on. And her, too, when she'd slunk to the floor and sucked him like there was no tomorrow. His hot, wet cum on her face. She trembled with pleasure at the recent memory and licked her lips.

He seemed to push all the right buttons and forced her to yearn for more. She could barely count the minutes until she'd see him after work today, after she'd finished her acquisition list and relished in her outstanding bidding prowess at the auction last night. Oh, the auction. Her pussy prickled at the memory of how he'd tied her up and paddled her bottom.

* * * *

Luc wasted no time getting dressed after Monique's departure. First thing first. He had to fix the disastrous effects of last night's auction. How could he have ever known Monique would go rogue on the bidding and gobble up his canvases meant for unsuspecting auction-goers? She was supposed to stick to the list they'd agreed upon. He was all too aware he was royally screwed by her going after the wrong paintings. A true vixen, she'd let the thrill of the chase capture her. He should have known better than to put her — an auction novice — in such a position.

He paced the hotel room, hashing out just how he could set things straight. He halted his frenetic pacing, went to the bathroom and popped out his contacts. Relief flooded him. As Luc, he'd had to wear them all night with Monique staying over. The last thing he needed was another close call like in the villa where she'd turned on the light and almost caught him without his contacts. Looking at his reflection, he wondered just what the hell he was doing falling for the fiery American, who had surprised him once again by confessing her penchant for voyeurism, then had given him the blow job of his dreams. He could still see his hot juices on her tits, just the way he'd imagined. *Focus, Alessandro.* He coached himself not to get carried away. There would be plenty of time for more of the vixen's American ass once he got this fiasco sorted.

After entering his sitting area, he looked out over his peekaboo view of the canal. The windows hadn't been cleaned in ages. He couldn't tell if it was hazy out or just the film. *Dammit.* He ran his fingers through his hair, reminded once again how short it was. He hated this whole hiding thing. Oh, sure, at first it was thrilling, the whole undercover thing, but that had worn thin as soon as Monique had inadvertently made things very complicated by being the unexpected alpha bidder at the auction. *Virgin, my ass.* He cracked a smile. That woman was born to succeed, and so she had, to his detriment.

Luc sighed and turned away from the window. There was only one thing to do — retract the works for sale. That way J wouldn't be ripped off, and Monique... Well, now that was a problem. How was he ever going to explain to her what was going on? She'd been hell-bent on getting those works, and he knew her well enough to know she wasn't about to let retracted items go quietly into the good night. He would have to tell her the truth — or at least a version of the truth. His real identity. Not the part about trying to shill the auction — that she didn't need to know.

Luc would see her tonight. He had to plan something very special for her and tell her. Perhaps he'd take her to Paris for dinner using his private jet. She'd love that, and he could have her all to himself when he told her that he was Alessandro Bonnard. Then he'd see how she took it. At least there would be the flight back to Venice with her, in case she didn't take the news well and he needed more time to convince her. For a moment, he fantasized about running away to Paris with her, lovers on the lam. *Oh, for God's sake, Bonnard, get a grip.*

After dialing Monique's number, he became frustrated when her line was busy at the office. He left a message for her in her room to meet him at seven p.m. sharp in his room and that he had a surprise for her, so for her to keep an open mind. When he hung up, he hesitated. Had he said enough? He wanted her to accept him as Alessandro and he hoped she would. *Shit, the woman has really gotten to me.*

* * * *

All day Monique tried to focus on her work, but her mind kept wandering back to her night of passion with Luc. Her sore bottom was a constant reminder of it as she sat at her desk, her pussy thrumming at the thought of what they might get up to tonight—what she hoped they might get up to. Then there was the breakfast maid, the reminder of just how close she'd come to losing her job for good. Not again, she pledged, and looked over her acquisitions list in earnest. No distractions, not during work hours. There would be plenty of that after hours for her brown-eyed hunk with a penchant for the kinky.

Having completed her list for the sculpture garden and a brief outline of placement for more items she hoped to acquire, Monique couldn't help looking up from time to time, hoping to see Luc's frame filling her doorway. Maybe he'd take her on the desk. Or by the window with her head hanging out and him fucking her from behind. Her ass cheeks burned with the thought of him paddling her again as he screwed her any way he wanted in her office. That was what she wanted — ached for.

A sound at the doorway startled her from her erotic daydream. She shouldn't have been surprised to see Marie scooting in with a tray, her four o'clock *caffé*, right on time. Monique could set her watch by Marie's punctuality. A pang of loneliness struck her when she realized she didn't even have a best friend, a girlfriend to confide in. She was a loner and enjoyed the company of men. In her bed. And theirs. It didn't lend itself to a lot of girl time.

"Oh, Marie," Monique greeted her, standing as Marie placed the tray in its usual spot. "Where did the time go?" she asked. She looked at her watch then at the delicious-looking biscotti next to the cup of *caffé* her confidante poured from the glass carafe.

"You looked deep in concentration, *Signorina* Monique. Almost hated to interrupt you, but espresso calls."

"I wish I could say I was working, but I'm afraid you caught me daydreaming."

Marie smiled and her kind eyes sparkled. "About *him*, I bet." Her double chin wobbled when she winked at Monique.

"Caught me red-handed," Monique confessed, glad to have someone with which to share the overflowing enthusiasm she felt for Luc.

"Seeing him tonight?" Marie inquired. "Shall I turn down your bed or...?"

"Oh, Marie, I *hope* I see him tonight."

"You're quite smitten with him, I can tell."

"More than smitten." Monique realized the feelings she had for Luc went further than her usual sexual attraction. She actually *liked* Luc. She missed him when they were apart. Shit, she might even love him. What was wrong with her?

"I'll make up your bed just in case," Marie told her as she headed for the door. "But I have a feeling you won't be sleeping in it tonight." She winked as she departed.

* * * *

Luc worked right through lunch, not even noticing the time, trying to put together an extensive stop list for the auction as well as mulling over just how he was going to explain himself to Monique. His ringing phone kept distracting him—Alessandro's encrypted phone. Finally conceding to tear himself away from his work, he answered it.

"*Monsieur* Bonnard." The voice at the other end was instantly familiar.

Fuck. It was Akito.

Alessandro gathered his thoughts in a split second. "No names," he reprimanded his assistant, even though they both were well aware the phones were encrypted. Precisely the reason Alessandro had insisted on using Blackberry phones in the first place.

"Forgive me. Red has been arrested," Akito informed him, referring to their code names.

"Damn." Red was the codename of one of his best bidders. His loyalty rivaled only Akito's, but then again, who knew what a man would say under interrogation?

"They're looking for you..." Akito said with urgency. "Apparently the *Carabinieri* has been on to you for some time. Last night's auction was the red flag they'd been waiting for." Then he hesitated before continuing. "You've got to get out of here. I already have everything in place."

Everything in place meant *the plan*. Alessandro rubbed the spot where his goatee used to be, instantly reminded of his debacle as Luc fucking Umbere.

"Sir?" Akito prompted when his boss was unresponsive.

His mind racing, he heeded Akito's warnings and knew he had to vacate the hotel immediately—and Venice. They had a backup plan for eventualities such as this, and his trusty aide would have prepared everything according to Alessandro's exacting specifications. Except for Monique, she was something Bonnard had never factored into his plans. Never one to involve his lovers with his work, he never considered their predicament if the shit hit the fan. But this time it had, and Monique had landed smack in the middle of it, thanks to him tangling business with pleasure.

Alessandro broke his silence. "There's something else I need you to do..." He hesitated, weighting the risks of staying on the line against telling Akito what he needed him to do. Soldiering ahead, he rattled out his instructions before promptly ending the conversation.

The line went silent after he'd hung up. *Those phones better be encrypted as promised or they'd all be in some deep shit.* With no time to reconsider his instructions to Akito, he frantically gathered his things as fast as he could, pausing to crash the laptop in case he was caught. *I damn well hope I'm not.*

After making double and triple sure he'd left nothing incriminating behind, he stopped for a moment and thought of Monique. What was she doing? How would she react to his plan?

Not able to spend a moment more in the room, he pulled the door shut behind him and headed to the fire escape. Almost skimming the steps with his rapid pace, he arrived on sub-canal level, deep below the water's edge. Occupied only by the maintenance staff and an impressive amount of mechanical equipment that serviced the hotel, Alessandro made his way through the maze-like basement to a tunnel under the canal that connected to a nearby business.

The tunnel was dank and dimly lit. Perfect for his undetected escape. Bonnard began to run because he was well aware there was no way for him to avoid the *polizia* if they got there first. Bursting through a metal door, he hurried up a small flight of stone steps and emerged at canal level in the haze of the setting sun.

As planned, Akito was waiting for him. Alessandro hopped into the waiting launch and ducked down as his trusted assistant throttled away from the mooring, forcing Alessandro flat to the floor of the boat with its thrust.

Hiding under the canopied portion of the boat, Bonnard couldn't help but feel like a coward. There was still Monique. Alessandro couldn't leave her behind. No doubt the police would be on to her at any moment. Double shit. And if he went to get her, to warn her, who knew what her reaction would be, and in the process, he'd lead the *polizia* right to her. Monique's very future — *their* very future — rested on whether Akito had acted as instructed.

The boat crashed over some waves, causing Alessandro to curse loudly when he banged his head on the bulkhead. Rubbing his head, he let despair overtake his racing adrenaline.

Akito tapped on the bullhead to signal the coast was clear. Alessandro emerged above deck and squinted into the searing sunset, leaving Venice behind in a stunning reversal of fortune from that fateful day when he had first laid eyes on Monique Le Bres. The woman he'd had no way of knowing would, in the course of four short days, become his vixen in Venice.

Chapter Twenty-Six

Monique stayed a little later in the office, hoping Luc would appear, but he didn't. After an extra hour, she decided enough was enough. She wasn't just going to sit there and wait for him like a love-struck teenager.

Monique walked into her suite and kicked off her shoes, cajoling her sinking spirits with the promise of a nice hot soak in the tub. Just what she needed to ease her tenderness from last night's paddling. Eager to get out of her clothes, she stripped as she went, pulling her top over her head, nearly causing her to walk into the bed. Her vision was restored when she tossed the top onto the bed. She eyed the flashing light on the phone. Could it be? She hurried over to the night table and sat on the bed, eager for any message from Luc.

"Monique." His message began softly and seductively. Like a round, juicy apple dipped into hot, creamy caramel. She gulped at the image, her pussy wet at the thought of just what he might do with a caramel apple. "Tonight, seven p.m. I have a surprise for you."

What kind of surprise, she pondered playfully. She could only hope it involved the apple she'd been fantasizing about.

"Keep an open mind," he added, before ending the message.

Replaying the message one more time, she could hear his breath heavy on the line and she could picture him on the other end. He was a man who took control and for once in her life, she liked it. She *loved* it.

Looking at the clock, she saw she had two hours until Luc's surprise. Plenty of time to get ready for him, her mind already whirring over what to wear, what he might have planned. Maybe she'd answer the door in just her thong and a sheer bra. He'd like that, wouldn't he? And if he didn't, he'd be sure to give her a good paddling. She quivered at the prospect as she practically scampered over to the bathroom, ready to prepare herself for her Luc and all his lustful intentions.

* * * *

The suds from her bubble bath clung to her slick skin as she stepped out of the tub. Monique brushed the bubbles away when she toweled off, paying special attention to between her legs and her sensitive behind. In the mirror, she saw her nipples were erect and rosy.

Already so turned on at the prospect of being with Luc and whatever surprise he had for her, she slid her fingers between her thighs. She felt how wet she was. Parting her outer lips, she stroked herself, her nipples growing more taut and tawny, turning darker and more erect. Her reflection conformation what Luc must see when he made slow, sensual love to her. She flicked her fingertip over her clit and was surprised how stiff it became with just a few touches. Easing her hand from her folds, she smiled, knowing she'd best leave the pleasuring to Luc. After all, he knew just what to do, and she couldn't wait.

Naked, she padded into the bedroom, where she slipped on her taupe lace bra and matching G-string. That ought to turn him on, the ass man that he was. Her pussy was wet again with arousal — her cunt, as Luc called it with admiration and lust. She loved it when he used such words, so raw and guttural. She felt like a naughty girl when he growled the words, like he couldn't get enough of her little cunt. Biting her bottom lip, she steeled her composure and readied herself for his arrival.

From the open windows, the haze of yellow and red streaked across her hotel room as the sun started to set. She switched on a few lights and listened. The canal traffic had slowed and now all she heard was the odd Italian chatter in the streets below and the occasional whoop or holler of a hot-blooded Italian man, most likely appreciating one the opposite sex as she walked by.

Checking the time, she flicked on the television — a chance to catch up on the days' news before he arrived. Not that she was interested in the news, but it was a good way to practice her Italian as she flicked channels and found a newscast she could almost follow.

A sound in the hall made her double-check the clock on the sideboard. It was seven. Hopping up, almost tripping over herself in her excitement to get to Luc, she gave the room a once-over as she headed for the door. Not that he'd care, the only thing he'd care about was her bed. They saw eye to eye on that topic.

She peered out the peephole then opened the door with a flourish. Her heart sank. Just a maid delivering room service to someone else's suite. Disappointed, she turned back into the luxurious quarters, sporting her G-string and bra, eager for Luc's arrival.

She spotted the image on the TV and stopped in her tracks.

Luc's image stared back at her, a small photo of him and some writing in Italian underneath it. The commentator raced along in machine-gun-fire Italian.

"What?" Monique stammered. She immediately reached for the remote to turn the volume up, as if that would help. She picked up a handful of words she knew as a few more photos flashed by and she struggled to keep up in Italian.

"Alessandro Bonnard," was one she knew immediately.

They were saying something about Alessandro Bonnard *and* Luc. They were friends — that much she already knew.

"Dammit, I wish they'd slow the fuck down," Monique snapped to the empty room, a sudden sinking feeling filling her. Something about the photo and the announcer's grim expression told her this wasn't a feel-good story. They flashed a photo of a man who was unsuccessfully trying to shield himself from the camera while entering an airport terminal in France.

Her jaw dropped. She peered closer. The man bore an uncanny resemblance to Luc. She shook her head to dispel off her disbelief.

"*Ricercate per l'arrest,*" the stern-faced announcer exclaimed.

Wanted for arrest flashed across the screen in Italian and English. Monique understood those words. Stunned, she just stood there, silent as the announcer rattled on and a series of pictures of Luc and some other people she didn't know flashed across the screen. Monique gasped at the television when they showed a picture of the Totally Five Star Venice then small photos of Alessandro Bonnard with his goatee, blue eyes rimmed with glasses and his chin-length blond hair. The photos were much clearer than the ones she'd seen on the Internet. They must be passport photos or some sort of official ID. She was one hundred percent sure that he was the man who had loaned her his hand so gallantly in the street. And now it looked like he was in some trouble, along with her Luc.

But why were photos of Luc side by side with Alessandro Bonnard's, Monique questioned, hanging on every word of the announcers and unable to understand the connection. Was it because they were friends? Were they in some sort of trouble? She was reminded why she'd thought they might be brothers. The likeness was quite striking, even more so with the better quality photos of Bonnard. The jaw, the shape of the eyes, the nose — *holy fuck!* — they were brothers after all. That must be why Luc was in so much trouble — Bonnard had to be his brother.

Monique inhaled so hard it hurt when another screen appeared on the TV, filled with photos of Luc in different disguises. Brown hair with brown eyes then red hair then blond hair, glasses, no glasses... Her head spun. This was utterly ridiculous. Monique stared at the screen. She barely understood the rapid Italian, but got the drift that whatever they were saying was not good. Definitely not good. She saw the villa on the island and understood the announcer to say it belonged to Alessandro Bonnard. Damn, it was so confusing. What the hell was going on? Just then they showed a video clip of the *polizia* roping off the front entrance as if it was a crime scene.

"I was there..." Monique shook her head in disbelief. At Alessandro Bonnard's house, with Luc.

A knock at the door turned her gaze from the TV. It must be Luc. *It must be.* She prayed it was. Maybe he was late because he'd been helping that Bonnard fellow, his brother it seemed, who was in deep trouble by the sound of things. And to think Monique had slept in his bed. Been helped in the street...by a wanted man. Had been blissfully bedded by his brother. Part of her thrilled that she had met Alessandro Bonnard and another part hoped he hadn't gotten Luc into too much trouble.

Hurrying to the door, she was eager to see Luc and find out just what was going on. Not bothering to look through the peephole, she just threw the door open.

But it wasn't Luc.

Teresa Stiles stood with her mouth agape for the third time since Monique had arrived at Totally Five Star Venice.

She averted her gaze from Monique's nudity, her gaze flitting to the TV then back to Monique. "I see you've seen Luc on the news, or should I say Alessandro." Her face cracked into a forced smile. Monique shivered in response to her unsettling expression.

"I was just watching it, but I couldn't understand what the hell they were saying," Monique said quickly, then realized she was barely dressed. "I don't know where Luc is, do you? He's late. He was supposed to be here half an hour ago." She rambled on, questions filling her head faster than she could voice them.

"Oh, he was, *was he*?" Teresa inquired, her eyebrows arching. A genuine smile graced her stony face as her gaze lingered on Monique. "I didn't mean to interrupt." Teresa smiled a smile that was anything but genuine. "I just wanted you to know that Luc Umbere is under arrest. That is, if they can find him. It seems your boss was a world-renowned art thief," she said, wide-eyed as if waiting for Monique's reaction. "He isn't Luc Umbere at all. Turns out *he is* Alessandro Bonnard."

"That's ridiculous," Monique countered in his defense and looked at the TV for some sort of proof. "Alessandro has blue eyes. Luc has brown," she said, grasping at straws.

"A master of disguise apparently, and a very good one at that by the sound of things. To a tune of forty million euros. Some of it probably swiped from right under your nose."

Monique felt faint as she stumbled backward onto a nearby settee. *Luc, an art thief?* Luc—not really Luc Umbere after all. How could it be?

"Don't get any crazy thoughts of leaving the hotel, Monique. The *polizia* will be here shortly to take your statement. That's what I came to tell you."

Monique only gazed up at the wicked bearer of the news in disbelief.

The nasty woman strode toward the door. "Oh, and you're fired," Teresa said with a noticeable lilt of satisfaction as she opened the door and looked back at her. "And for God's sake, put some clothes on you before you embarrass Totally Five Star worse than you already have—if that's possible."

Chapter Twenty-Seven

Running to the toilet and heaving up what had been a perfect lunch before the day had turned on its ear, Monique shoved tendrils of hair away from her face.

Queasily, she gasped as she moved away from the bowl and sank to the cold tile floor. She wiped the sticky remnants of acrid puke from her lips.

Alone and shivering, the rancid aftertaste of vomit still lingering in her mouth, she rose shakily. The overwhelming realization that she'd been duped yet again by a man seized her. But this time it was even worse — she must have gotten herself involved in some sort of art smuggling ring. That was if what Teresa had translated was correct.

"Shit, double fuck," Monique cursed and sobbed into her hands before her despair turned to anger.

Wiping her tears, she tried to stand. Her body was stiff from sitting on the floor for so long. After rinsing her mouth in the sink, she looked at herself. What a wreck. The dark smears of mascara under her eyes made her look ten years older. Not the glowing reflection she'd become used to seeing these past few days with Luc. Or should she say, Alessandro Bonnard. She didn't know who the fuck the man she'd been sleeping with was. The man she'd been falling for despite her resolve not to give in to her lust and the deeper feelings of trust and even love.

Throwing her hand towel down onto the counter, she glared at the sad-looking reflection. She was better than this. Stronger than this. She was Monique Le Bres. Once, in a place a long time ago, she'd been Monica Don from trailer thirty-one on the outskirts of Wichita.

There was no way she was going to let this man, whoever he was, undo her.

* * * *

Ready to find out just what the hell was going on before the *polizia* got to her, Monique dressed. She packed haphazardly, throwing in whatever she could collect in a few minutes. She grabbed her passport from the in-wall safe inside the closet. Thank God the hotel hadn't taken it when she'd returned to her job. Somehow, that had eluded them when she'd been reinstated to her old job, thanks to Luc.

Glancing around her suite one last time, Monique tugged her luggage behind her and opened her door carefully before venturing out into the hall. No doubt the police would be here momentarily, and she had to get out of there before they arrived. While she had a chance to find someone who could tell her just what was really going on. Someone who understood Italian better than she did and could translate it for her.

Deciding against the elevator, which created too much risk of running into someone, Monique opted for the stairs. Awkwardly she descended the steep flights, bumping and banging her bag all the way. Her luggage nearly knocked her down while she descended to one level below the lobby to the busy basement area. The one Donovan had told her about. An underground sort of an upstairs-downstairs reprieve for the staff, far from the watchful eye of hotel brass.

Monique hoped to find Marie among the many staff members off duty or on their breaks. She poked along discretely, searching the big kitchen mess area and the dozens of uniformed employees who were eating, drinking and playing cards.

No sign of Marie. Shit, now what? Head to the airport and hope she got on a flight to somewhere before her passport was flagged? Before she was pulled over and what? All those years on the wrong side of the tracks had taught her one thing—anytime the police wanted to talk you, you were already in trouble. She didn't even know what she was guilty of, if anything. Just falling for the wrong guy.

The hoots and hollers of the late-night workers tipping back shots and playing cards faded away as Monique left the mess area.

Monique heard someone call to her from down a darkened hall. The tone was insistent and urgent. She followed the sound.

Much to her relief, Marie stood at the end of the corridor, motioning for her to hurry. Her friend said nothing as she ushered Monique through a doorway and double-checked to make sure they weren't being followed. Reassured, she shut the door to the small supply room stocked with cleaning products and propped a mop under the door handle to keep anyone from coming in.

"Oh, *Signorina* Monique, I was so worried." She took Monique's hands in hers and squeezed.

"You're worried? I don't even know what the hell is going on. I saw it on the news about Luc, but I didn't understand the Italian. They rattled on so quickly…"

Marie smiled nervously and soothed her by patting her hands. "It's not good." Her usually jolly expression was replaced by a serious frown. Her narrowed eyes made Monique shiver.

"Tell me what you know. I don't know what to do, Marie," Monique pleaded.

"I only know what I heard on the news and what they are saying upstairs." The maid motioned upward with her eyes.

"And?" Monique prompted. "Tell me anything you know, please. The police are coming, aren't they?"

Marie nodded. "*Si*, the *Carabinieri*. I've already been interviewed, and some of the others who knew Luc. I mean, *Signor* Bonnard," she corrected herself.

"Oh, dear," Monique said, realizing this wasn't only affecting her. It was bigger than that, whatever it was. Interviewing all the hotel staff. That was serious.

"Apparently Luc was not who he said he was. He is Alessandro Bonnard, an art thief. Some sort of smuggler."

"I don't believe it," Monique said, shaking her head, unaware she'd spoken the words aloud until she saw Marie's eyebrows rise.

"You have to, it's true. It's all over the news. There are pictures and everything. He just smuggled a whole bunch of art at that auction last night, the one you two went to…" Marie's voice quivered.

Monique felt her stomach drop down to her knees.

"No, no, no…" Monique stumbled backward against a rack of cleaning supplies, causing some to fall off the shelf, liquids spilling open on the floor.

Marie paid no attention to the disaster, quickly reaching for Monique to steady her. "It's true. They don't know what happened, and I'm sure you have nothing to do with it, but they *are* looking for you. They asked me if I knew where you were and when I last saw you."

Monique's eyes widened at the realization that this was really happening. Something very big was going down. Shit, it just like her to get her big break and walk headlong into a shit sundae. That's what her mama had always called something that looked too good to be true. And this was a shit sundae with whipped cream and a cherry on top.

* * * *

Several minutes later, Marie stood guarding the door as Monique slipped out. Her loyal maid had bought Monique's line that she was going back to her room to wait for the police. She hated to lie to Marie. She'd been a good friend, Monique's only friend, really, since she'd come to Totally Five Star, but Monique couldn't jeopardize Marie's innocence if she told her the truth. Monique was fleeing Venice before the police found her. And nothing was going to stop her from getting out of Dodge.

She lugged her cleaning solution-soaked suitcase out of a back passageway and up some old stone steps, the musky scent of the canals a reminder that she was indeed in Venice. The perfect city for getting lost and evading the police, if she could just figure out where to hide for a bit while she figured out what to do.

Monique emerged from the hotel into the mild night air. She glanced nervously over her shoulder every so often to make sure she wasn't being followed. It was difficult to get her bearings in the dark. She had to stop more than once to double-check which way she was headed. The canal shimmered on her right as she tried to keep track of where she was going, eagerly looking for some remote spot where she could hole up for the night until she got a plan. Or maybe it was better to head for the train station right away and hop on a train to...to...to where? Where *was* she going to go with no money to speak of? She couldn't very well walk up to Totally Five Star demanding her paycheck after the fiasco with Luc. *Or should I say, Alessandro.*

The night air grew damp. Monique felt the slight chill, her trench coat obviously not doing its job, and tugged it tighter to her throat. After aimlessly wandering, her mind rushing through scenarios and rehashing any clues she might have picked up on with Luc, she became weary. Like some sort of street urchin, she tugged her belongings behind her. She rounded a corner and stopped in her tracks.

The Totally Five Star.

Damn. Monique was right back where she'd started. She'd gone in a complete circle. What an ass she was. She couldn't even run away from the hotel properly. Tears of frustration pricked her eyes as she turned away angrily and pulled the damn suitcases over the cobblestone, hurrying off again as fast as she could.

"*Signorina?*" a man's voice called out from the dark.

She panicked. Damn, the police. Monique kept her head down and she carried on, hoping they were calling to someone else.

"*Scusi,*" the voice called out again, then a hand reached for her arm. Monique almost fainted. She was so scared when she was forced to turn and look at whomever it was who had caught her.

Her eyes widened in surprise.

The Asian man from the auction. She recognized the unusual tortoiseshell glasses. He said nothing but gripped her arm firmly as he pressed her into an alcove. Alarmed, Monique was speechless as a million thoughts went through her mind at once, none of which were good.

"From *Monsieur Bonnard*," he said while he reached in his breast pocket. He handed her an envelope.

She looked down at the envelope then back up at him.

The messenger had disappeared as quickly as he'd appeared. Alone in the dark, she just stood there, the envelope clutched in her hand.

Monique stumbled backward on the cobblestones and leaned against the alcove wall for support as she held the envelope in her hand and looked out after the man. She assured herself that he had just been there in front of her, even though now there was not a soul in sight. But there was nothing, just the flicker of the eerie light from the street lamps.

She glanced at the envelope then turned her back to the street, shielding herself from anyone's view. She opened the envelope, tearing recklessly, aware of the wax seal on the back that was making it difficult to open. Shards of the paper fell to the ground as she forced the envelope open and pulled the contents out—a folded note of some sort.

Monique opened it slowly, her heart pounding in her ears, almost afraid to read it.

An audible gasp slipped from her lips as she looked over her shoulder to see if anyone had heard her. Still, no one was around, so she looked back down at the paper and began to read in the dim light of the street lamp. The note was handwritten in ink, the script perfect, something she'd always tried to achieve herself, but never had.

Dear Monique,
Forgive me.
It was not my intention for any of this to involve you. You have done nothing wrong. I can explain – if you let me.
Please, I cannot leave you like this. My love for you was genuine from the first day I met you. I hope yours for me is the same.
In my bond,
AB

Under the AB, which Monique figured stood for Alessandro Bonnard, there were strikes through the initials where he'd also initialed LU. For Luc Umbere, she assumed. So it was true he was Alessandro Bonnard in disguise. Her mind dizzied at the thought.

Studying the note again, she then turned the page over. There was some scribble, the script not as perfect as the other page, but she could make out the words.

Fondamenta Santa Lucia.

Monique studied the penmanship, noting the author was definitely the same as the other side. She flipped the letter over then back again. She knew by the way he made his F with a unique swirl at the peak of the character and a strike right through the middle of the F. It was Luc or Alessandro or whomever the hell he said he was – the man who she'd fallen for despite her better judgment.

The Fondamenta Santa Lucia. She recognized the name of the train station she'd arrived at that first day of her new job, before she'd gotten lost in the streets and stumbled into Bonnard's path—Luc's path. *Oh, damn, this is so fucked up.*

What did it mean, the name of the train station on the back? What did he expect? Was it a clue? Did he think she'd blithely follow his suggestion that she go to the train station? For what? For her to get on the train? With what money and to where? With whom? Would he be there? And just who was *he* anyway? Luc or Alessandro? Was he fleeing the police? What was going on? What was he asking her to do?

Her head swimming with questions, Monique read the note again and again. Her gaze kept lingering on his confession of love on the third line. In a note no less, while on the run from the police. This was mad. She threw the note down in disgust then quickly grabbed it as it drifted to the cobblestones. Her heart tugged with regret as she stood there wanting more than anything for things to have worked out differently between them. For him not to have been a thief. She snorted at the ludicrousness of it all before a tear cracked her tough exterior façade. Slinking down the side of the wall for support, she sobbed.

Chapter Twenty-Eight

It was now pitch-black, the light from the street lamps little help as she navigated her way along the empty canal ways, the letter safely tucked into her pocket. Not knowing what she was doing or where she was going, Monique repeatedly mulled the letter over in her head, every so often glancing over her shoulder to make sure she wasn't being followed. She felt more like a criminal on the run on one of those TV shows than a woman from Kansas who was as lost in Venice as her heart was.

"Blast it," she sputtered. She neared the train station, well aware that she had found her way there despite her inner self scolding her for being so gullible.

Her heart sank when she approached the steps to the deserted terminal. What exactly did she expect to find there in the dark on the steps leading up to the station? Luc on bended knee confessing his love for her and telling her all it was big mistake? That the whole art thief thing was a fiasco, a bad joke gone wrong?

Monique looked around warily. There was no one but an old man passed out on the steps near the stair railing, a bottle drifting lazily from his hand before bouncing nosily down the steps. *Tink, tink, tink.* The glass rattled as it tumbled from stair to stair, the man still in his own world, completely unaware, as the bottle hit the bottom step and shattered — just like her heart.

She shivered and continued up the stairs, baggage in tow, into the train station, not knowing why, just thumbing the letter in her pocket. She had to get out of Venice. Perhaps that was the message he was sending her. Run for it. Romanticism reared its ugly head as she wondered if Luc might be there waiting for her on the train platforms. Hoped was more like it.

But there was no one there as she entered the eerily vacant terminal, the long platforms stretching out with a few parked trains that had no signs of going anywhere soon in the middle of the night. Who took a train at twelve p.m. anyway? She looked at the clock and decided this had been a colossal waste of time.

Disappointed, she turned away from the trains. Monique instantly spotted the Asian man out of the corner of her eye. He leaned casually on a pillar and nodded. She checked over her shoulder to see if there was someone else he was looking at, but the place was clearly desolate. Shivers spiked up her spine as she glanced back at him and saw he was moving toward her. Did he have the police in tow and was it some sort of trap?

He reached into his breast pocket again. Her heart skipped a beat. He pulled out another envelope and walked straight to her. Rooted by fear, she did not move. His path did not alter. He passed right by her, making her reach for it as he passed. Once again, she was left standing there clutching an envelope. *Now this is getting creepy.*

She hurried the opposite direction, eager to read what was inside, double-checking no one was following her as she ran encumbered by her luggage back down the front steps of the station. The drunk was still dead to the world as she stepped over the broken glass and strode quickly to a nearby canal way. To a place she could read the note unnoticed by prying eyes that might be watching her.

The same wax seal was on the envelope as Monique ran her fingers over it. The sensation made her feel closer to Luc as she opened it with more ease than the last note.

Standing under a street lamp, she was disappointed there was no note, just one line.

You've made it this far. It's your choice now.

And two tickets.

One to Kansas. In her name, Monique Le Bres.

And the other a train ticket to Switzerland in the name of Celeste Beaumonte.

Switzerland? Is he fucking for real? This was like something out of a James Bond flick. Attached to the ticket for Celeste Beaumonte was an ID card with Celeste's name.

The note fell from her hand as she saw the photo on the ID and a wad of euros that looked like a few thousand bucks by the thickness of it. She bent down to retrieve the fallen note, looking at the picture on the ID. *Her* picture stared back at her from Celeste Beaumont's ID. *Holy shit!*

Monique immediately dove into the front alcove of a storefront, desperate to avoid anyone as she clutched the fake ID and ticket in her shaking hands.

What the hell? What did Luc—or should she say Alessandro—want? She stood there thinking.

The ticket to Kansas in her name. *A safe bet.* She could return to the US then what? Back to her normal life, not that she had one to return to, but he didn't know that.

With the wad of bills he'd enclosed, she could make a fresh start somewhere. Not Kansas, that was for sure. She wasn't ever going back there. Maybe California. She'd always wanted to rub shoulders with movie stars and bask in the warm sun. Shit, who was she kidding? She'd never get a job after this fiasco, and who knew how much trouble she was really in if the police followed her back to America. Either way, the ticket to Kansas looked like a dead end. No Luc or Alessandro in her future, that was for sure.

Then there was the train ticket to Switzerland. *Under an assumed name. A fake name, for God's sake. Like a criminal on the run.* But it was a chance, a mere possibility to see Luc…Alessandro…and get answers, if that's what this all meant. But then what after that….he was a criminal….maybe she was an accessory… What the hell *was* she doing?

She studied the note again.

It's your choice. You've come this far.

Of course, he was watching her. Someone had to be to set up the Asian man handing her the first envelope at the hotel and now following her to the train station.

She knew she was in a heap of trouble. If Luc was watching her, then maybe the police were too. But there was no one. No sign of anyone following her, as she looked around suspiciously, unable to resist imagining he was there. Wanting him to be there was more like it.

Dammit, she missed him. Criminal or not. And rather than be mad at him that he'd seduced her under a fake persona, she couldn't help remembering the fire she felt whenever he touched her, the sense of being alive and desired that she never had before—a connection that had rocked her to the very core.

A train blasted its arrival into the station, jolting Monique back from her reverie. She listened from her hiding spot, thinking just what to do next. She watched for a few minutes as passengers eventually made their way down the same steps she had climbed not that long ago. They passed the drunk and staggered out into the night.

Monique tucked the ID and wad of money into her purse, feeling exposed by the arrival of the passengers. Her mind reeled with the choice before her.

Go back to Kansas, broke and out of a job, or hop on a train to Switzerland under an assumed name. She could at least let Luc have a chance to explain, couldn't she? Well aware that she was bargaining with the devil when she let her heart rule over her head, Monique stepped out onto the platform.

Chapter Twenty-Nine

The train headed for Switzerland sounded its horn and swiftly departed Santa Lucia train station—with Monique onboard. Or should she say Celeste. Oh, this had to be the riskiest thing she'd ever done, and there was steep competition for that, given her past, but something inside her needed to see Luc again. If only to put the pieces of his deception, not just of her, but of the art world as well, under scrutiny. But as she gazed out of the window into the empty night, she knew it was more than that. Her heart yearned for some resolution, some hope that this was all one big mistake and he was not an art thief, not some mastermind who had lured her into his web. She ached for his touch, the sound of his voice, the expression on his face and in his eyes when he looked at her. It was official—she was royally screwed. Not that she hadn't been in plenty of unsavory predicaments before. She was no saint, that was for sure.

The chaotic day caught up with her and Monique soon drifted off, lulled by the soothing jostling and shaking of the train as she leaned her head against the glass.

Monique awoke with a start as the motion stopped. Her eyes flashed open, the glare of the overhead lighting an assault on her doziness. Confused, she peered out into vastness.

Where the hell were they, and why had they stopped? Looking around the compartment, it dawned on her there was no one else there. No other passengers. How had this detail escaped her when she'd boarded the train? She'd been so consumed with boarding as Celeste and relieved when no conductor had come through to check her ticket and ID, that she hadn't given any notice to the fact she was the only one in the car. But now, her senses heightened to the unusual stopping of the train, she took in every detail of the compartment.

A sharp jolt startled her as the train lurched forward and she felt a thunk, then sudden movement.

The train was moving again. That was a relief.

The lights in the cabin grew dim. So dim she could barely make out the shapes of the rows of seats as the train surged along, the speed evident as she tried to rise to look around in the darkness. Bracing herself with her hand on the headrest of her seat, she stood, holding steady against the movement of the train as her mouth dropped open in disbelief.

The door connecting her compartment to the next car opened.

Luc stood at the far end of her cabin, his silhouette unmistakable. Shaking her head to make sure she wasn't dreaming, Monique saw he was still there. Cautiously, steadying her racing heart, she started toward him. Her eyes adjusted to the light as she stepped closer and she was now able to see he was actually inside the connecting car.

He said nothing but motioned for her to continue to him. Almost in a trance, she said nothing, just stepped slowly toward him, sure that at any moment the realization her eyes were playing tricks on her would shame her back to her seat. But as she stepped nearer, Monique could tell her eyes were not betraying her. It was Luc, looking every bit as handsome as ever, his hair somehow different, tousled, his expression beckoning as she stepped across the bridge that connected the cars, only vaguely aware of the tracks visible below as she moved closer to him.

She bit her lip in trepidation and expectation. He was a man on the run, a criminal. An art thief, no less. Her pulse raced. Her heartbeat so loudly she could barely make out what he said when he spoke her name.

"Monique, you came—"

"Celeste," she corrected him. The bite in her words defied the relief she felt at seeing him alive and in one piece, aware now of all the horrible scenarios she'd run through her head of him meeting his demise.

"*Touché*, I deserve that."

He smiled that same sexy smile that had melted her whenever he'd flashed it. But this was different. Things had changed. He'd deceived her. She bit her bottom lip, resisting the urge to rush into the refuge of his arms and hide from the reality of what he'd done. What *they* had done.

"I am still very glad you came," he repeated.

"I did, although I don't know why." She glanced behind her nervously, still anxious the police might have followed her.

"You made the choice to come, to give me the chance to explain..."

"So explain," she said, only too aware of the effect the hypnotic pull his gaze was having on her, his eyes different somehow than she remembered.

Looking into his striking blue eyes, she realized what it was. Even the brown eyes had been fake. What a fool she'd been. Her head whirled with a million thoughts and sensations. She battled the urge to be swept up in his arms and pretend things were different.

"First thing first..." He reached for her.

Their lips met instantly, both hungry and desperate. She clung to him, taking in his scent, the taste of his lips on hers and the feel of his strong, muscled form pressing against her, protecting her, wanting her.

Only a whoosh of air made her open her eyes as she looked back and saw the compartment she had just come from detach and disappear into the night.

Disbelief racked her. He pulled her into safety and away from the racing train tracks below.

In the light of the cabin, she gazed up at him in surprise. His eyes were brilliant blue. But that wasn't the only thing different, as she quickly scanned him, noting his hair was different and there was something else that she couldn't put her finger on. Overwhelmed, she stepped away from him, the surroundings awing her as much as the fact that the compartment she'd been in and her belongings had just disappeared into the night. Now standing alone with Luc in what looked like a private train car, she glanced quickly around then back at him.

"Let me explain," he said and took her in his arms again.

"Not so fast," she protested. Her mind spun when she noted the luxurious velvet-upholstered couches, the rich, oriental carpet and the Andy Warhol's and Picasso's on the walls that were far from decorator art. Oh no, these were the real thing—authentic.

This is his. Some kind of private train car. Alessandro's private car...on his own train. It shouldn't surprise her, but it did.

"*Avere fiducia in mio,*" he soothed. Believe. He was asking her to believe. Believe in what—in him?

He pulled close. His embrace was distracting as she struggled to make sense of what was going on. "I never meant for you to wind up in the middle of all this," he told her. "You must believe me."

Again with the *believe.* "Why?" she snapped.

"I hoped you'd give me another chance, and you did by coming here. I can't tell you how worried I was that you wouldn't."

He brushed a tendril away from her face and the tenderness irritated her. Not because of the gesture itself, but her feelings for him made her feel weak. Weak against her desire to touch him, to kiss him the way she wanted to.

She held a hand up only to make space between them. "I don't understand any of this," she said.

"Please," he requested.

The tone of his voice appealed to her as he motioned for her to sit on the couch.

"I'm fine standing," she said. The train bounced along, setting her off balance and into his arms again.

"Me too." He didn't yield to her challenge.

"On second thought, I'll sit." She stepped away to plant her bottom firmly on the couch, where she didn't have to worry about falling into his gorgeous arms again. She needed to keep her head on straight, not go all gooey at his touch. And he needed to tell her the truth.

"Your confusion and mistrust are completely understandable," Alessandro reassured her, gathering his composure as he moved toward the bar cart in the center of the compartment. He started to make them drinks.

"Make mine a double," Monique said with no hint of emotion as he poured the scotch from the decanter into the crystal glasses.

He nodded. Of course, she'd need a double. How insensitive of him not to realize she was having trouble taking it all in. Obviously she was struggling to accept his explanation and trust him, as he wanted her to. He'd been so anxious she wouldn't come at all, that he'd misjudged her moxie, when she'd actually gotten on the train and chosen not to go back to Kansas. He'd mistakenly assumed that meant everything was fine between them, but nothing could be further from the truth. In her eyes, and probably the eyes of the law, he was a criminal on the run. No doubt she would have questions, reservations and second thoughts.

He stepped toward her with their drinks in hand, knowing he had to take the bull by the horns. Showing her his private bedroom in the back of his private train would have to wait until later. That was, *if* there was a later. He damned well hoped there was the way she was making his cock stiff when she tilted her chin at him as he approached. Her gaze lifted to his, her lips perfect and dewy. Just like when she'd slipped his dick between those rosy red lips. Control, dammit, he reprimanded. He didn't want to scare her off. She'd come this far, and he wanted a chance with her — to explain.

Monique said nothing, just sipped the scotch as he watched in appreciation when the liquor beaded on her bottom lip. He fought the urge to reach out and kiss it off her lips.

"Well?" she said impertinently.

He'd had what he was going to say all planned, but now that she was there in front of him, he was having trouble knowing where to start.

She exhaled impatiently when he said nothing, stammering in his mind with the first words he might utter.

"So you're an art thief," she stated flatly before taking another long swig of Scotch.

She'd surprised him with her forthrightness. Although why such a vixen being forward would surprise him, he didn't know. It was one of her traits that had first attracted him when she'd leaned over her desk, her tweed skirt pulling over her ass, practically begging his palm to paddle the perfect specimen of womanhood.

"And you're not Luc Umbere, that I am quite sure of," she said.

It made him realize how very bad this looked from her point of view.

He stilled his thoughts. "I am Alessandro Bonnard, but I can explain why I was undercover when I met you."

She arched her eyebrows. "Undercover?"

"I was working for J. It was all planned out."

Monique took another big sip. "I don't know who the hell this J is!"

He noted the way her glass shook in her hand. She was either afraid or pissed, and his vote went with pissed.

"James Conroy," he clarified.

"Alessandro Bonnard doesn't work for people. He doesn't need to. You'll have to do better than that if you want to convince me of your innocence."

Great, she thought he was lying. It was in the telltale narrowing of her eyes.

"Oh, I'm not handling this well, am I?" he asked her and saw her expression soften. "Look, I am definitely not an art thief, of this I assure you." He gestured around the cabin. "This is all mine, as is my fortune that I built myself with hard work, buying and selling art. I never stole anything. Everything has been acquired, and I have all the receipts."

"I don't care about receipts. Tell me about James Conroy and what the hell you're talking about, being undercover. Are you a cop or something?" she said, backing away as if recoiling at the thought.

He couldn't help his smile, as she seemed so disgusted that he was an undercover cop. "No, no, I am not a cop. J and are friends. Good friends."

"James Conroy?"

"Yes, James Conroy. And because I am an art collector of some repute, J asked me to come to his newest hotel and oversee the art collection."

"You mean me," she said.

He could see her struggling to put the pieces together. "Exactly, you."

"Then why the fake name, why the brown eyes... They were brown, weren't they?" She seemed confused. "And the disguises, I saw them on TV. Why the disguises?"

Her cheeks flushed and her eyes flickered frantically. She darted her gaze about as she processed what he was trying his damndest to tell her.

"Ah," Alessandro said, "good question. J and I knew everyone would recognize me, so we decided I should take on the fake name and the disguise, so to speak. All I really did was wear contacts, change my hair color and shave my goatee. But I didn't mean to deceive you, please believe me. I couldn't tell you who I was. I was planning on it, but then all of this happened."

"Umph," was all she said.

He wasn't sure just what she was thinking.

"And the stealing part?" she prompted, not giving him a moment of reprieve.

But her posture softened somewhat, giving him a glimmer of promise that she was indeed listening to what he was saying.

"You are persistent," he said with admiration. He hoped the softness in his tone told her he was happy to answer her questions all night long if that's what it took to win her back. "Monique, I promise you I am not an art thief. What I *am* in trouble for — and the jury will be out on whether I am guilty or not — is something called shilling. Rigging the market, so to speak, but that's a crude term. I prefer the term 'market value' when discussing my auction techniques."

"I know exactly what shilling is," Monique replied quickly. "The carnies did it back in Kansas. It's driving up the price of something by using fake bidders."

"Yes. Well, not exactly. I have people who work for me who bid up art at auctions. It's not entirely black and white whether it's a crime, but for now, we can call it that if you need to know why I am retreating to

Luxembourg, where I will be exempt from further interrogation by the police."

"Luxembourg?" she queried, "but my ticket—I mean, Celeste's ticket—is for Switzerland…"

He shook his head at her astute attention to detail given how confusing the situation must be for her. "I didn't want anyone following me to Luxembourg—"

"You mean if I got caught, you wanted them to think I was following you to…"

"Switzerland." He filled in the blank and beamed at his smart little vixen.

"Okay, so you've explained that, but back to the topic at hand. There was something on the news about the art from the auction you and I were at. That the Asian man…you must know…the one who gave me the envelopes."

"Yes, that's Akito. He works for me, and yes, he bid up the art that night at the auction. You were never supposed to bid on it, Monique, that's why I was so cross that night."

"I remember, you paddled me."

His cock strained in his pants at the preciousness of this woman. "You know full well I did that to bring you pleasure, and myself too. I was not cross with you then. And, as I recall, we both quite enjoyed my paddling your beautiful, round ass."

"Don't change the subject, Luc," she said, then caught herself. "I mean, Alessandro. I don't know what the hell to call you."

"Call me anything you like, my fiery little vixen, as long as you're here with me, that's all I need."

"And what about me? What about the police coming after me? Am I guilty by association?"

"Absolutely not," he said, seeing the alarm in her eyes. For all her bravado of being a ball-buster, the little lady was just that—a lady. And she was afraid. And he was a total shit for having put her in this position. Thank God he'd had the wits to phone J the minute the shit had hit the fan and clear her name. "I can assure you that the police want nothing to do with you. I called J the minute all this broke and made it clear under no circumstances are you responsible for any part of this. The art you bought that night does belong to Totally Five Star, but I immediately wired J the funds to reimburse him."

"What?" she said, moving her hand to her chest protectively. "That was over thirty million euros!"

"I don't think you realize the extent of my wealth. It was merely to keep honor between gentlemen that I reimburse J for any mix-up. And clear your name, of course."

"What about the other people you must have profited from illegally?" She broached the subject tentatively.

Her eyes cast an uncertain gaze. He suppressed the urge to reach out and show her just how little he cared what others thought—only what she thought. He'd pay millions more if it meant having her by his side.

"Well, only time will tell that, but I am quite secure in my assets. I doubt it will be much of a problem, even if they are able to reach me in Luxembourg."

"You really think you can escape there and not be persecuted?"

"I know I can. And that's if I'm even guilty. That hasn't been determined yet. Now, back to paddling your gorgeous, little ass, which is much more interesting than debating my innocence." He paused deliberately, like a lawyer in a courtroom for effect before proceeding. "You had a choice to make, to follow me...and you did. Now you have another to make—will you join me in Luxembourg?"

She gulped. He saw her throat constrict when she wet her lips. That tongue that would be the undoing of him if only she would say yes, then he'd show her just how deep his feelings for her went. The love he felt for her, not just the lust. The need to be with her, the pain at the thought of being without her.

The rattle of the train car was the only sound as she looked up at him. He could almost see the wheels spinning in her head. The fight between good and evil, between lust and love. He hoped—no, prayed—that she felt it too.

"Please, Monique, forgive me and give me a chance." He took the drink out of her hand.

"Not so fast," she said, crossing her legs tighter. Her pussy thrummed at the memory of the night after the action. "If you are this Alessandro Bonnard that you tell me you are...then what about our meeting that first day?"

"In the street?" he ventured, his gaze softening. "The *Calle Ostreghe* when I caught you as you fell, when your heel snapped off. Your ridiculously high heel, if I may say, but ever so sexy."

It was him. Only Alessandro knew of the shoe. She'd never had a chance to tell Luc. *They are the same man.* He was telling the truth about that at least.

"Do you believe me?" he asked.

"I think so," she said with hesitation. It was as if speaking the words aloud would break the spell of her belief.

"You said to me that day, 'one down, ten to go'."

No one would know that but Alessandro. Her Luc was Alessandro. No doubt about it.

"I still remember that saucy, little smile you gave me," he continued. "It was so intoxicating, all-consuming, but I had to leave you there in the *calle* for fear of being caught. I knew at that moment that you had to be mine, then when I walked into that office and saw your pert little ass in the air, wriggling it in frustration at whatever had fallen under the desk, I knew I had a second chance. And I took it."

Her eyes brimmed with tears of relief.

He smiled at her, his blue eyes sparkling as she looked deep into them just like she'd done that first day they'd met on the *calle*.

"You were a vision that day, and you still are. You're my vixen in Venice," he said, then plucked her glass from her hand and placed it on the table.

"Luc," she said softly, her voice hoarse with emotion. She loved it when he took control, and right now, she ached for him to show her just how much he wanted her. Needed her. To know if his feelings for her matched the intensity of hers for him.

Her gaze became riveted to his, taking in their striking blue depths, even more revealing than his brown eyes had been.

"Your eyes, they were brown," was all she could think of to say. Ridiculous she knew, but he placed his hand back on her thigh, sending shockwaves of delight throughout her body. She gulped when he began slowly trailing his fingertips up from her knee to between her legs. She was well aware she was hanging on by a thread.

"Contacts. They were contacts." He leaned in and kissed her fully.

Scotch and passion mingled on their tongues as she parted her lips and allowed him access to her mouth, to explore her with his hand sliding more forcefully between her legs. Unable to resist, she parted her thighs.

"I'm so glad you didn't run away," he said, pushing her back onto the couch, kissing her forcefully and eagerly.

He lowered himself onto her, his erection rubbing between them as she reached around his neck and pulled him closer. The glorious sensation of being taken by him was irresistible when he kissed his way down her neck, across her breasts, removing her clothing as he went. The uneven jostling of the train made his kisses undulate when he slid between her legs, slipping her stockings off while she lay there, her thoughts vanishing when he parted her legs. Her bare pussy waited for him.

He blew hot caresses along her mound. Monique squirmed at the pleasure.

She flung her head back. Oh God, this man was too much. "I'm glad I didn't run away either..." she uttered, unable to finish her sentence when the heat of his mouth teased her.

Alessandro licked a smooth path from her clit to her entrance and he whimpered in pleasure.

"I've missed you," he said, finding her erect nub. Circling her clit with his tongue, he teased then sucked hard, grabbing her ass. He dug his fingers into her flesh, helping support her hips when he delved his tongue into her channel.

"Luc," she gasped. Not just her voice, but also her whole body trembled as she fought the wave of orgasm that built with each divine stroke of his tongue.

"Alessandro," he corrected her. He stopped his kisses and looked at her over the bridge of her hips, his eyes flickering with fire, his mouth wet with her juices. "Say it," he commanded.

"Alessandro," she uttered, wanting more than anything for him to take her to the place that she knew only he could.

"Alessandro what?" he prompted. His blue eyes shimmered with naughtiness.

He dipped his tongue lower. His eyes remained on her. He lapped at her clit and her hips bucked in response to the exquisite thrills of his kiss. She quivered in near release.

He stopped. "Tell me what you want."

"I want you to kiss me, make me —" she begged just as he circled her clit with his tongue. He was unrelenting in his attention. He sucked her sensitive nub and slipped his finger into her wet channel at the same time, his finger pressing just where he knew it thrilled her.

"Come, baby, come for me," he coached as he kept up with her rhythm.

Monique careened into orgasm, a guttural groan escaping her lips while she exploded into release. Her legs shook with the aftershocks of her bliss as he lowered her hips to the couch and then crawled up along her body.

"Oh, Luc—I mean, Alessandro," she said breathlessly when their lips met with her musk on his tongue.

"I hope this means you'll be giving me a second chance," he said with a wry smile as he fell next to her on the couch.

"I think everyone deserves at least one second chance," she said, rolling him over onto his back. "It's not like I haven't made mistakes too," she confessed, thinking just how alive she felt when she was with him.

"It might not be easy, I'm warning you. We might have to live in Luxembourg awaiting extradition," he said.

She glided provocatively down his torso and dragged her palm over his crotch. Loving the feel of his hard shaft under her touch, she unzipped his fly. "We?" she asked in mock surprise.

"Yes, we are a team, remember?"

"I remember. But that was when you were Luc."

"I've always been Alessandro."

"Well, Luc Alessandro. You can go by any name you like as long as you make me feel the way you do." She swirled her hands along his cock, feeling it swell when she stroked it, long and slow, watching his body twitch in arousal when she rubbed her slick pussy on his legs.

"Deal," he gasped.

She lowered her lips to take him fully into her mouth. He reached around and gave her bottom an appreciative squeeze. First, soft then hard. With each deep lick of his cock, he gripped her ass with even more intensity. She mimicked his pattern of soft then firm grasps. She sucked him hard then soft, loving the feel of his rhythm under her when she took her sweet time blowing him one delicious lick after another.

Chapter Thirty

Monique and 'Luc Alessandro', as she had become fond of calling him, spent many long winter nights in a villa in Luxembourg awaiting his extradition hearing. They barely noticed the chill of the nights as they explored their passion in exquisite thoroughness. Monique often suspected the slow, low murmur of their absolute pleasure carried through the rambling villa while she and Luc Alessandro kept their promise to take a chance on each another, one sumptuous, erotic night at a time.

When winter turned to spring, Monique found herself immersed not only in her love for Luc Alessandro, but also in the art collection she helped him to catalog while he waited for his judgment day. Monique, ensconced in the villa, no longer worked as a curator, but she helped Luc Alessandro manage his vast art collection for his homes around the world. Tiring of the game of collecting and selling to the highest bidder, he and Monique preferred pursuing more thrilling ways to stave off boredom.

J remained a loyal and trusted friend to Alessandro, despite the unfortunate art acquisitions debacle at his Venice hotel. Recently, he'd rung Alessandro in Luxembourg to tell him that he'd decided to keep the paintings acquired by Monique for the Venice hotel. A shrewd hotelier, J opted to have the works continue to grace the walls of his hotel. Aware that not only would the art appreciate, but also the collection would attract a notable tourism crowd each year, all eager for the guided tour the hotel was soon offering of the unusually acquired art.

One March afternoon, a fire smoldered in the massive stone fireplace, taking the chill off the impressive study at the far end of the sprawling villa during the Luxembourg spring. Immersed in her work, Monique, with a stack of files tucked in her arm, walked over to the ledger she kept on her desk—a desk Luc had brought in just for her and placed only a few feet from his.

Monique placed the folders down on the leather-inlayed desk and went about her duty of entering yet another name for one of his paintings into the ledger, complete with documenting all its lineage and margins. She was always careful to make doubly sure to account for every detail so there would be no doubt the work was acquired legally. It was a painstaking job, but one that Monique enjoyed while she and Luc Alessandro waited in his Luxembourg fortress for his innocence or guilt to be determined. She was far from Kansas, but not so far from her dreams of being an art curator.

It was the best of both worlds, assisting Luc by day, and by night, he helped her explore her ever expanding sexuality. A match made in heaven as the elusive man in exile and the woman who was once

Monica Don from a dusty trailer park pursued their love of art and their love for each other, as they awaited a verdict.

Leaning over her desk, Monique finished a time-consuming entry into the ledger, then moved on to the next. She flipped the page so she could start fresh with a new category — the impressionists. Her lover had a soft spot for the impressionists, she reminded herself, so she'd need more than ten pages to catalog his personal favorites.

Monique reached for a Post-It Note pad to mark off the required pages in advance, in case Alessandro came in and tried his hand at cataloguing. Luc Alessandro had many talents, but cataloguing was not one of them. She chuckled to herself and remembered the way he'd tied her to his big four-poster bed last night. Their lovemaking had caused such a ruckus when she'd crescendoed into the crush of orgasm that his night maid had come running to make sure they were okay. Luc had been straddling above her, his muscles hard and rippling, his cock slick with her juices as they quickly shushed the maid away. He'd wasted no time getting back to the task at hand.

Distracted by the recollection, Monique leaned too far over the desk to get the note pads and they fell to the floor, along with a few files. Bending to look under the desk, she quickly reached for them. She stretched to grasp the sticky squares of paper, bonking her head on the desk when a firm hand caressed her ass.

"Ah, my vixen in Venice."

His voice sent a flutter of arousal right through her as she righted herself and rubbed the sore spot on her head.

He pulled her into his grasp and kissed her along the nape of her neck. "I have good news, my vixen," he said, then feathered more kisses along the exposed flesh of her décolletage.

"Good news?" she asked, intrigued.

He swayed his hips against her. His stiff cock pressed against the softness of her thighs, even through the fabric of her skirt.

"Very good," he said.

She murmured her appreciation when he dropped his hands lower, circling over her breasts then fondling them through her silk blouse. Next, he traced the outline of her now erect nipples.

"How good?" she teased and then giggled with anticipation.

He spun her around and pushed her down onto the desk.

"This good," he answered.

The rasp of him undoing his zipper made her quiver when he held her down with one hand, and she soon felt his cock on her ass after he lifted her skirt up roughly and swiftly pulled down her panties.

He ran his hand along her ass, kneading then gently caressing her exposed cheeks with the tips of his fingers. Her pussy ached with need when he teased her mound, making her beg deep inside for more. Waiting for his touch, for him to invade her, she held her breath. He slid his hand farther down to her folds, spreading her slit, readying her for his cock.

Hard and deep, he drove his rod into her. She slid forward on the desk with the impact of his thrust, biting her lip from the pure pleasure of his abruptness. He placed one hand on her shoulder and held her steady as he spread her legs apart with his, her face still flat on the leather and wooden surface of the desk. The ledger and papers crashed to the floor when he thrust deeply in and out of her tight, slick channel. She gasped and moaned at the exquisite invasion. He reached around her waist, tweaking her clit at just the right moment to send her quivering into release. He pumped even harder into her, his grunts of pleasure echoing throughout the cavernous room.

"Oh Luc...Luc...Alessandro," she cried out. He moved his other hand to her ass cheek and circled his fingertips around her anus, teasing and testing her. She murmured her approval. He wasted no time and slipped one finger deep into her rear hole, still hammering his cock inside her. She groaned and buckled forward, unable to contain her grunts of ecstasy that beckoned with each thrust. He reached down and sent her over the edge of the abyss, patting her clit until she screamed out in surrender. The wave of a second orgasm was so strong her inner walls clenched tight, and she felt his cock pulsing and throbbing when he spurted his cum inside her.

Collapsing over her, he lay on top of her while she remained face down on the desk, her skirt hiked up over her ass and her legs still parted with his hips nestled perfectly between them.

He kissed her shoulder softly. "We won the case, Monique. Now you know you're free to leave here anytime you want."

Shocked, she craned her neck to look at him, trying to conceal her horror that he'd think she'd actually leave now that he was exonerated. There was nothing but her love for her mystery man from the *calle* that kept her with him.

"That's wonderful news," she congratulated him. "And just so you know, I have no intention of leaving just because you won," she added feistily.

"*We* won," he corrected her. "We're a team, after all."

"Yes, *we* won," she conceded, well aware that he was a self-made man and no one got that way as a team player. "I always knew you would be exonerated," she said confidently. But deep down she'd been scared all winter that the judge would find him guilty. Not that she would ever have told him just how terrified she'd been that her lover would be locked away.

He stroked the sensitive spot along her spine then trailed his fingertips over the crest of her bottom. "I think you were worried that I might be sent away." He paused and eased his weight on her.

She could hear the tenderness in his voice and feel it in his touch when he stroked her ass cheeks and bent over behind her to kiss her bottom.

"I could see it in your eyes...when you would be working away in here, cataloguing our collection... sometimes when I would carry you upstairs, you'd have that look in your eyes then too."

"The only thing I was worried about was that you'd paddle my little bottom," she countered back with humor. She couldn't reveal her true feelings of worry she'd had for his future, for her future. She glanced back at him, knowing they both loved nothing more than for her to get a good paddling.

He rubbed her butt cheeks appreciatively. "A beautiful ass if I ever saw one, but back to the win — *our* win."

Monique was so touched by his unwavering insistence that they were a 'they' that she turned her gaze to the roaring fire so he wouldn't see the tears pricking her eyes. "It's really your win, Luc, and your collection."

"It's our win and you know it." He spanked her ass playfully and nipped at her neck.

She smiled over her shoulder at him. He reached down between her legs. She was sure she heard him open the desk drawer as she watched, intrigued.

The drawer shut and he smiled. "What's mine is yours—just like if we were married."

Monique gasped when she stared back over her bare ass and saw him holding a dark burgundy and gold ring box. Her eyes brimmed with tears when he cracked the lid open with one hand to reveal a stunning diamond solitaire. The stone sparkled in the firelight like a star in the midnight sky.

"I told you I always know what you're thinking. Your eyes are indeed the windows to your soul," he said, adjusting his stance to allow her to roll over underneath him. Struggling to right herself from the desktop, he extended his free hand and helped her to her feet.

She wobbled nervously and smiled widely. Monique gazed up at him but said nothing. A tear rolled down her cheek and he kissed it away with his lips.

"I think that is a yes...?" he ventured.

"What was the question again?" she said cheekily, recovering her sense of humor with the realization he was really truly proposing to her.

"You saucy little vixen." He swatted her ass before lowering himself to one knee. Slowly, he extracted the ring from the box, the band so tiny in his strong hands, the gorgeous gem laden with sparkles.

Extending the ring to her, he asked the question she had longed to hear. All those nights of pleasure and joy and worry now merged into one when her newly freed man kneeled for her approval.

"Monique Le Bres, will you marry me? Will you be my wife, my lover, my friend, my confidante?"

Her heart quivered. She looked down at him and smiled.

"Who is asking, Luc Umbere or Alessandro Bonnard?" she taunted. She enjoyed making him squirm a little as he kneeled there, ring in hand.

A smile lit his face. "Both."

"Oh, ménage, I like it," she quipped with a wicked laugh.

"Very well, my vixen, I'll ask you again. Will you, Monique Le Bres, marry me? I mean us — Luc Umbere and Alessandro Bonnard. Will you be my, I mean, *our* wife, our lover, our friend, our confidante?"

"I will be all those and more," she said, accepting the ring as he slipped it onto her

finger. Luc Alessandro swept her up into his arms and carried her to their bedroom.

About the Author

A die hard romantic and former wedding planner, Kate has been writing stories about romance, from the sensual to the sinfully sexy, since she was in college. When she's not writing or reading, Kate can be found on the tennis court—yes, there's even "love" in that game too! And she found a sport she can play and still wear a dress. Born in England, Kate now lives in Arizona with her wonderful and very patient husband. Kate enjoys travelling and dreaming up new exciting stories. She'd love to hear from you.

Kate Deveaux loves to hear from readers. You can find her contact information, website details and author profile page at http://www.totallybound.com.

Totally Bound Publishing

www.ingramcontent.com/pod-product-compliance
Lightning Source LLC
Chambersburg PA
CBHW021520240626
47154CB00002B/715